MURDER WILL OUT—

Governor Tellegen's eyes opened. "You've kept silent for twenty years, Mr. McCandless?"

"Yes, but I can't any longer. If I want to save my boy, I have to tell what I know. I'm sure you'd welcome a chance to destroy the power of Joel Tilley in this territory, Governor."

"Yes, of course, but—"

"Well, you give me my boy's life and I'll give you Tilley's!"

"Do you realize you'll be leaving yourself open to severe reprisals?" Tellegen asked.

"They'll be reprisals against me, not against my family. I'll get only what I deserve."

"I can't interfere with the trial, Mr. McCandless, but if the verdict goes against your son— I'll pardon him!"

FRONTIER LAWYER, a novel about a lawyer who was the territory's last hope for justice, is a PERMABOOK original.

FRONTIER LAWYER

Lawrence L. Blaine

Permabooks · New York

Frontier Lawyer

PERMABOOK edition published June, 1961
1st printing..April, 1961

This original PERMABOOK is printed from brand-new
plates made from newly set, clear, easy-to-read type.

•

PERMABOOK editions are distributed in the U.S. by Affili-
ated Publishers, Inc., 630 Fifth Avenue, New York 20, N.Y.

•

PERMABOOK editions are published in the United States by
Pocket Books, Inc., and in Canada by Pocket Books of Canada,
Ltd.—the world's largest publishers of low-priced adult books.

L

Frontier Lawyer

1.

AN ICY WIND had been blowing in from Canada for days now, turning the ground to rock, bringing winter to the whole Territory of New Mexico. It was going to be a long, bleak winter. Everyone could see that. Summer had been brutally hot, and now the other side of the coin was uppermost with a vengeance.

Shortly after dawn, in the small, lively city that was San Carlos in the closing decade of the last century, a burly, heavy-set figure made his way uncertainly toward the red brick building that faced the old plaza. He was Jake Kilgore, attorney-at-law, and nobody hated the cold weather more than he. Kentucky-born, an inhabitant of the Territory for the last two decades, he lacked the Northerner's fatalistic attitude toward bitterly cold weather. He despised it, pure and simple, and the thought that two or three months of it were still ahead filled him with despair.

He peered through the plate-glass window on which the name of the firm was lettered in gold leaf: JAKE KILGORE, ATTORNEY-AT-LAW. After a moment, he kicked open the door, and blinked owlishly into the empty room. Lying on his secretary's desk was a pile of memoranda typed during the night. Kilgore shuddered.

He ran a furry tongue over the inside of his gums, nodded thoughtfully, and made a beeline through the inner office to the privy in the back yard. After an interlude of meditation in the morning chill, he returned to a leather chair which stood, imperious and high-buttoned, beside a rolltop desk of many pigeonholes. He stuck a pair of dusty boots in a lower drawer and almost instantly was deep in slumber. Beyond the window, the sun inched up into the sky, the frozen earth began to thaw, a mission bell tolled in the older quarter of

1

the city, and precisely on the half hour Kilgore opened his eyes, completely refreshed. He swung about as the door opened. He found himself staring at the implacable, ruggedly ugly face of his spinster secretary, Sarah Hilleboe.

"I swear, Kilgore, I don't see where you find the brass to get into this condition the night before a case," said Sarah Hilleboe in a discouraged voice. "Aside from constituting a standing insult to the dignity of the court, I'll bet your head's no more orderly than the inside of a slaughterhouse. How can you expect to make a decent argument this morning?" With a gesture of impatience, she ran up the shade and threw the window open to the bitter breeze.

"Would you give me pneumonia, Sarah?"

"This place could stand some fresh air in the morning!"

"The temperature is under twenty. Fit only for Eskimos," Kilgore growled.

"It'll clear your brain," she ~~she~~ retorted. "Carousing the night before a case—"

Kilgore fixed narrowed, reddish eyes on the woman. "Sarah, I was at my post of duty," he said solemnly, scratching his deep, powerful chest. "In a few hours I might have to pick a jury in a case where there's lots of feeling against my client. The saloonkeeper's no bargain, and people tend to feel he was a mite rough on the old man. Under the circumstances, it's been my legal obligation to influence public opinion—and if the call takes me to the Cantina Royale, why, that's where I aim to turn up. Aside from all that, Ben Weingarten kept drawing all night to inside straights, and I couldn't pass up the chance to share the wealth of the dry-goods trade."

It was hopeless. Sarah gave up. "Understand once and for all, Kilgore," she said strongly, "I don't give a damn where you spend your nights, or how, just so long as it isn't Laurie Morgan's sporting house. Now you better clean up that mess before a client shows," she added. Returning to her post of duty, she began to type the finishing touches of a fancy cover for the legal brief she had done the night before.

A small shed in the yard served as a washroom for the law firm and its employees. Kilgore laid out a cake of yellow soap and went to work on the thick stubble sprouting from his pugnacious chin. A cock was crowing on a distant dung heap, and the shrill, defiant sound touched a responsive chord in the Kilgore temperament, but he was more interested in the tough-looking face that stared back from the mirror.

"By God!" he murmured admiringly. "Kilgore ain't pretty, but he's sure formidable! That's a lawyer's face in those silvery depths—and a deadly eye that's qualified to hypnotize the most recalcitrant jury and strike terror in the heart of the most audacious witness! Kilgore," he went on appreciatively, "just remember that you're in your prime. You may not be the greatest trial lawyer in the whole damn country, but you sure look the part!"

And indeed it was a bold and striking head that had provoked the outburst of rhetoric. He drew the straight razor across bold, prominent features, flushed and handsome. A thick mane of lustrous black hair sprang boldly from a low, broad forehead, now wrinkled with the effort of concentration. His heavy brows were like thickets, casting into shadows the small, deep-set eyes which could in moments of anger flame like rubies. It was a powerful face, defiant with latent wrath, and altogether suited to the purposes of his profession.

The razor was scraping at a jutting larynx—that resonant voice box famed throughout the Territory—when there was a tap at the door. Kilgore drew a towel about a hairy chest and stared out at Sarah.

"Waiting room is filling up, Kilgore. Young man to see you. Name of Clem Erskine. Just got off the stage, and he looks kind of peaked and hungry."

"What's his trouble?"

"No trouble. He's looking for a job. Got a letter of introduction from Joe Anslinger."

Kilgore reluctantly drew his attention from the mirror. "What's the boy look like?"

"Mournful, serious. Kind of eager, I guess." Sarah considered the matter further. "Raggedy, too. But dress him up and he could make an asset to the firm."

"Or a shill," Kilgore grunted. "Let him wait in the office, Sarah. Mebbe we could use a good spittoon cleaner. From the looks of that item, it's been seriously neglected by that damn Mexican. Is that brief done?"

"I finished it last night. Want to read it before you submit that memorandum to the court?"

"Why should I?"

"It might have mistakes."

"I dictated it myself. You transcribed. You've got my confidence, Sarah." Kilgore paused. "Still and all, you might let this boy go over the text while I finish this shaving. It'd give me something to question him on."

Sarah Hilleboe lingered. "They's someone else waiting."

"Yeah! Who?"

"Laurie Morgan."

Kilgore frowned. Laurie ran a sporting house up in Santa Fe, and Kilgore considered himself a friend of hers. From time to time he went to Laurie's place for consolation when the world was too much with him. But there had been a fuss last month, when Kilgore, in his cups, smashed up some furniture and insulted a couple of the girls, and he hadn't seen Laurie since. He wondered what had brought her to San Carlos, to his office. He had made good the damage, hadn't he? He had apologized most handsomely when he sobered up. Laurie could be vindictive at times, but he didn't think she was here to tax him with last month's fracas. But why else would she have come?

"Laurie, hey?" he repeated. "And no idea why?"

Sarah shook her head. "I'll tell you this, Kilgore. She looks mighty nervous."

"Let her wait. She's got plenty of time." He dipped his head over the basin and poured a pitcher of cold pump water over his head. "I'll see that Erskine boy in a minute," he said.

When Kilgore returned to his office, he found a travel-worn young man at the window reading a legal brief. The sun picked out the lines of a square, pleasant face that seemed thoughtful and intelligent. The boy was completely absorbed in the typescript he was reading.

"You Erskine?" Kilgore demanded.

The brief was lowered. "Yes, sir."

Kilgore flopped into his chair and favored the visitor with a penetrating stare. "Well, sit down!" he growled. Clem Erskine had a raw-boned and diffident air as he sank into the wooden chair and faced the older man. The lines of his face were dark and thoughtful. A lock of yellow hair tumbled rebelliously over a round, high forehead.

"Tired?" grunted Kilgore.

Erskine nodded. "Some, sir."

"How far did you come?"

"All the way from Leadville," said Erskine, and added, "sir." He shrugged. "I picked up the stage at Sweetwater. I had the middle seat all the way down, and I was hanging from that center strap, and my back is almost broke." Kilgore remained silent. "I'm not complaining, Mr. Kilgore, about anything except the cold. I near froze before I got to San Carlos." He broke off uncomfortably under the probe of the lawyer's searching eyes.

"That stage line ought to be abolished," Kilgore agreed finally, with no trace of a smile. "One of these days Dan McCandless will put the railroad through and these relics of barbarism will retreat into the unmourned past. Or mebbe he won't." The lawyer leaned back and stretched a pair of gaudy galluses. "You know why the woolly West has bred a race of superior men? Simple. The weather and the cooking kills off the weaklings. Only the supermen survive." Kilgore lit his first cigar for the morning—harbinger of many yet to come. "I gather you want to be a lawyer?"

"That's right, Mr. Kilgore."

"I won't ask why," said Kilgore grimly, "because it's an irrational desire, not subject to explanation. Either you'd feed me some highfalutin lies, or you'd give me the debased truth, neither of which would mean a damn thing." He pointed a cigar. "You think you got the makings?"

"If I didn't think so, Mr. Kilgore, I'd have stayed in Leadville and tried my hand at prospecting. I'm willing to work, and I think I've got a fair understanding of the profession."

"It's a tough business."

"I know."

Kilgore puffed meditatively until the office was filled with a rank smell. The younger man's face was drawn in thin, sensitive lines, but a dogged, obstinate twist about the strong mouth was a recommendation. A pair of gray eyes were alert and intelligent.

"You read that brief?" Kilgore asked.

Erskine nodded.

"What's your opinion?"

"The law says a bartender's obliged to eject anyone who's drunk and disorderly on his premises. This old man had a gun and he was dangerous. It wasn't your client's fault that the old man fell and broke his leg after he was ejected."

"Around here they don't like my client too much, because he's tight with credit," Kilgore said. "The other side claims he used unnecessary force on a harmless old man in his seventies. What's your answer?"

Erskine shook his head. "Right at that moment the old man wasn't harmless. And everyone admits he fell down himself. There just isn't ground for a complaint except if you're sentimentally involved."

Kilgore grinned. "Exactly. It don't matter that the defendant is a son of a bitch and the complainant a friendly old geezer. The law's the law, and we can't go awarding damages against folks we don't like." Kilgore took a puff and said, "Let me give you another proposition in legal ethics, Erskine. About ten years ago I had a call from the lockup where this prospective client was languishing in the toils. We've got a police force, you know, but the culprit had been picked up in the hills, so that made the offense the sheriff's case. Mike Duer had been freshly elected on a reform ticket, and he was hot then—hotter'n a cheap mail-order pistol. I don't care for Duer, nor him for me, but I've always made it a point to be polite with him, just in case I might have to turn my back on him some night in a dark alley. Also, it's important in this business to keep on a talking basis with sheriffs in general.

"Well, Duer was kind enough to advise that this was one case I wouldn't take. Aside from being hopeless, it was too smelly, he said, even for Kilgore. This was a case of parricide —the fiendish killing of an old man by his degenerate son. I gathered that the prisoner had been wandering around town proclaiming that he had killed his daddy back in the hills with an ax. Duer took him into custody and got a complete confession. Or so he claimed. He told me the case was so ironclad the criminal was yelling for Kilgore—the only lawyer in the whole damn territory that could save his miserable neck. Naturally I was interested."

Abruptly Sarah Hilleboe opened the door and looked in. "Kilgore, I think you ought to see Laurie," she said in worried tones. "She's getting awful itchy out there."

"Tell her to hold her water," said Kilgore calmly. "Just now I'm tied up with this young man."

Sarah sniffed, and slammed the door. Kilgore resumed his story. "Well, I never saw a more miserable, scrofulous, slack-jawed, vacant-eyed, trembling example of humanity at its worst. However, it was my duty to question him, and I did, and I put it straight without even first casually discussing the ancient doctrine of self-defense. I don't like to put a thought in a client's head unless the man's intelligent and reliable enough to handle it, which this one wasn't.

"He said, 'Counselor, I just can't lie to your face. That is the ax that killed the old man, and this is the hand that done it!'

"Disgusted though I was, I asked his motive. He said, 'Fact is, the old man was sickly and I just didn't think it would pay to carry him through the winter.' Then he asked me to represent him in court. Now, Erskine, here is my question," said Kilgore, pointing his cigar. "Assuming that the man can pay an adequate fee, is he entitled to a lawyer, and would you take the case?"

The younger man had been following with intense concentration. As the final question was put, he relaxed in visible relief. "Why, Mr. Kilgore," he said reproachfully, "I don't think there's any two ways about it. That exact case came up in Kentucky in 1847 and it got consideration from the American Bar Association when the Canon of Ethics was formulated. They said it was an extreme example, but every man is entitled to legal representation, even that one. In fact, the more guilty a man seems to be, the more he needs skilled help. I can give you the citation if you let me think on it a moment." Erskine paused. "In fact, I suspect you're giving me a reported case and not one of your own."

"Oh, it was my case, all right," Kilgore said, grinning at the thrust. "Question is, how far do you go in defending him?"

"I'd do everything in my power," said Erskine earnestly. "A lawyer who can't think that way has no business hangin' up a shingle."

"Even where the client personally confesses full guilt in unmistakable language?"

"Mr. Kilgore, a confession don't necessarily mean a thing. I would examine a confession with the utmost suspicion unless I knew the circumstances under which it was made. I say that a lawyer's job is to defend."

"You seem to be all worked up about this," said Kilgore curiously.

"I am."

"Why?"

"Because I've got a criminal record up in Colorado, Mr. Kilgore, where I wouldn't stand a chance of getting admitted to the bar," said the young man simply. "That's why Mr. Anslinger gave me this letter of introduction. He felt sure you'd be sympathetic to my problem."

There was a long moment of silence. Kilgore listened to the steady pounding of hoofs in the street.

"So you're a jailbird?" he growled finally.

"I've done time," Erskine admitted.

"And you expect—"

"I was only sixteen when I fell in with this thief," Erskine interrupted. "I was charged with stealing an overcoat from the Hotel Carleton."

Kilgore resumed smoking. "A petty thing to do."

"Yes, sir," said Erskine humbly.

"What was the coat worth?"

"Five dollars."

"How much time did you get?"

"One year in the state pen."

"What was the name of the judge?"

"Duquesne," Erskine said bitterly. "Forrest Duquesne!"

Kilgore nodded thoughtfully at the rancorous tone. "I heard all about Duquesne. He's a miserable son of a bitch. But I've got one question to ask. Did you actually steal that overcoat?"

"No, sir!"

"Did you tell that to the court?"

"I never had the chance, Mr. Kilgore. I pleaded guilty."

"You *what?*" Kilgore bellowed.

Erskine drew back at the passionate shout. "I—I told the court I was guilty," he faltered.

"You just told me you were innocent!" Kilgore stormed, leaping to his feet. "Now you admit you stood up in court and confessed to theft. Boy!" he went on in a deadly whisper, "are you trying to insult my intelligence?"

"No, sir!"

"Were you trying to insult the intelligence of that court?"

"No, sir!"

"Or to flout justice?"

"God damn it, Mr. Kilgore," said Erskine, rising hotly, "I didn't come down here to face these kind of tactics. I can explain—"

Kilgore stared with contempt. "Explain? You don't have to explain. You're about to tell me some cock-and-bull story you devised during that year you spent in the pen. I'm willing to bet you're out to claim some hotel dick caught you red-handed, probably wearing that coat—"

"Why, yes," said Erskine, taken aback.

"—and you told him you bought it in good faith from some

thief you met in a poolroom, and then— Sit down when I'm talking!" Kilgore bellowed, thrusting a meaty finger at the younger man's chest. "Only you didn't know the name of this thief, and the hotel clerk picked you out from working in the kitchen, and then you saw the jig was up and you broke down. Now, that's the truth, ain't it?"

"No, it ain't!" shouted Erskine, flaming with anger. "You've got no right calling me a thief till you know the facts!"

"No right? Ain't there a prior record of conviction?"

"Yes, but—"

"Ain't that conclusive in law?"

"Yes—"

"Are you asking me to go behind the record just on the unsworn say-so of a senile old fool like Joe Anslinger?"

"Yes, I am," said Erskine. "Mr. Anslinger's no fool, and he's not senile. He's still the best conveyancer in Colorado. He sent me here because he felt you'd be understanding and sympathetic."

"Now, why would I be sympathetic?"

"Because you once got the same raw deal yourself," said Erskine hotly, "an' you ought to know how a young boy might fall into a trap, and be conned by a smart detective into a false confession to suck up to the court! Everybody knows you got a record yourself—and how you got it!"

"Oh, they do?"

"Yes!"

Kilgore received the outburst with unusual mildness. He returned to the desk and opened a drawer. With deliberation, he took out a comb and a pot of perfumed grease, which he applied liberally to the thick black mane of his hair. When it gleamed in splendor, he faced the excited Erskine.

"If Kilgore's the kind of lawyer that's got a spotty and criminal past, will you kindly advise him why you're so anxious to hitch onto his coattails?"

Erskine hesitated under the baleful scrutiny of the older man. "Well, Mr. Anslinger felt I didn't have a chance in Colorado," he muttered, lowering his eyes. "But aside from all that, he told me you were the finest trial lawyer in the whole country and the best all-round man this side of Arkansas."

"He said that?"

"He sure did!"

Kilgore's chest swelled visibly. "Well, it's true enough," he mused. "I'll tell you what—"

The door opened with a bang. A bony woman of middle years strode into the room shaking her fist. "Kilgore! You son of a bitch! When I come down here to see you, I don't want to be kept waiting like some cheap trollop! That woman of yours kept telling me to sit tight, but—"

Sarah Hilleboe appeared at the door, panting. "I'm sorry, Kilgore. I just turned my back for a minute—"

"It's all right, Sarah. I don't mind talking to Laurie, long as she's here now."

The secretary withdrew, muttering. Kilgore looked at Laurie Morgan. "Well, what's so all-fired important, eh?"

Laurie Morgan was wearing a floppy bonnet and an ornate silk frock with white gloves and parasol to match. She had once been pretty, but the drooping pouches under her eyes showed the advance of the years.

Erskine rose uneasily and said, "I guess I'd better leave—"

Kilgore held up a paw. "I ain't finished with you, Erskine. Stick around. This anything you wouldn't want my young friend to hear, Laurie?"

She shrugged. "My daughter Honey's missing," she said simply.

"Honey missing?" Kilgore repeated. "Well, I'm not the constabulary, Laurie. When did you see her last?"

Laurie was twisting a handkerchief. "Not for about a month. That's when she sneaked away to visit Dade Rawlins here in San Carlos and I've been writing and writing her to come home, I've been that worried. And finally I decided to come and fetch her. But she's been gone three days."

"What does Dade say?"

"That's just it!" Laurie stood biting her thumb in distress. "Dade said she went off, and he didn't think to worry when she didn't come back at all. Somebody's keeping her out of sight."

"Who would you say?"

Laurie hesitated, and shot a glance of suspicion at Clem Erskine, who was watching the storm of mounting emotion with embarrassment. She drew a breath and answered, "Harry McCandless!"

Kilgore swung about and toyed a moment with a letter opener on the rolltop desk. The woman's face, he saw, was dead white, and the patches of rouge were like flame.

"Why tell me?" he asked slowly.

"Because you're that thick with his daddy," Laurie replied. "You'd know! And you might be covering up for that boy."

"You figure I'd do a thing like that?"

"I wouldn't put it past you!"

"That kind of reasoning is ridiculous, Laurie," said Kilgore with contempt. "I got better ways of spending time than participating in abductions. Kilgore's reputation and character refute that charge *eo instanti*—and what's more, you know it."

"Reckon so," Laurie said. "I didn't really mean it, Kilgore. But I'm so panicky I don't know what to do."

"Harry McCandless is practically a stranger to me," Kilgore said. "Just because I do legal work for his father don't mean I'm an expert on the boy's scrapes. What makes you so sure that Harry McCandless knows where she is? It might be any one of a hundred men, or women, in this town."

Laurie shrugged bewilderedly. "I'm only guessing."

"Did you get in touch with Harry?"

Laurie shook her head miserably. "You know what chance I stand to get on McCandless ground," she muttered. "I been sending in messages, and begging, and using the telephone, but I can't get any satisfaction out of any McCandless, there or here in town. Kilgore, I'm sick with worry."

Kilgore rose. His expression was one of concern—both over the woman's agitation as a mother, and because of the sudden stabbing pain lancing through his ear. He had some sort of infection in there, he figured. His gruff voice fell to a kindlier level as he motioned the woman to a chair and offered a tumbler of whisky. Erskine resumed his seat and tapped out a cigarette.

"Mind if I smoke, ma'am?" Erskine asked.

"Hell, no," said Laurie, coughing on her liquor.

Kilgore made small talk of a reassuring nature. When the woman's agitation had diminished, he said quietly, "Look here, Laurie. You get yourself back up to Santa Fe and go about your business. The police will find Honey, and if I have to I'll light a firecracker under Police Chief Valdez myself. Don't go off half-cocked about Harry McCandless. Honey could be off on a joy ride with anybody in town."

"She's a good girl," Laurie muttered.

"She'll turn up, in any case." Kilgore assisted Laurie to the door. "I'll be in touch with you. Maybe I'll ride up to Santa Fe next week and pay your place a little visit, if I'm still welcome there."

"Hell, Kilgore, I'm not holding a grudge."

"Glad to hear that. And don't worry about Honey."

When Laurie was gone, Kilgore turned to the younger man. "Erskine," he said solemnly, "that rolltop desk and that high-button sitting chair has just seen a morsel of the human drama that parades through a lawyer's office. Laurie Morgan's about as tough as they come in these parts—but I wouldn't take the load of misery that's in her heart for that little girl of her'n for all the tea in China."

"How old is her daughter?" said Erskine.

"Eighteen," said Kilgore. "A pretty little thing. Red hair and green eyes and a dancing little figure and the spirit of fun. Well!" he sighed. "She's probably off to some ranch house for the cold spell. Only way to keep warm this time of year." He shook his head. "Honey Morgan's bound to turn up with a new dress and a ribbon in her hair. Meantime, I've got to straighten out a legal argument in my mind. What about breakfast?" he concluded with feeling.

2.

To THE HUNDREDS of *campesinos*, the mountain peasants who lived in the lands surrounding San Carlos, a single Catholic priest was assigned to bring the comforts of a faith that had supported them and their fathers in a hard life. He was a young man, tall, thin, with sharp and sensitive features. A cold wind whistled about him as he rode his mule through the steep hills to the settlements that made up his parish. A shawl was gathered about his shoulders and neck. His mule was a fair animal, a gift of the commanding officer of Fort George, several hundred miles to the north. The priest's cassock sheltered the animal's brown flesh against the cold.

A box of toys rode the mule's back behind him—toy pistols, dolls, tops, jacks of Anglo manufacture—and in the same box, carefully wrapped, an inner box with bell and chalice for the ceremonials that lay ahead in small mountain villages that had been old when Coronado first came to the land. His breath came out in plumes, and his thoughts were inward, upon a young mother who had died a week earlier of pneumonia. He had had no medicines to give, only blessings, and she had died.

The dead mother was in the thoughts of young Father Enrique Crespin as he rode north into San Carlos to replenish his supplies. And because his thoughts were inward he failed to see the girl who lay supine on the ground, staring upward. Passing the body unknowingly, he rode on, thinking of the coarse hot food and straw pallet that he might expect for the night. He was deciding whether or not to press on to San Carlos when a boy came running barefoot, throwing pebbles at a mongrel dog. At the sight of the priest, the boy put a finger to his mouth and halted bashfully.

14

"God be with you, Manuelito," said the priest with a tired, kindly smile. "Will you tell *los padres* that I would like to rest the night?"

The boy turned and ran off. Turning, the priest followed him with his eyes, and caught a glimpse of red in a thicket of brush near the road. "*Ai de mí!*" he groaned. "*No es posible!*"

But it was, he saw, entirely possible. The girl lay on a rise of the hill overlooking a turbulent, shallow river. She seemed entirely at peace. Her legs lay sprawled and apart; one arm was thrown back in a helpless gesture, the other crossed at her breast. Her dress was pulled up to her hips, exposing her body. Her tongue peeped from between bruised, purplish lips.

Automatically the young priest pulled down the dress to cover the nakedness before him. He brought his hand over the corpse and with pity began to intone the liturgy of death as the sun dropped behind the mountain. He became aware that a man and woman stood behind him, muttering to themselves.

A twinkling of lights appeared in the distant city, and a change of the freezing wind attracted a coyote. A howl arose in the night. The priest led the way toward the small cabin, his face a weary mask.

"*Padre*, let me bring her into the *casa*," his peasant host pleaded. "It is not decent that she should lie out there like a beast."

"No, Manuel. This is something that must be reported to the authorities. It is clear that the girl was brought here after her death for a purpose. She is not to be moved."

"Will they suspect me?" asked the man fearfully.

"Of course not," the priest replied, vexed. "If you were responsible, you would have hidden the body in some *arroyo*. You would not have left her to be found so near the road on your own land."

"But they will question me," the man wept.

"Indeed, they will question you," the young priest agreed

grimly. "*Yo lo creo!* But if you move the body, they will surely arrest you, or something worse."

"Father?"

"*Si?*"

"Take the body with you?"

"Be quiet!" cried the priest. "And be sure of one thing, you foolish man. You are to watch the body for every moment of time until the authorities come."

Something in the young priest's tone was dangerous. The man bowed his head and swore the body would be guarded.

Suddenly his wife nudged him fiercely. "*Di la verdad!* Tell the truth!"

The priest glared suspiciously. "*Qué verdad?* What truth is this he is not telling?"

The man glanced venomously at his wife, then began to quiver in fright. Sternly, the priest pressed him with questions. Piecemeal, the true story emerged.

Three days before, a buckboard had appeared, driven through the night along the rutted road. Manuel Sanchez, the *campesino,* had observed and wondered at the distinctive sign painted on the buckboard—a brand in the form of the *crux ansata,* the looped cross, which told him that the buckboard came from the great rancho of the McCandless family, which stretched out below. That the *crux ansata* was an ancient symbol that went back to the Stone Age he had no idea. Nor would he have cared.

The buckboard had stopped not far from the Sanchez cabin. The driver, a man in sheepskins, had descended and taken out a bulky object wrapped in a woolen blanket of Navajo design, dragged it to a thicket of mountain laurel, then returned empty-handed to the buckboard and driven back toward the distant rancho. For two days the trembling Sanchez had avoided the thicket. On the third—no more than an hour or two before the priest's arrival—he had gone to it, and had found the body. He had told his wife, but the simple people had not known what to do. And then the *padre* had arrived, and himself discovered the body.

There was no point rebuking the people for their attempt

to conceal the story. Father Crespin said regretfully, "You should not have let her lie there these days. If the weather were not so cold she would have changed and become hideous. And the law should be told."

"We fear the law," Sanchez said hollowly.

The young priest retired. Before dawn he arose, said his prayers, ate the corn-meal preparation offered by the woman, and washed it down with hot coffee. He gave the shivering mule its head and followed the main road deeper into the valley. Sometime toward noon, he looked up to find himself before the brick building that housed the offices and lockup of San Carlos County.

It was a building he knew well. Almost as well as the courtyard in which twice he had mounted a scaffold with desperate men who had accepted his offices with resignation and defiance. Almost as well as the tall, hulking, cold-faced man who received his report.

Sheriff Mike Duer listened without a change of expression on his stony face. "Sanchez said there was the looped cross on the buckboard?"

"Yes. The McCandless brand."

"That's real interesting," Duer mused. "Yeah."

"The girl is from San Carlos, I am sure," the young priest said. "The hands are too soft for a girl from any rancho or farm out there. The nails have been cared for, and the dress is silk. I am sure she is from the city."

The sheriff made no direct reply. "The country ends a few miles past Sanchez' place. Maybe she was brought across the line from Croghan County."

The priest frowned in perplexity. The long ride had tired him, and even now, the warmth of a stove blazing with piñon logs, the wine and sweet biscuits and hot coffee brought by Pepita Duer, the sheriff's wife, had not brought ease of strain. He could not understand the sheriff's odd reluctance to take action.

"This is all nonsense," he said. "It does not matter where the girl came from, whether from Croghan or not. I am reporting this matter to your office, and the fact remains that the body was found within your jurisdiction. It is important to take action as soon as possible." He paused under the stare of cold, expressionless eyes. "I will tell you another reason why I think that girl came from this city."

"Yeah?"

"Her cheeks were painted with rouge. I cannot imagine where she might have come from except the American section of San Carlos. One more point. If she were Spanish, I would have recognized her. I did not. Now, how soon will you ride out?"

"I'm arranging for a buckboard," said the sheriff. "Given this cold snap, it don't matter how long that takes. She's been there awhile already, and she'll be waiting when we get there."

The priest arose. "I have told you whatever I know. Have you any idea who this girl was?"

"Mebbe," said the sheriff after a pause. He added, "But until I'm positive, I don't want to say more. This ain't the first body that's been dumped out in the hills, and it ain't the last. But I'll ask you to keep this to yourself until I notify you. I don't even want it known that the body was found. Or anything about that looped cross on the buckboard. Keep shut till I'm ready to move. Is that too much to ask, *Padre?*"

"No, it is not. Perhaps. In any case, I am on my way to Santa Fe, where I can be reached through the Archbishopric. I will be at your service. Remain with God, Sheriff Duer."

The young priest left, wrapping his shawl about his neck. Dry snow crystals swirled stingingly through the streets of San Carlos as he trudged across to the mission grounds.

San Carlos had a telephone system, one of the earliest installed in the Territory, and when Duer had finally put his thoughts in order he made a call to the police station in High Street. The phone rang half a dozen times. A poker game would be in progress, the sheriff knew, and his brother-in-law, Police Chief Valdez, would be reluctant to throw in his hand and come to the phone. On the seventh ring someone picked up.

"This is Joe Valdez."

"Mike."

"What can I do for you, eh?"

"You still got a feeler out for the Morgan girl?"

"*Naturalmente*. Kilgore told me yesterday that he wanted to see the girl back. He will keep bothering me. Why?"

"I might have a line on her."

"So?"

"You don't sound interested. I thought you just said Kilgore was personally bothering you about the disappearance."

"He is, and I don't go out of my way to cross him," Valdez said. "Nor to please him. It ain't the first time Honey's lit out. She'll come back. I figure she's warming her toes someplace out in the country. Or someone else's toes. What kind of line you think you have?"

"Maybe you'd better get over here."

"I'm supposed to be on duty here," Valdez complained. "I can't come running every time you snap your fingers, Mike. You don't run the police."

Duer glanced at the window and sighed. The noonday snow was piling up on the ledge. "All right, Joe," he said ominously. "I'll come over to your place, but I want to talk in private. Keep this to yourself."

Duer hung up and reached for his sheepskin. Within minutes he was at the police station. The poker game had resumed, but with an impatient nod Duer called his brother-in-law away and into the inner office, where in terse sentences he repeated the priest's narration.

Valdez was aghast at the news. "*Pobrecita!*" he murmured, shaking his head in dismay. "You're sure of this description?"

"I'm giving you the story the way I got it," Duer said. "That body is a good twenty miles out in the country—just waiting to be picked up. Frankly," he added sourly, "I'd normally go out on this myself, but you're the coroner, and I need your help. Let's keep the trip small. You, me, Doc Hewlitt, and Sam Dodge."

"The newspaperman? What for? And why the doc?"

"Because," Duer said with thinly veiled impatience. "I want Dodge to be along. I owe him a favor, and I know he can keep his mouth shut when he has to." Slowly and distinctly, knowing that his wife's brother had none of Pepita's wits, he went on, "Somebody took that girl out there on some purpose. I got no idea why that was done, but it smells weird, even from the description the priest gave me. If that buckboard really was a McCandless buckboard, this is gonna be a noisy case, and I want Doc Hewlitt to testify in your court from direct examination of the ground." He paused a moment. "While we're at it, get that Apache trailer and keep him sober long enough to do a job. He can examine the tracks."

"Charlie Bear? Ain't he at Fort Train?"

"Charlie's here in town." Duer paused. "Now what?"

Valdez scratched his head unhappily. "I don't know, Mike! You say this was a McCandless buckboard? Is any one of them involved?"

"Might be. The little girl was fooling around a lot with Harry McCandless." Duer went on stolidly. "I don't know where this is going, Joe, but we might—we just *might* find ourselves knocking on Dan McCandless' door with a warrant for that boy of his."

"Ah!" said Valdez with a look of pain.

"Just keep your mouth shut, and let's be careful each step of the way. Bringing a charge against any McCandless is easy enough, especially now with the way feeling is running against him. Making it stick is entirely another thing. How soon can you move?"

"I don't understand, but—"

"Don't bother understanding, Joe. Just remember this is big, and a lot of capital could be made in court of a sloppy investigation. Now get out and find that Apache, and the doc."

It was freezing in the hills, but the wind had died and the sun was brilliant on the sparkling landscape. The small group of men stamped against the cold, and blew on their fingers, and cursed softly to themselves. Charlie Bear, a fat old Apache from the Mescalero reservation, huddled in sheepskin, labored up the rise. His breath was blowing like steam in the dry cold.

"I'm that sorry, Sheriff," he said in fair American, rubbing his knuckles, "but it ain't much I can give you. The ground was wet and soft before the body got pulled off the road, and then it froze over. You can see the drag marks where the twigs snapped off."

Duer said, "How was she brought out?"

"Hard to say," the Apache replied, squinting toward the mountain road. "There's two or three tracks made by some wagons before the freeze-over, but also a couple of boot tracks in the mud that look like somebody from the city. Sure ain't no cowboy made these tracks. But whether they belong to the man or men who brought this poor girl, I couldn't say."

Duer and Valdez exchanged glances. Dodge, the editor of the San Carlos *Journal*, remained silent.

"Is that all?" Duer asked.

"Just about. You got to expect wagon tracks on a road, Sheriff, so they really don't tell too much about what took place."

A voice called from above. "Sheriff!"

Dr. Spencer Hewlitt had been crouching in the thicket, carefully studying the white, frozen body of the girl. Bits of turf were stuck in the mass of hair, and the silk dress was torn. But it was not these things that attracted attention. It was the pale scurf that spotted the mouth. Delicately, mastering his trembling hand, the physician picked up a morsel of friable consistency with the point of a knife.

"Plaster," he remarked.

"So it seems," Duer agreed. "Something she picked up from the ground, maybe? While she was being dragged?"

Dr. Hewlitt shook his head. "I wouldn't think so. The girl's mouth is filled with this stuff. I'll examine it more carefully when I get back to my office. But you wouldn't find builder's plaster like this out here in the country. They'd have wood or adobe houses here."

The sheriff crouched and poked a finger between the frozen lips. The thrust was resisted by teeth and stiff jaw muscles, but the effort extracted a sprinkle of crumbs. The sheriff glanced at the Apache trailer. "Charlie, why would a man stuff the girl's mouth with plaster?"

"Beats me," Charlie Bear said. "It sure ain't Apache."

"It ain't a white man's trick."

"That don't make it Apache," said the trailer stubbornly.

Duer ran a hand over the girl's clothing, studying the open eyes and the pieces of builder's lime strewn on the dress. "All right, Charlie," he agreed. "But what about some other tribe? Could this be some special kind of medicine? Ute, say? Or Navajo?"

The Apache shook his head. "They're so damned scared of the dead, they wouldn't linger. Besides, what would be the point?"

"Don't rule out the possibility," Sam Dodge said suddenly. "The idea might be to keep the spirit in the body. Like a plug, I mean. It would be consistent with tribal customs."

The Apache turned stolidly toward the newspaper editor. "It might be to choke the girl to death. Besides, there's something else right under your nose, and it sure don't point to any Indian."

"What are you talking about?" Duer asked.

The Apache knelt and picked up a pin with a curious design from the ground.

"These letters are Greek," said the doctor with surprise.

"Like a fraternity pin from college," Sam Dodge put in. "A fraternity pin—"

"Let's see," said the sheriff, snatching the pin and examining its gold texture with an intent expression.

Police Chief Valdez' slow mind had been following the conversation with some difficulty. But now he brightened and said, "Hey, there ain't but one college man in these parts, I mean who might have been in one of them Greek fraternities. And he's—"

"Sure. He's Harry McCandless," Duer said. "Now we don't need tracks of that buckboard. We got better proof that it was from the McCandless ranch." He glanced up with satisfaction. "I guess we got enough here, Doc. Suppose we get that corpse into the wagon and roll. You can do your cutting when we get back to town." He frowned. "A fraternity pin, a bloody Navajo rug, a dead girl with her mouth full of plaster. And the *campesino* who saw the brand on the buckboard. I bet Dan McCandless will come running back from New York in a hurry when he finds out what kind of a mess his boy's in *this* time!"

3.

THE SNOW had stopped, but the wind was still strong and afternoon gloom had descended as the corpse-laden wagon crept slowly into San Carlos. It came to a halt at the Lucero barn at the outskirts of the city. At a gesture from Duer, Charlie Bear dismounted and shoved open the side door of the barn. The Apache went in and turned on a kerosene lamp. Valdez and Doc Hewlitt lifted the frozen body down from the wagon and carried it inside.

Mike Duer stared meaningfully at the newspaperman. "Sam, you'd better get back to your office and proofread tomorrow's paper."

Sam Dodge frowned. "What about the autopsy?"

"I'll let you know, Sam. You go about your business now."

The newspaperman accepted the dismissal and moved away. Turning, Duer slowly went into the barn, his face a study in concentration. This was going to be a testing time for him, he knew. He had always been confident of his strength;

he was head and shoulders above men like Hewlitt and Valdez, and he knew it. But now the time was coming when he'd have to stand up against Dan McCandless himself, the most powerful man thereabouts, and probably against Jake Kilgore, too. There was no sense wishing none of this had ever happened, Duer thought bleakly. It *had* happened, and as sheriff of San Carlos County he was duty-bound to see it through to the end.

On a pair of rough planks lay the girl's body, extended and rigid, the long red tresses trailing to the straw-colored floor. Alongside, the doctor was opening his case of surgical instruments. The kerosene lamp flickered balefully overhead.

"Get the dress off her," Doc Hewlitt said.

Valdez and the Apache stripped the dead girl. She had been a lovely little thing, but there was nothing appealing about that frozen nakedness now. Duer eyed the small dead breasts, the slim hips. He turned suddenly to Charlie Bear, realizing the Apache tracker had no place here, and said, "Charlie, you get yourself back to the fort now." The Apache looked unhappy about being sent away. Duer flipped him a silver dollar and said, "Here. Get your guts warm before you go."

"Thanks, Sheriff."

"Ain't that a little foolish, Mike?" Valdez asked after the Apache was gone. "He'll get loaded and spout the story all over the place."

Duer regarded his brother-in-law thoughtfully. "I think he might," he replied, "but it might take a bit of time before the story spreads around. You can expect Charlie to get drunk, but he won't babble until it becomes convenient. A little public sentiment can't do the cause of justice any harm."

Dr. Hewlitt let his long, trembling fingers smooth back the dark-red tresses of the dead girl. "I could use a drink myself," he muttered.

"Afterward, Doc," Duer said. "What's wrong?"

"Don't know," said Hewlitt. "But I feel right badly. I remember this little girl."

"Go on," said Duer. "You just give me a criminal cause of death and that's all I ask."

Hewlitt was another who wouldn't spill information when boozed up, Duer thought. The doctor was a wreck, a shameless alcoholic, drunken graduate of the St. Louis Medical School, abortionist, discredited refugee from complaints of the Medical Society of Missouri. But he was the best San Carlos had at the moment. They would have to make do with him. He knew his trade, after all.

Hewlitt blew on his hands, then searched in his bag for his bone saw. "I'm going to open up her head," he announced. "She's got a fractured skull. I want to see what it looks like inside there."

Long minutes passed in silence as Hewlitt sliced into the cadaver, pausing from time to time to rub his hands together. He looks like a cadaver himself, Duer thought. The doctor was six feet three, and probably weighed no more than one fifty, if that much. Instead of eating, he drank. It gave him energy, but no fat.

The sheriff stared with fascination at the interior of the girl's skull. Joe Valdez muttered an inaudible prayer and turned his eyes away squeamishly. Hewlitt nodded in satisfaction, talking to himself at a steady clip.

"Well?" Duer asked finally.

Hewlitt looked up from his task. "She was hit on the head, that's what killed her. Fracture of skull caused rupture of the dura mater—that's this, here, the tough lining around the brain. An effusion of blood from the dura compressed the brain, causing death. You can see extensive hematoma—blood clots—yourself. Of course, to be sure, I've got to examine the other vital organs, but the blow to the skull would be a competent producing cause of death."

Joe Valdez crossed himself. *"Pobrecita!"*

Mike Duer nodded grimly. "I want a thorough job, Doc. But we'll take that for now. Was she raped?"

"That isn't so easy, her being dead three or four days and all. But with this cold spell, the signs might hold and I could tell with a microscope. Best I can give you is an educated opinion."

"Go on."

Hewlitt indicated a series of bruises and scratches on the face and neck. "She was attacked, and she defended herself."

"Good enough," the sheriff said. "Now you can fill in the details—but I've got a strong hunch that you're going to find that this poor little thing was treated like an animal before she was killed. Joe," he added, turning his back, "tell your woman to fix dinner for you pronto. You're going to take this news to Santa Fe yourself. I want you to tell Laurie Morgan that we found her little girl and that she can come and bury the body. Doc, you finish up and I'll send a deputy to watch the body when you're done until we figure something out."

Valdez paused at the barn door, staring into the freezing cold. "You going to make an arrest tonight, Mike? This is shaping up to quite a case."

"Not tonight," said Duer. "This is one case I want to be very careful about. Tomorrow morning I'll ride up to Wa-po-nah and ask Harry McCandless some questions. Maybe he can answer, maybe he can't. I want to be fresh and rested when that moment comes. I've got a simple question to ask. What was this fancy little pin on the poor little girl's body doing out there in the cold?"

"Honey?" said the old man.

The strong knocking continued at the door of the wooden shack on the far side of the city.

"Honey?" the old man repeated.

"It ain't Honey," a deep voice replied. "Open up, Dade! We're freezing our ears off."

"Sure, sure," said the old man hastily. He paused a moment on the edge of an unmade bed, panting from the exertion and breathing out the fumes of cheap whisky. After a moment, he arose and drew about his shoulders a tattered shawl and shuffled across the splintery floor to the door.

"Come in, Sheriff," he muttered. "What in the world brings you here? I was hopin' it would be Honey. You ain't got any news?"

Mike Duer strode in from the black night, bringing a gust of cold air, and stood in the center of a slovenly room that smelled of sweat and beans and cheap whisky. Visible beyond was another, smaller room decorated with portraits of actors and actresses and a devotional picture of the Virgin of Guadalupe. The old man stood blinking in the presence of his visitor, and both were conscious of a blue frock thrown across the bed in the little room.

Dade Rawlins was a drifter, a man who lived without any apparent means of support. He was in his late sixties, probably, and it was said that he had made a pile in the Seventies in prospecting and had stashed it away, living like a miser on his hoard. A more plausible theory was that a brother in San Francisco sent him a small check every month to keep him alive and far away from California.

"You got some news about Honey?" Rawlins repeated.

"Yes."

"She's found?"

"Yes."

"Oh, where?"

"Out in the country."

Rawlins took a deep breath. "I'm that relieved, Sheriff," he said earnestly. "I was beginning to get that worried. The girl's mother has been writing, and wiring, and pestering, and I just didn't know what to tell her. Oh, now! Where was she found?"

"A *campesino* found her twenty miles out of town a few days back. Took his time about letting anyone know."

Rawlins stared at the sheriff, and as the import of the message sank in, he began to tremble. "Oh, my, Sheriff!" he muttered. "Something's happened to that little girl? She's dead?" He drew a shaking hand over a whiskered face. "Oh, my! Oh, my! I can't believe it. I was that fond of the child." He looked up in the dim light of a smoking kerosene lamp. "Does Laurie know?"

"She will," said Duer grimly. "I sent Joe Valdez to Sante Fe to give her the news. Now, Dade, I'd like to ask you a question."

Rawlins seemed in a daze, and the question was repeated before he shook himself and motioned the sheriff to a chair. Duer said, "Which bed did she use?"

Rawlins pointed dumbly to the inner room. Duer studied the trembling chops, the rheumy eyes, the blinking and gummy corners of a shaking mouth. He asked, "Were you messing with that girl?"

Rawlins raised a trembling hand. "As God is my witness, Sheriff!" he said earnestly, "she was just a pretty little thing I liked to see around the house. I'm old enough to be her grandfather. It's a terrible question to ask an old man."

"It's important to know."

Rawlins was struck with a horrible thought. "Why? What difference does it make?" He paused, aghast. "Somebody killed her?" he whispered. Duer nodded. "Who? Who?"

"I don't know. I'm trying to find out. When did you last see her, Dade?"

"About a week ago."

"A week? Lord, man, and you didn't tell anyone she was gone that time?"

"I wasn't worried," said Rawlins defensively. "Wagon come down from Wa-po-nah to get her, and she lit out when she heard the jingle bells. I figured she was going to spend a few nights with Harry McCandless. No reason for her to report to me."

"And that was the last you saw?"

"Yes, sir!" Rawlins drew a trembling hand over his face. "Sheriff, I feel responsible—letting her go off like that with Harry McCandless. He's got a lot of book learning, but he's a wild one. I don't know what I was thinking about. Sheriff—" He paused, not daring to utter the thought.

"Go ahead," the sheriff invited.

"Do you think Harry McCandless had a hand in this thing? Excuse me," he added hastily, "maybe I shouldn't ask a terrible question like that."

"Why not?"

Rawlins looked aside, unable to meet the sheriff's penetrating stare. "Don't know," he said in a low voice. "Harry McCandless has done a lot of wild things in his time. But I don't know of any harm in him. At least, not from the stories I hear going around. His nose is too much in books— Excuse me!" Rawlins looked aside and suddenly burst into tears, wiping his eyes on a dirty bandanna and rocking with grief. "That child! That poor little child!"

"All right," Duer said finally. "Get some clothes on, Dade. I'm going to keep you in my nice warm lockup where I can have a comfortable talk and get all the details. I give you two minutes to get ready."

No sleeping was being done by Jake Kilgore that night. His civil case had been decided during the day, speedily and without recourse to jury, when counsel for the plaintiff had admitted he didn't have much of a case. The defendant, out of his own generosity and relief, had offered to give the plaintiff a few dollars, not as damages but merely as an expression of sympathy, and it was understood that the old man was welcome in the saloon when he recovered from his broken leg, so long as he behaved himself. Kilgore collected his fee and walked out of the courtroom with his new assistant, Clem Erskine.

"A whole lot of work wasted," Erskine said. "A brief prepared, lawyers kept busy, and the case should never have come to court in the first place."

"Agreed on the latter, but not on the former," Kilgore said. "Work is never wasted. Without me, they might have hung damages on my esteemed client simply because he's an unpopular bastard. This way I forced everyone to admit that there was no case, and we've upheld at least a tiny shred of the law around here. I propose we walk over to the cantina and see if there's any card playing action tonight."

Erskine smiled. He had been covertly warned by Sarah Hilleboe to try to keep Kilgore away from his cronies, but he saw there was no use trying. He went along, staked to a hand by Kilgore. Within an hour, Clem had won clear his stake and had paid the lawyer back. By midnight, a substantial stack of silver dollars and even a gold eagle or two reposed on the table in front of Clem. Kilgore beamed with paternal pride, even though some of the money was his own. His apprentice was a good man with the cards. That bespoke potential skill at the law, too. It was a good sign.

Morning, cold, bright, and clear. And first thing in the morning, Sheriff Mike Duer was at the brick building in the center of town whose façade proclaimed it to be the headquarters of the San Carlos Irrigation and Development Company—the main enterprise of Dan McCandless.

Perhaps a dozen men were at work at the lower floor as the sheriff entered. He strode quickly past bookkeepers and clerks, and up to the second-floor office that overlooked the plaza. Ornate gold letters declared the office to be that of Frederick Hicks, the general manager.

The door was half open. Duer knocked anyway. Frederick Hicks glanced up from a welter of letters and slipped back a pair of arm garters.

"Can I help you, Sheriff?"

"I suppose you might," Duer said, entering the office. He glanced significantly at Hicks's secretary, a plump, good-natured woman named Flora Bowen. "Like to talk to you alone, Hicks."

Hicks was a slim, long-faced man with a waspish air about him. An underling by birth, Duer decided. Hicks had authority, but he was really only Dan McCandless' puppet.

"If you insist, Sheriff. We can go into Mr. McCandless' office."

"McCandless senior?"

"That's right." Hicks led the way into an adjoining office, large and expensively furnished. Green shades threw the room into shadows, but a rich glow was cast up by the colors of a large Navajo rug. A Gainsborough gazed at a full-length portrait of Dan McCandless, across a scene more suited to scholarly pursuits than to commerce. Rich woods and marble sculpture were distributed with flamboyant taste.

"Now, Sheriff, what's the trouble?"

"Nothing very much. I don't suppose the vice-president of this firm is around here this early in the morning, by any chance?"

"Harry?" Hicks smiled. "We don't see too much of Harry around here."

"Oh, really?"

"He comes in every now and then. Smokes his father's cigars, snoops around a little, reads a little, then leaves."

"I thought he took a more active part in running the business," Duer said. "After all, he's the heir."

Hicks nodded. "His father's unhappy about that. But Harry's not cut out for business, I'm afraid."

Duer glanced around the office. He had never been in Dan McCandless' private office before. The desk was of intricate design, inlaid in gold leaf. Ornate crystal fixtures dangled from the ceiling. The room reeked of money, disbursed with a lavish hand.

Duer said easily, "You mean he's just in and out of here, eh? When did you see him last, for example?"

"I'd say about a week ago," Hicks replied.

"As long ago as that?"

"Yes. He came in and wanted to have a look at the books. Nobody but old Dan is supposed to have access to the books. Dan never said anything about letting Harry see them, so I refused. Rather rudely, I'm afraid. I told him to go back to his own office and cut out paper dolls, because that was about all the good he did around here."

Duer laughed. "I bet he didn't like that."

"I bet he didn't," Hicks agreed. "But he knows I'm in charge here when Dan's away, and he's afraid to buck my authority. So he went out. He hasn't been back since. That was—let me see—yes, at least a week ago. But I'm sure you didn't come here to discuss the inadequacies of the heir to the business, Sheriff. What exactly is it you'd like to talk to me about?"

"Precisely what we've *been* talking about," Duer said. "And you've been very helpful. Thank you most kindly, Mr. Hicks. Much appreciate the time."

And he turned and left. Down below, in front of the building, he called a deputy over.

"Pete, go round up half a dozen men or so, and make sure

they're armed. We're going to ride up to Wa-po-nah and take Harry McCandless into custody."

The deputy nodded and rode quickly away.

Upstairs, Frederick Hicks gaped in bewilderment for a moment in Dan McCandless' office. Then his brain started to function again. If the sheriff had come here to ask questions about Harry, then Harry must be in some sort of trouble. Hicks knew where his responsibility lay. He had to phone Wa-po-nah and warn the boy.

He reached for the telephone.

 4.

HARRY McCANDLESS had awakened at his usual time that morning and lay in bed before breakfast. He could hear the whinnying of a horse in the stables. A cockerel crowed in one of the outhouses. He heard the stirring of the servants.

A light tap at the door. "Mr. Harry?"

"Yes, Julian?"

"You want to sleep this morning?"

"No, why?"

"You were up kind of late."

"How late was that?"

A moment of hesitation. "I'd say past two."

Harry considered the matter. "I've got too much to do this morning, Julian. I'd better make an appearance at the office. I'll be down in ten minutes."

"I'll have breakfast ready," said Julian.

Harry closed his eyes, waiting for the dull ache of the hangover to pass. How much had he been drinking? Not much at all. It was the other two who had gone for that bottle of bourbon—over his protests, he reflected. The whole idea of that party had not been his.

Or had it?

He threw back the covers and stalked into the marble bathroom that projected over the east wing. Deep lines rimmed his flashing, intelligent eyes as he prepared to shave at the open window. A tank on the roof gave him running water—a luxury in the Territory. But, then, the great mansion of dressed stone with its scores of guestrooms and murals and vast hearths and rare wooden floors was rather fabulous. Wa-po-nah had been built ten years before, when Dan McCandless had moved the family down from Colorado to take up residence permanently in the Territory of New Mexico.

Dan (he never thought of his father except in this way) had acquired the old Lucero ranch property of ten thousand acres at a time when it seemed that the governorship of the Territory lay within his grasp, subject only to the consent of the President of the United States. The great castle had been erected not far from the old Lucero headquarters ranch house, and surrounding the huge structure were hundreds of acres planted to pears and apples in new and improved strains imported from New York, California, and England. Since that first day several hundreds of thousands of acres had been annexed to the original purchase.

A kettle of hot water had been brought earlier by Julian to the marble sink. It was still steaming gently as it ran into a soap cup, a gift from Dan McCandless to Harry on his sixteenth birthday. The cup was pure gold.

He did a bad job of shaving. His skin was tender and scratchy, shredding easily. Blotting the oozing blood on a towel, he returned to the bedroom. His clothes were neatly laid out for him—a suit of fine worsted made in Bond Street, with the deep pockets and long lines of the period; soft shirt, wing collar, bow tie. On the dresser were gold cuff links and a slim watch of Swiss import attached to a fine gold chain.

Julian smiled approvingly as Harry came down the winding stairs, rubbing his eyes blearily. "I say!" the Negro remarked. "You surely would pass on Wall Street, Mr. Harry!"

As usual, Julian was waiting for his arrival, serviette over his wrist, glancing reproachfully at the grandfather clock, which proclaimed that Harry was five minutes late.

"This isn't Wall Street," said Harry with a grin. "And this rig isn't my idea of the way to dress out here."

"You are every inch the businessman," said Julian, inclining his head in a courtly gesture. "I am sure Mr. Dan would be more than pleased."

Letters and the Santa Fe paper were waiting at the breakfast table—a long refectory table in Chinese Chippendale, which stood in a great, vaulted dining room paneled in costly woods. Harry lifted the uppermost letter. It had been postmarked in New York City five days earlier. The bold scrawl was more than familiar. He looked up as Julian returned from the kitchen with a silver platter heaped with rashers of crisp bacon and a mound of scrambled eggs.

"How did this letter get here?" he asked.

Julian paused in serving the food to explain that the driver of the stage from Sweetwater had recognized the handwriting and had given the letter to one of the Wa-po-nah *rancheros* somewhere along the road that skirted the McCandless property. McCandless mail got special handling. It was a federal offense to circumvent the post office this way, but the drivers risked it for Dan McCandless.

"I guess he expects a handout at Christmas," Harry said.

"Quite likely," said Julian gravely. They exchanged glances. The McCandless enterprises had not been going well this cold season. Harry's laugh was harsh and unpleasant.

"This may be a hard Christmas all around, Julian."

"Yes, *senorito*," said Julian, returning silently to the kitchen. Harry finished breakfast, letting the envelope remain unopened before him, propped against a pitcher of cream. A shudder went through his body. It was the thought of Julian, he told himself; or rather, the silent tread that took the old man through the great house like a specter. Had there ever been a time without Julian? he wondered.

Finally he opened the letter.

Dear Harry:

No one suggested to me that you leave the university and come into the company. The idea was my own, because I wished, under the extraordinary way in which you have been conducting yourself, to make sure that you followed a course of action that would build that strength of character and knowledge of people and the intimate details of business methods that will enable you to carry some of the heavy responsibilities that will one day prove too much for me.

Of course you are a free agent. Have I ever said or done anything to indicate the contrary? The fact is that you have always enjoyed perfect freedom—and from the earliest age you have been encouraged to make your own decisions. I don't know what part of me you have inherited, but you have the brilliance of your mother's family, and there is nothing you could not achieve if you were to set your mind on goals worthy of your gifts.

But what have you done? You went back to the university last fall only after President Hawkes had listened to the most desperate pleading on my part. I suppose he expects some gift for his endowment fund, and one day I will meet that obligation. Even so, I had the greatest difficulty persuading him to overlook your disgraceful marks in courses that you had picked out yourself. *Philology. Medieval French poetry.* I almost suspect you chose these courses to challenge every sensible plan I ever tried to devise for your benefit. I must admit that calculus will be useful to you as an engineer—but when will you take the solid courses in that field that will benefit you when the time comes to assume greater duties in connection with the business?

I am not easily hurt, but I was wounded, really wounded, to learn that you had virtually ceased to be a student during this semester. I was told that you cut classes, spent your time in taverns with low women, and depended on your native wit in the few classes you saw fit to attend. Your expulsion hardly seems unmerited.

I daresay I expected nothing else when I left you at Wa-po-nah for this trip to New York. I can hope only that you are attending the office, using your brilliance for something better than your customary debaucheries. It is breaking my heart.

Now, enough scolding. I don't enjoy it—and it keeps me steeped in gloom. New York is cold today, with a damp fog blowing in. Our hotel is only a short distance from Wall Street and the offices of Mr. Gould, on whose pleasure I dance attendance every day. I have never found myself in such difficulties before. After years of pouring hundreds of thousands of dollars into the company—the soundest enterprise in the Territory—these vultures in Wall Street will not advance one hard nickel to a land of riches. I hardly mind for myself. I have made millions, and I have lost millions, and I'll make them again. What hurts is the evidence of hatred and mistrust from all those who have backed the company with hard cash.

Money is there, but Frick and Gould are using this terrible depression as an excuse to close the door on me. I am so extended that I have been pinched at times for pocket money. Silver has gone down, and my resources are lower than they have ever been since I left Canada for the States. I am even embarrassed to leave this drafty hotel for fear that the bill will prove more than I can pay—and I dare not seek to borrow a cent in this town. It would be quite disastrous if my position were known.

I have a feeling that Joel Tilley is somehow responsible for this loss of credit. I am sure he is working in the background, spreading rumors and capitalizing on the general dissatisfaction, but these smiling bankers never mention his name, and of course I must preserve an appearance of indifference against the tactics of that guttersnipe.

Now one last word. I have never before gone into these difficulties. It is not my policy to discuss matters of adversity, but I must tell you that the present situation can well be disastrous. I have many enemies in the Territory. Long before you were born, I participated in events that all of us want to forget, but people have long memories and the first sign of weakness will cause them to turn on me like wolves. You must keep these revelations to yourself—and above all conduct yourself like a man of character and dignity as a representative of the family.

Should you involve yourself in any difficulties while I am away, the man to consult is Kilgore. He is a difficult man, and disapproves of you, but he is fundamentally honest and can be trusted. I prefer, of course, that you do not require his services in any matter. Now, Harry, enough. I am pleased that you are punctual in attendance at the office, and I hope that the shock of your expulsion from the university will persuade you to take a new course of action.   .

> Your loving father,
> DANIEL McCANDLESS

Harry read the letter through with a growing frown, and by the time he was finished his hand was shaking. The crisp, ringing tones of his father's voice seemed to be echoing in the room, and then the silent tread brought Julian and there materialized a silver pitcher at his side.

"What the hell!" cried the surprised Harry.

Julian said with dignified reproach. "You always take a third cup, Mr. Harry."

The telephone began to ring. Harry rose and went past the smiling servant into the library, where the telephone stood on a desk of its own in the big room filled with rare and valuable books dealing with the history of Mexico and South America. It was the first telephone introduced in the Territory, strung on a private line from Wa-po-nah into the office of San Carlos years ago, preceding the first public telephone exchange in the Territory by some six months.

"Yes?"

"Hicks, Mr. McCandless. Thought you'd like to know that Sheriff Duer was just up here. Asking a lot of questions about you."

"About me, eh? What did you tell him?"

"The truth. That I hadn't seen you in a week."

"And what did he do?"

"Thanked me and left. I don't know how to interpret his visit, Mr. McCandless."

"All right," Harry said slowly. "Thanks for telling me. Is that all?"

"Yes, Mr. McCandless."

"Very well, Hicks. I won't be in today, either. I guess maybe the sheriff will come to visit me."

He hung up and turned to stare into Julian's deep-set, wrinkled visage. Julian seemed to be awaiting orders.

"Mike Duer may come here this morning," Harry said. "See that he gets shown in without any trouble. I'll be in my study."

"Very good, Mr. Harry."

Harry's own study was a smaller one adjoining the library. Its walls were lined with books in a dozen languages, for in his intense way Harry had become quite a linguist. Spanish, French, Italian, Portuguese, Latin and Greek, German, a smattering of Dutch, a bit of Hebrew, even Rumanian had . come within his ken. He selected a book at random—Antonio Herrarra's *Histórica general de los hechoes de los castellanos en las Islas i Terra Firme del Mar Oceano*, a leather-bound volume three hundred years old—and leafed through its stiff pages, waiting for Duer.

The sheriff arrived an hour later, with a posse of seven. They were shown into the study, all of them—blunt, rough-looking men, obviously awed by the splendor of the Mc-Candless home. And there was a sense of relief on their faces, too, relief that they had not encountered gunplay from the Spanish *rancheros* and *vaqueros,* who were loyal followers of the household. Not even the sheriff of San Carlos County could bluster into Wa-po-nah with impunity.

Harry faced the men, staring at the hard-eyed sheriff and

avoiding any direct contact with Duer's gaze. Harry was conscious of his own dandified appearance, contrasted with the rough dress of the men who confronted him. But he managed a smile and said lightly, "May I offer you a cigar, Sheriff? And your men? These are my father's best *habanos.*"

"I'm here on business," said Duer. "Ain't you interested to know what it is?"

Harry sank into a brocaded chair and nodded pleasantly. "I'm intensely curious."

"I want to talk to you about Honey Morgan, McCandless."

Harry noted the dropped title of respect. He finished lighting his cigar and blew a cloud of smoke to the ceiling. "Sheriff, you're not going after the church vote, are you?" he asked with an air of amusement. "I could name a dozen women you ought to be asking about. What's Honey done to interest you?"

Duer exchanged glances with Levi Hughes, his chief deputy, before making a considered answer. "She's dead, McCandless, that's what interests me."

"Dead?"

Harry looked about at the circle of glum men. "This is some joke!" he exclaimed. "Honey can't be dead. Why would she be dead? How could that possibly have happened?"

"We're trying to find out," said Duer quietly.

"Oh, this is awful! Awful!" said Harry in a shocked tone. "What happened?"

"She was murdered," said Duer.

"Murdered?" Harry echoed. "How? Who would do a thing like that to Honey?" His boyish face was suddenly ashen. Duer got up heavily and eyed the younger man with thoughtful skepticism. "McCandless, it's a pretty good act you're giving me," he said appreciatively. "Under other circumstances, I might admire it, but the fact is that Honey was last known to be alive right here in Wa-po-nah. She was here on your invitation. I'd like you to come along with me to town and answer a few questions."

"Do you think I have something to do with it?" Harry asked curiously.

"I'm just asking you to come and answer questions," Duer replied stolidly.

Harry backed away. "Now, just a moment. Is this an arrest, Sheriff? Do you have any grounds to arrest me?"

"Some," said Duer. "I'm just asking you to come along in a peaceful way. In any case, you're going to come along. I'll have to decide whether or not to make an arrest."

The two men exchanged glances.

"Sheriff," said Harry finally, "I don't know why you would want to take this line. I haven't even *seen* Honey Morgan in the past two weeks. Isn't that right, Julian?" he added suddenly, turning to the house servant who had stepped quietly into the room.

"Mr. Harry—" Julian began.

"Save your alibi for later," said Duer heavily. "If you won't come quietly, I'll put you under arrest. Are you coming?"

Harry McCandless stood for a moment in the middle of the room, thinking deeply, and a grim, lurking smile finally formed. "May I take a book with me, Sheriff?"

"You'd better take a nightgown and a toothbrush," said Duer. "It may be a while before you get back."

"I wonder if you know what you're doing," said Harry with amusement. "Is it really a wise thing for you to do? To walk into McCandless property clanking those guns and muddying up our fine hardwood floors? You're the sheriff of San Carlos County and I'm Dan McCandless' son. And when this is over, I'll still be Dan McCandless' son—but you may not be the sheriff of San Carlos County."

"Pick up your book," said Duer. "All this foolish talk is being remembered. At the right time, we'll see what it means."

"If it weren't so tragic," said Harry, "it would be amusing. I'm sorry only that Honey Morgan should be the pretext for this farce." He put a slim hand to the bookshelf and reached up to the German section and drew out a volume: *Wilhelm Meister* by Goethe, and turned with a smile. "Some day, Sheriff," he said lightly, "you ought to read a book. *McGuffey's Reader*, First Grade, if it's not too difficult. You would find it an experience. And now, let's see if you can make this stick."

5.

"Dad?"

Carlotta McCandless stood at the door, listening to the sounds of a heavy man pacing in confined quarters. She frowned and knocked again. The footsteps came to a halt.

"Yes, Carlotta?" said a deep voice.

"Getting late," she said with concern.

"Just got to put on these studs," said the voice. "Look after your mother."

Carlotta waited as the footsteps receded and then turned to the full-length mirror swiveling in a walnut frame. For all her independence of mind, she had a healthy interest in her feminine appearance. She went into a low curtsy, keeping an eye on the neckline of her gown. It struck her as amusingly frivolous—more Newport and New York than San Carlos and Radcliffe. The whole problem of womanly modesty was too tiresome, she thought, in the light of social issues of crucial importance, which were more her concern. However, she reflected, unmarried girls were supposed to show some modesty, especially those with Spanish blood as well as American. With a grimace, Carlotta brought together the revealing lines of her attractive silk gown. She was not in the marriage market, she reflected, with a toss of her head, and she could afford to show reserve.

She was almost ready to leave now. In the adjoining rooms of their suite at the old Waldorf, Dan and Isabella McCandless were dressing also. The trio would eat at Delmonico's with Mr. and Mrs. Jay Gould; then, over to the Metropolitan Opera House for a performance of *Faust*. And finally home around midnight. Carlotta was growing weary of New York high life, with its pretensions and its hollow pomp. She was reluctantly

41

debating the question of a dab of face powder for the occasion when she heard the knocking at the outer door.

Frowning, she closed the door and turned the telegram over in her hand. *Bad news from home.* The conviction sprang immediately to her mind. It could be nothing else. A fire at the ranch? Some new financial squeeze at the irrigation and development company? Did it involve Harry?

"Oh, Dad—" she began.

She started toward her father's room. Then she stopped and shook her head. He had enough worries at the moment. He was counting on this evening with Jay Gould to effect a change in his fortunes. But Dan McCandless would need to be in full possession of his powers if he wanted to impress the New York railroad magnate. Dan McCandless had the cold eyes and impassive face of a man whose life had been devoted to the financial world and its struggles and he could well carry off any bad news. But what if it involved Harry?

The telegram, short and brief, was from Julian DuVivier:

MISTER HARRY ARRESTED BY SHERIFF DUER IN CONNECTION WITH DEATH OF GIRL NAMED MORGAN STOP WIRE INSTRUCTIONS

Carlotta sat and considered the telegram with disbelief. Its very terseness was eloquent. It was cryptic, reserved, warning. It bespoke an incredible intrusion on the McCandless power, a blow struck at the face of authority, the violation of a legend. Harry had been troublesome before—but on a schoolboy level, never anything like this. What lay behind the action of the sheriff?

At twenty-three, three years Harry's senior, Carlotta had come to expect almost anything of her brilliant wastrel of a younger brother. She knew about his affair with Honey—knew much more about it than her parents did. She knew other things he had done—women and girls he had seduced, money he had stolen from his father, everything. He confided in her as much as he did in any human being. She knew Harry to be moody, unpredictable, arrogant, self-indulgent. But she also knew that he was a weak person, unable to defend himself. Whatever trouble he was in now, he needed help—and needed it from someone in San Carlos, not from family thousands of miles away.

She hesitated. Then, picking up the room telephone, she asked for Western Union. The telegram she dictated to Julian was terse. It instructed him to hire Jake Kilgore to represent her brother. It added that the McCandlesses would return from New York as soon as possible.

Folding the telegram from Julian, she thrust it into a dresser drawer. Her father would understand why she had kept it from him, and he would approve of the action she had taken. It would be a bitter homecoming tonight after the opera, she thought.

"Carlotta?" said Dan McCandless from behind his closed door. "Are you ready?"

"Just about, Father," she said as calmly as she could.

"Go knock on your mother's door, then, and tell her I'm ready to leave."

"Yes, Father."

The estrangement between her parents had deepened while in New York, she thought. Her father and mother scarcely spoke to one another now, except in public. Carlotta wondered whether the danger to Harry would tend to pull the family together once again. She hoped so. She went down the carpeted hall to knock on Isabella McCandless' door.

It was the following morning, another cold day in San Carlos. News was not yet in circulation of Honey's murder or of Harry's arrest. Jake Kilgore had noticed much activity in the vicinity of Sheriff Duer's office, but as yet he had sought no explanation for it. His curiosity was dulled by the ceaseless cold and by the painful throbbing in his ear.

"Mastoiditis!" said Sarah Hilleboe with concern. "If you don't call the doctor, I will!"

"God Almighty," Kilgore protested. "It's just an earache. A common, run-of-the-mine, garden-variety earache! I don't want

Doc Hewlitt poking around in my hearing organ with those infected fingers."

"If the infection spreads," she retorted, "you won't live to see the next cold spell in these parts. You call him or I'll drag you over by the nose!"

Lawyer and secretary eyed each other with determination, and for once the formidable, steely gaze of the advocate was lowered before that of a woman.

"If it don't improve," Kilgore agreed, "I'll run up to Santa Fe and get one of those fancy sawbones to look into it with an instrument. While I'm at it," he added wickedly, "I'll pay a social call on Laurie Morgan and find out about that little girl of her'n."

"You're sinful and wicked, Kilgore," said Sarah acidly, "but you're a liar by training and a hypocrite by preference. I don't believe a word you say! I just hope that bragging never catches up with you in court. Suit yourself!"

Kilgore was breakfasting now with Clem Erskine at Sam Yee's, the best restaurant in San Carlos, located in an adobe store on the plaza. A sense of gloom swept over him as he considered the fly-specked menu, which he knew by heart. A decision had to be made.

"Damn this ear," he muttered, wincing at the hot needle that stabbed into his skull. "What's your pleasure, Erskine?"

Erskine smiled uncertainly. "I guess hominy grits and maybe griddle cakes and sausage."

Kilgore brushed this aside with contempt. "Sam!" he said loudly to the smiling owner. "Bring this boy a rare steak with mushroom sauce for a starter, and when that's done, maybe some quail fried in butter, with hash-brown potatoes, and a bowl of canned fruit. I'll have the steak with lamb chops, but skip the quail."

"Are you sick, Mr. Kilgore?" asked Yee anxiously.

Kilgore shrugged. "I just ain't feelin' too hungry this morning."

When the food arrived, Kilgore emptied a bottle of ketchup on an enormous steak and shoveled potatoes while meat juices ran down his chin. He kept up a steady line of talk, hardly letting the younger man get in a word. "The one thing I miss," said Kilgore, belching and sticking a toothpick between his teeth, "is seafood. Fact is, I got a taste for bluepoints on the shell from ridin' the Santa Fe express across Kansas some years back on this trip from New York I made with Dan McCandless on business. We et like hogs, and lived like kings, and I still remember those fillets of whitefish with Madeira sauce. Let me tell you, Erskine, it's an experience to cross this great land in a private car with all luxuries provided by a crowd of railroad men who'd cut your throat if they thought they could get away with it. I never was so stuffed. And that Santa Fe crowd would've cheerfully poisoned Dan and me, only they didn't have the guts. Or decided to wait for another day, I guess." Kilgore grinned. "You know anything about Dan McCandless?"

"Everybody knows Mr. McCandless," said Erskine, "from here to Boise. He's the big noise in this Territory, isn't he?"

"It's an open question. Moot, as we say in the law." Kilgore poked a finger into his mouth and searched for a shred of meat. "McCandless is in serious money trouble now, and it's no secret around here. And people have a lot of reason to hate him. Dan did his share of land-grabbing in the old days, and the people haven't forgotten it. And a lot of them have money in his railroad enterprises, money which they might be about to lose. They blame Dan. And then there's Joel Tilley."

"How does he get into this?"

"He was Dan's law partner, years back. But they had a falling out, and they've hated each other like poison ever since. And Tilley being a big influence in the Territorial government, why he could hurt Dan real bad if he ever got the chance."

"But if they were partners, what came between them?"

"Nobody knows that but Tilley and McCandless. Oh, they's a lot of stories about them. That they were mixed up in some old murder and quarreled afterward. I don't know the real story, and if I did I'd keep it to myself. McCandless is my client when the occasion arises. I kind of enjoy representing the most hated man in the Territory. It's zestful when things get monotonous in this peaceful country town. As they are right now, for instance. Things are so quiet now that I don't even know why I took you on. Oh, yeah—you're taken on. Forget about the one-week trial period."

"You mean that, Mr. Kilgore?"

Kilgore grinned. "I've decided you'll do. You got a nice way of expressing yourself, Clem, and of standing up under fire. I respect your potentialities. It ain't every boy of twenty-five who can get a recommendation out of Joe Anslinger. He wrote that you read and digested every book in his library, including all of Gildersleeve's reports, plus the Compiled Statutes, and also the 1856 version of the Kearny Code adopted by Congress for Kansas. He says you're a born lawyer. You think that's true?"

"I've got ability, Mr. Kilgore. And maybe a special calling for the profession. When I got out of the pen, I had a hard time locating a job. I got a real taste of feeling like an outlaw, and I drifted up to Leadville, hoping I might get lost in the shuffle. It's a tough town, Mr. Kilgore, and lots of riffraff are running things, and some of 'em are wearing badges. Well, Mr. Anslinger got me to read his lawbooks—and then, when I began to get the hang, I got the notion I might do something about injustice. Not just bellyache the rest of my life about the tough break I got from Judge Duquesne in Denver.

"Now that's exactly why I'm here, Mr. Kilgore," Erskine concluded. "Mr. Anslinger warned me you were kind of crude in your manner, but he also told me this was only put on for show. He told me you were a remarkable lawyer, outstanding in ability, with a great passion for justice. He says in twenty years you defended over two hundred men accused of murder in this jurisdiction, and others. Of these he says you got all but twenty acquitted—and not one of the rest got himself sentenced to death—"

"There was one," said Kilgore. "I got him pardoned on the showing that he was a halfwit. Otherwise that's the record." He beamed. "Okay, Erskine. If you want to clerk in my office, I'll have you. I can teach you law, but from here on you ain't likely to win any popularity contests. I'm just puttin' you on notice that around here a lawyer can be a mighty unliked man."

"That's no matter, Mr. Kilgore. All I want is a chance to learn."

Kilgore nodded. "First thing to learn is who's who around here." He pointed through the window. "See that tall Nigra coming toward us—the one who looks like he's eight hundred years old and smarter than any of us? Well, that's Julian DuVivier. He's Dan McCandless' steward, and a mighty strange hombre himself. Used to be attached to the House of Lucero before Dan married into it. Been in the Territory since Coronado's time, if you believe the stories."

"He seems to be coming this way."

"Damned if he isn't," Kilgore mused. "Julian don't eat breakfast out. He must be on an errand to see someone for Harry. Me, maybe."

Kilgore was right. Julian entered the restaurant, looked around for a moment, then made toward Kilgore's table. He walked with a floating, unearthly grace.

His voice was gentle as he said, "Might I see you privately a moment, Mr. Kilgore? Sorry to disturb your meal, but this is rather urgent."

"Sit right down here," Kilgore said, wondering how his Confederate officer of a father would take the idea of his inviting a black to join him at table. Probably would kill old Captain Lew Kilgore, Kilgore thought, if he weren't dead already. "This is my new clerk, Clem Erskine. You can talk in front of him, Julian."

The old man remained standing. "As you wish, Mr. Kilgore." His voice was barely audible. "Perhaps you have heard that Mr. Harry was arrested yesterday by Sheriff Duer?"

Kilgore had been trained in the cockpits of the law where the ability to keep a straight face under all circumstances was part of an honorable pursuit. Indeed he had not heard the news, but torture could not have wrung this admission from him.

"Why, yes," he said carelessly. "I heard something about that. Can't be too serious."

"I suppose not," said Julian, noting the look of surprise on Clem Erskine's face.

Kilgore lit a cigar. "What brings you to me, Julian? I'm a leetle surprised it ain't Fred Hicks from the irrigation company."

"I wired to New York for instructions," said Julian, lowering his eyes. "I was instructed this morning to bring the matter to your attention."

"Fair enough," Kilgore agreed. "What's the charge again? I seem to remember some rumor last night."

"Murder, Mr. Kilgore," said Julian quietly. "Honey Morgan was found out in the hills."

Kilgore half-rose and in his surprise let his voice rise to an uncontrolled bellow. He struggled with the simultaneous blows of learning of Honey's death, of Harry McCandless' arrest, and of the delay in consulting him. He said, "God damn it, Julian! You mean to say you let that poor, defenseless boy spend the night in the lockup, the prey of an unconscionable and ruthless pack of enemies, without telling his lawyer?"

Julian waited quietly, as if to tell Kilgore that he had lived a long time and never rushed about anything. "I telegraphed New York. Miss Carlotta replied instructing me to engage you in Mr. Harry's defense. Her wire did not reach me until very late last night. I did not think to disturb you at that hour. I am sure Mr. Harry will come to no harm in custody."

Clem Erskine looked bewildered at the sudden explosion of events.

Julian said firmly, "You will handle the case?"

"I want to know a couple of things. How'd they pick on Harry as the suspect?"

"I'm sure the sheriff could tell you that."

"And what do you know about Harry and Honey Morgan?"

"It would be better if you spoke to Mr. Harry before questioning me, Mr. Kilgore," said Julian significantly.

Kilgore was silent a long moment. At length he said, "I'll talk to Harry, and then I'll decide if I want the case. If I take it, I'm not going to be cheap. It'll cost Dan McCandless five good figures if he wants his boy to go free."

Julian's lips puckered, as though the idea of discussing a fee at a breakfast table revolted him. "Mr. McCandless will remunerate you generously, of course. You have never had occasion to complain in your dealings with him before."

Kilgore grunted. "Mebbe not, but this case is going to be expensive," he said grimly. "I don't know the facts. But it's one thing sure. Mike Duer wouldn't have made an arrest without seeing to it he had a lot of backing. Certain things stand to reason."

Julian nodded and left.

Clem Erskine waited as the lawyer stared out at the cold blue sky, frowning in thought. "*Are* you going to take the case, Mr. Kilgore?"

Kilgore came back to the younger man. "Oh, I guess I'll take it," he said slowly. "Only it ain't too simple, the way things are shaping in the Territory. I ain't worried about the case. I can't imagine any reason why Harry McCandless would touch a hair of that poor little girl's head. He's done a lot of wild and unprincipled things, but I don't see that he's got the makings of a murderer. However," he said firmly, "if moral scruples stand between you and a large fee, Erskine, take the fee! In a confused and bewildering world that's one rule that stands out like a beacon in the night to guide the weary advocate in his toil." He gulped his coffee and rose. "Let's get over to the lockup."

They stepped out into the cold. Kilgore winced as the icy gale doubled the pain in his ear. Dully he realized that a murder trial would keep him from tending to the infection for many weeks. Too bad all this had not come up a couple of weeks from now, he thought. A nuisance.

As they trudged across the plaza to the sheriff's office, Kilgore said, "A lot of people in New Mexico would like to see Harry McCandless hanged. Some of them because they despise him personally, and others because they know it would break Dan McCandless." He shrugged. "Mike Duer's an ambitious man. If he could make a murder charge hold against Harry, there'd be people in Santa Fe to reward him liberally."

"Would Duer deliberately try to build up a fraudulent case?"

Kilgore grinned appreciatively. "Sound thinking, Erskine. It shows the earmarks of the born lawyer. I'll be surprised, *mighty* surprised, if the exigencies of the law won't make some such argument convenient and necessary. As far as I'm concerned," he added, stamping the frozen earth, "Harry McCandless is the victim of prejudice and violence and the trampling of all his legal rights—by the tool of an unscrupulous clique of politicians prepared to use any means to tarnish the name of McCandless. But I promise one thing, Erskine! Dan McCandless will never see the day that boy of his goes to the gallows. This is Kilgore—for the defense!"

On this note of determination, they reached the lockup. Kilgore rapped on the door peremptorily and when the bolt slid open applied his shoulder and made his entrance.

6.

LAWYER FACED SHERIFF for a long silent moment in the narrow, cramped office, while Clem Erskine stood uncomfortably to one side. Both he and Duer were well over six feet tall, and Kilgore, standing between them, seemed even squatter and thicker through the shoulders than usual.

Kilgore said, "I hear there's been a lot going on in this county behind my back, Mike."

"Do you figure you've got a right to know everything that goes on here, Kilgore?"

"The daughter of a friend of mine's been murdered, and the son of a client of mine has been arrested. I figure somebody ought to have told me a little about it all. The other day

I spoke to Valdez about the disappearance of Honey Morgan. How come he didn't come tell me she'd been found?"

"Because I sent him up to Santa Fe to tell Laurie, that's why. He stayed over there an extra day because she wasn't fit to travel. He's coming in with her on the morning train. It's none of my job to keep you posted on the news around here, Kilgore."

"I suppose not," the lawyer admitted grudgingly. "Have you met my new clerk, Clem Erskine? Clem, meet our illustrious sheriff, fearless in all save the pursuit of dangerous criminals. Michael Patricio Duer. If there's any flaw in his character that you may suspect, Erskine, you name it, because he's got it. But at least there's one thing to be said in his favor. He's been faithful in the pursuit of his own interests through a long and devious lifetime."

"One of these days," Duer said heavily, "I'm going to stick a pin in you and let all that hot air out, Kilgore. Are you representing the McCandless boy?"

"I might be."

"I figured as much. Well, you better prepare to have your string of successful cases broken. This boy's gonna hang."

"We'll see about that," Kilgore said. "But suppose you give me at least a glimmer of the case against him."

Duer turned and aimed a globe of juice at a rusty spittoon. "Oh, now, Kilgore," he drawled. "I've been up and down that hill before. Anything you want to know you'll find out in court just as soon as I'm ready. I'll tell you this much. I've got good and sufficient evidence, circumstantial and eyewitness, enough to hang him higher'n Haman! And I'm just beginning to put my case together."

"Just don't be too sure," Kilgore advised. "When does the boy get to be arraigned?"

"You in a sweat?"

"Not particularly."

Duer nodded thoughtfully. "Just as soon as Joe Valdez gets back from Santa Fe, I'll suggest he convene a coroner's jury to hold its inquest. But I can advise you right now, Kilgore.

They're going to bring in a finding of murder. That's time enough for me to swear out a warrant against the boy."

Kilgore rocked slowly on his toes, eying the sheriff. "It's my opinion," he said slowly, "you ain't got a case, Mike. There's a furtive look in your beady eyes that tells me this is a highhanded act of legal violence without sanction in law and completely based on total lack of evidence. Otherwise you'd have had this boy before the justice of the peace first thing this morning. It's just a typical legal outrage, Mike, and I'm going to expose your methods in open court."

Duer yawned provocatively. "I'm not interested in keeping any prisoner without due process, Kilgore. I run a clean operation. But if you think you've got a point, tell it to the justice of the peace. Or you know where else you can go for relief!"

"Where's that?"

A slow grin spread. "Judge Hazledine sits in this circuit, Kilgore. And he's back in Santa Fe! Any extraordinary relief you want, you know where to go." Duer struck a sulfur match on his desk and lit a pipe, staring complacently at the lawyer.

Kilgore's scowl grew darker. Judge Abraham Hazledine of the Supreme Court of the Territory had jurisdiction here, in the Fifth Judicial District. But he was a henchman of Joel Tilley. He wasn't likely to make any decisions favorable to Dan McCandless' son.

"Never you mind that," Kilgore grunted. "Just get about your arraignment, if you can. Now I'd like to talk to the boy."

Harry McCandless was seated on the bunk bed of his austere cell in the rear cell block reading a book. Either he was thoroughly absorbed in it, or else he pretended to be; he did not look up until the cell door clanged.

Kilgore said, "All right, Duer. I'll call you when I'm through talking with him."

"No, you won't. I'm staying right here."

"Like hell you are!" Kilgore grunted. "I've got a right to consult with my client in private."

"Talk to him all you like after the arraignment," Duer said stolidly. "Right now any conversations will be held in my presence. You've got five minutes."

"Never mind, then," Kilgore said. "I'm not minded to question him in front of you."

Harry, who had remained aloof and silent from the moment Duer, Kilgore, and Erskine had entered his cell, suddenly came to life. "I've got nothing to hide," he said excitedly. "I've already told the sheriff I haven't seen Honey for over two weeks. I haven't laid eyes on her."

"This isn't the time—" Kilgore began.

"It's the fraternity pin," Harry went on, disregarding the lawyer's raised hand. "It doesn't prove I murdered her, or even that I saw her. There's no indication when I gave her that pin—"

"Shut up!" Kilgore said, bluntly and forcefully.

Harry raised his voice. "There's no case against me," he said with an edge of hysteria. "I've denied seeing the girl, and he's got no witness to contradict my statement!"

Kilgore stepped forward and seized the younger man's wrists in his powerful hands. "Shut your mouth!" he said with deliberation. "Mike Duer is drinking all this in. He doesn't care what you say—just so long as you say something, Harry! Don't admit anything, and don't deny anything. You keep silent. Is that absolutely clear?"

Harry looked aside. "I guess so."

Kilgore turned to the sheriff. "All right, Mike. I'll just note for the record that counsel was denied an opportunity of a confidential interview in the manner prescribed by law. You'll answer to me in court. Come on, Erskine."

"I'll answer, all right," said the sheriff with a small grin. "But I'll answer with something better than a hair-splitting argument. I'll answer with a solid case."

Kilgore turned and left, followed by his assistant. In the plaza, a small knot of curious onlookers eyed their progress as they picked their way to the warmth of the piñon-log fire blazing in the Franklin stove in the office. The lawyer was silent and thoughtful as he poured two whiskies, and only when he felt comfortable did he express his misgivings.

"I could cut that fool boy's tongue out," he observed. "He was talking like a child."

"Why's that, Mr. Kilgore?" Erskine asked. "All I heard were some denials. I thought he was pretty convincing."

"I suppose," Kilgore agreed. "Harry's always convincing and plausible, but he's just about as smart as they come, and he understands legal principles and the problems of proof better than half the lawyers in the Territory. Which ain't much of a standard, I'll admit. A man in his spot shouldn't even sneeze."

"You think he's guilty?" Erskine asked.

Kilgore shook a troubled head. "No," he said, considering a gnawing doubt. "Harry's high-strung and impulsive, but I can't believe he'd do anything like this. No, what bothers me is something else. The only course is silence. A general denial can be harmful, but specific denials can always trip you up. He knows that just about as well as anyone. What makes him so talkative?"

Erskine put another log into the stove. "I guess you're officially on the case now?"

An expression of pain crossed the lawyer's face, and his hand went toward his ear. "Erskine," he muttered, "I'm going to need intelligent help. I guess you can start by making a study of the relevant sections of the Compiled Laws of the Territory. You'll find 'em next to that edition of *The Federalist Papers*. There's nothing fancier, or more persuasive, than a fat quotation from the Founding Fathers of our country to make an impression on a jury."

"Yes, *sir!*" said Erskine.

Westward out of New York sped the train bearing the McCandless family. They had left the morning after the arrival of the telegram. Now Dan McCandless stared out over the empty farmlands as they whizzed by. Carlotta was at his side, Isabella across the aisle. No one had spoken for hours.

McCandless was a big man, close to six feet four and carrying his fifty-three years well. The last weeks, though, had aged him, and the telegram Carlotta had shown him after the opera had been the crusher. He clenched his fists, tightening the big, hairy fingers around each other. His empire—his world—was falling apart.

Isabella, he thought. Proud daughter of a proud line. She was still beautiful, at forty-five. And he loved her as deeply as he had a quarter of a century before. But a gulf had sprung up between them, and he knew she hated him. He could hardly remember when she had last allowed him to sleep with her. He had gone elsewhere for that, but the loss of her physical love wounded him deeply.

Carlotta. A good girl, he thought. Intelligent, beautiful. More beautiful than her mother had been. Isabella's beauty had been of the lean Spanish kind, while Carlotta was full-bodied and abundantly feminine. But self-willed. At twenty-three, she should long since have been married. Yet she tended to frighten suitors away with her ruggedly independent ideas. She read too much. She thought too much. Of the three of them, McCandless thought, she was the only one with any love for him, but for all that he knew she disapproved of his ruthlessness, scorned his involvement in the predatory world of finance.

Harry. Ah, there was the deepest wound. His only son, his heir—and his shame. If he did not know Isabella so well, he might suspect Harry's paternity. For Harry was certainly not created in his father's image. Eight inches shorter, a hundred pounds lighter, Harry was foppish, handsome in an effeminate sort of way. And he had a woman's mind, too, unstable and skittish, unable to pursue any single line of activity for long. McCandless recognized his own stubborn strain in Carlotta, but there was little of him in the boy. Harry was a waster. And yet, to him would the McCandless empire descend if the vultures failed to destroy it in McCandless' own lifetime.

And now the murder charge. For the first time in his life Dan McCandless felt fear—fear that they would take his son away from him. Harry disliked his father, cleaving instead to Isabella and taking her side in family disputes. But he was still Dan's son. Dan would never have another. To destroy Harry would be to destroy the McCandless name.

Dan McCandless chewed viciously on his cigar, wishing he had his enemies between his molars instead. He wondered whether this present crisis would serve to unite his disunited family. Perhaps some good would come out of this all. He signaled to the car steward for another drink. He had been drinking steadily since the train left New York, but to no effect. Not even a gallon of whisky could anesthetize him now, could halt his relentless brooding mind. Moodily he gulped his drink, feeling no surcease. The train sped westward.

The following morning, Kilgore was waiting patiently for an expected report that Laurie Morgan had arrived from Santa Fe on the morning train with Joe Valdez. He remained in his office, fighting the pain in his ear, considering rumors brought to him by tipsters—rumors circulating in the bars and cantinas of San Carlos that the noise of the local murder was being heard in the Territorial capital and beyond. The great newspapers of New York and Chicago and Boston and Washington were sending inquiries to Sam Dodge as the local representative of the Associated Press for more details on the legal battle shaping up in the Territory—and the visitation of special correspondents was promised for the future. The Territorial newspapers, from Roswell's *Record* to the *New Mexican* at Santa Fe, had already swung into action with shocked editorials, commenting on the political implications of a charge brought against Dan McCandless by the sheriff of San Carlos County, Michael Patricio Duer. A Denver newspaper had gone so far as to speculate that the Territorial Attorney General, Pierre Beaudoin, might openly intervene to supersede the local prosecutor. The undercurrent of an ugly mood was beginning to circulate throughout the territory.

Toward noon Kilgore began to put on a sheepskin coat. Sarah Hilleboe confronted him firmly. "You're not going out into the cold with that ear!" she announced. "Any errands can be run by me or Clem."

"Sorry," said Kilgore. "This is one thing I've got to do myself."

Laurie Morgan was waiting in the Presidential Suite of the Marshall House—which consisted of two large rooms made hideous by mohair and tassels of velvet. She was dressed entirely in black and for the first time in decades was without a painted look. Her eyes were red-rimmed as she welcomed the lawyer.

"They say you're defending Harry McCandless?" she began without preamble.

"That's right," Kilgore said. "Mind if I take off this coat?"

"Why, no," said Laurie. "Can I get you a whisky?"

"I'd be mighty grateful," Kilgore replied. He waited quietly while the woman went to the hall and called down to the clerk to send up a bottle and two glasses. It was clear that Honey Morgan's mother was holding herself in tight control.

"Well, Kilgore?" she asked finally. "You got some reason to be here?"

Kilgore nodded. "I just want to make sure Harry Mc-Candless gets a fair trial, Laurie. I don't want the general prejudice against Dan to influence the situation. I think you might help."

"You think I would help?" Laurie asked after a pause. "Now, why?"

"I don't think you'd want the wrong man to swing for it," said Kilgore. "You've got character, Laurie. If your little girl's death means anything, you'll want justice to come out of it. Not injustice."

Laurie paused. "I guess that's a compliment, Jake Kilgore. What makes you think Harry McCandless is innocent?"

"What reason would he have for such a thing?" Kilgore replied. "Honey had a good thing in Harry. He had a good thing in her. What's the point?"

Laurie Morgan had been sitting quietly, staring at the massive lawyer whose rugged face, illuminated by the wintry sun, bore an expression of pain. A bitter look accumulated on her face.

"I've got a lot of respect for you, Kilgore," she said quietly. "We been good friends and I understand your position. You're a lawyer and you got a duty to your client. But I'll tell you this. Harry McCandless killed my little girl. He broke her head open for no reason at all except his own cruelty. He looks like a milksop but he's one of those men who take it out on girls like Honey. I saw the body at the funeral parlor. A man who could do a thing like that deserves to die."

Kilgore closed his eyes. "What makes you think Harry McCandless would ever want to hurt your little girl? Could you tell me, Laurie?"

Laurie shook her head. "I'm under instructions not to say anything, Kilgore. I've got good and substantial reasons for knowing he had an important motive, and you'll hear them at the trial. I don't want to give you any handle to twist my testimony when I tell my story to the jury. I want Harry McCandless to hang."

Kilgore sighed. There was no point in answering the embittered woman. "That won't bring Honey back to life," he said mildly.

"It'll keep him from doing the same thing to some other poor girl. I don't see how you'll find it in you to defend him."

Oh, Lord! Kilgore wished he were a thousand miles away. It was the most difficult and distasteful aspect of the case, this matter of dealing with the family of the dead. There would also be the family of the living to consider. He arose. "Even if I thought for sure Harry killed her, I'd defend him somehow. I'd find something to say in his behalf—if it's only a plea for clemency. That's fundamental to our system of laws."

Laurie said with wonder, "Even where a man is proved to be a murderer?"

Kilgore nodded. "Laurie, this is a tragic moment for you, and I know it. But that's the test. Anybody can speak up for an innocent man. A child knows enough to make that kind of argument. In your own moment of sorrow, looking back on your own life, you ought to know that every human being is shaped by mysterious and wonderful forces which he's got nothing to say about. He don't ask to be born and he don't ask to die. Every one of us is guilty of something and human justice is imperfect. I'll try to get Harry McCandless off because that's my obligation as a lawyer. But if I can't make the court see that as a proposition of justice—I'll plead for mercy. And if I can't get justice, or mercy, why, then, Harry McCandless will hang—unless I figure out something else. I figure everybody needs a defense. All I ask is a fair trial and a chance to sum up to an unprejudiced jury." The lawyer paused. "What are your plans?"

Laurie Morgan walked to the window and stared at the frozen ground. "I'll bury my little girl in the churchyard here and I'll go back to Santa Fe. Mike Duer has promised to let me know in good time when I've got to get back for the trial."

Kilgore waited in the silence and opened the door. "Don't be bloodthirsty, Laurie," he said in a troubled voice. "There's things about this case I can't understand. Harry McCandless is a waster, but he's got a father and mother and sister and you've got to consider how serious to them any testimony you give will be. I'm that sorry we've got to meet in court, Laurie."

There was no reply, and he left for his office. Light flakes of snow were beginning to spiral through the overcast as he strode across the plaza to his office. It was brutal weather, he thought, with worse to come. The entire Territory seemed locked in the stiffening cold of winter. And there was a different sort of cold, too, the cold in the hearts of men. Mike Duer was a cold man. Joel Tilley, another. And Dan Mc-Candless a third. Kilgore strode on, conscious that his labored breath was blowing great plumes of steam in the icy air. The cold men were at each other's throat. And it was his task —as a man with a warm heart—to carry the burden of justice to a bitter conclusion.

Clem Erskine was waiting in the office as Kilgore strode in, shivering and rubbing his hands. When they were settled in the office, Sarah Hilleboe was dispatched back to her type-writer and Kilgore invited his assistant to make his report. Erskine was glowing with the excitement and importance of having covered the courthouse during the afternoon.

Kilgore smiled through pain. "Well?"

Erskine hitched forward. "Coroner's jury rendered a ver-dict while you were at the hotel, Mr. Kilgore. It was just what you expected."

"Death by murder at the hands of parties unknown?"

"That's it."

Kilgore grunted. "Any indication when to expect the

arraignment? I haven't been able to raise any information out of McCartney."

Kilgore was referring to Hugh McCartney, district attorney of San Carlos County.

"No, sir," said Erskine. "I had some trouble picking up information, but I did overhear talk that McCartney expected to be superseded by someone coming down from Santa Fe."

"Expected," Kilgore grunted. "Who?"

Erskine paused, having held back the important morsel of news for the end. "I was told that Attorney General Beaudoin is coming down for the arraignment himself."

If there was any element of surprise, it was not evident in Kilgore's manner.

"Why not?" Kilgore asked. "This isn't some Indian they're trying to hang. It's Dan McCandless' son and Kilgore for the defense. They're going to pull out all the stops." He poured himself another whisky. "This damnable ear is going to drive me out of my mind," he muttered. "That is, if Sarah doesn't. Sarah screams when I go into court with liquor on my breath, and my ear plagues me when I don't. There's a lesson for you, Erskine. Man's life is a bunch of conflicts, seriatim. *Thou must* is always warring with *thou cannot*. But I guess it's necessary that way. We'd die of boredom otherwise." Kilgore managed a shaky smile. "Get me that newspaper, Erskine. And then see if you can't shine up the spittoon. There is no greater reproach to a law office than a rusty spit bucket. If a lawyer can't keep a brass pot clean and shining, what can he keep?"

It was a joke, but all the same it came with an effort.

7.

JUSTICE of the Peace Tom Harrell sat in a shabby courtroom housed in a decrepit building that also housed the district court of the Fifth Judicial District. He was a flabby old man who had held his political position for many years without benefit of legal training or the qualifications of more than moderate training. He banged a gavel, and the murmur of voices came to a halt.

"We waited just about long enough," he announced. "I'm going to grant an adjournment—"

"Hold it!" said Kilgore dramatically.

Kilgore had timed his entrance for best effect, gauging nicely the moment when the justice would grant the application made by the sheriff to postpone the hearing upon the arraignment. All eyes turned toward him, and there was a general shift and murmur of excitement as he strode into the crowded courtroom and made his way to the bar. Harry McCandless was seated to one side, manacled, with an air of pale excitement, quite different from the detachment of the day of arrest. Also present were Laurie Morgan, quietly dressed in a skirt and severe blouse of black, and Police Chief Joe Valdez, who wore an air of excitement and importance. Mike Duer stood apart in a corner, earnestly in discussion with a lean and elegantly dapper man in his late forties—Pierre Beaudoin, attorney general of the Territory. Sam Dodge, editor of the *Journal*, was in conversation with an artist he had hired for the occasion to make line drawings for a special edition of his paper.

"Somebody might have had the goodness to notify me that this case would be called first on the calendar," Kilgore complained. "Is there a conspiracy going on to keep my client from having his day in court?"

"No conspiracy," Tom Harrell replied. "You're expected to know when the court starts. You're no privileged character, just because this is a court of limited jurisdiction. It's still a court of law. This here is just for taking the arraignment."

"Fine and dandy!" Kilgore announced. "Let's get on with it. What's the stage of this travesty?"

Harrell banged his gavel. "Jake Kilgore, you behave, or I'm going to test out the limits of my power to hold you in contempt. This is no chicken-stealing case we're dealing with. This is an important murder case, and you're not going to suck me into making any mistakes. We're honored by the presence of the attorney general, and I'm going to demand some respect."

"Naturally," Kilgore said. "I apologize. Hello, Pete," he added, grinning broadly as he turned to the attorney general and stuck out a meaty hand. "I couldn't ask for a better tribute to the weakness of the case against Harry McCandless than your presence. Let's get on. Call your first witness."

Beaudoin smiled. "Thanks, Kilgore, but if you don't mind, I'll have an application."

The attorney general's voice was powerful and controlled like that of a Shakespearean actor, touched slightly with the accent of Louisiana and Creole ancestors. His eyes were cold and his mouth cruel.

Mike Duer stepped forward. "Judge, I'm handing up this sworn affidavit setting forth my reasons to believe that Harry McCandless—"

Kilgore interrupted. "Let's have the prisoner to the bar while this conversation takes place. He's entitled to hear the content of this mumbling."

A bailiff stepped forward and nudged Harry McCandless to the bar. Kilgore stepped to the side of his client and said hoarsely, "This is all just a formal pack of lies, Harry. The real perjury comes later. But it's useful to have it committed to paper."

A warning gavel brought silence, and the sheriff continued to explain the nature of his application. The inquest of the coroner's jury had resulted in a verdict that Honey Morgan had met her death at the hands of parties unknown. On his own affidavit, he had previously obtained a warrant of arrest and now presented his prisoner before the justice of the peace for pleading.

Kilgore waited with folded arms as the proceedings went on. "Oh, now!" he complained finally, "all this is just a waste of time. We plead not guilty, and now I've got an application."

"What application, Mr. Kilgore?"

Kilgore gazed stolidly at the array of faces. A hostile atmosphere hung over the crowded court. Murderous hate was expressed against the son of Dan McCandless. Duer—Laurie—Beaudoin—Valdez. He turned back and pointed an expressive finger.

"I ask that the prisoner be admitted to bail pending his appearance before the district court," he said quietly.

"Bail!"

A dozen men seemed to be talking at once, until Harrell made himself heard. "I can't do that, Mr. Kilgore," the justice of the peace protested. "This here offense is a hanging offense. It's above the grade of felony. I don't have the power."

"No power?" Kilgore roared suddenly. "Why, you've got to be satisfied from the papers that they've got the right man. It don't matter the grade of offense. Mike Duer hasn't got a shred of case against this boy. Matter of fact, I move to discharge him entirely on the ground that all the affidavits taken together don't show any probable cause to believe that Harry McCandless was involved in this poor girl's death. Set bail or set him free!"

For a long moment the storm of protest raged. Kilgore stood at its center, the waves of sound beating painfully against his swollen eardrum. Tom Harrell pounded his desk and tried ineffectually to regain order.

Silence returned. Tom Harrell said in his weak voice, "The papers are all regular, Jake. It would exceed my authority to grant bail."

"Pardon me, Mr. Kilgore," said Pierre Beaudoin suddenly. His voice was as elegant as his posture; he spoke with a purr, but yet it was a purr that could carry to the farthest reaches of a courtroom gallery. "You seem to be operating under a fundamental misunderstanding of the function of Mr. Harrell here. As a justice of the peace, he's not empowered to set bail in a murder case. That would certainly exceed his authority, as I am sure you must have been well aware when you brought the entire matter up."

Kilgore put one hand behind his throbbing ear and glanced with narrowed eyes at Beaudoin. "Am I to understand that the attorney general will remain with us to provide legal advice during the trial?"

"The attorney general," Beaudoin said with a flickering smile, "has been named to prosecute the case. It was felt that he would more efficiently serve the Territory's purposes than the local district attorney, Mr. McCartney. So we will be adversaries once again, Mr. Kilgore. At the moment, though, I ask you to talk to my point. Is the justice of the peace empowered to set bail? And if you think he is, can you cite proof of your contention?"

"I realize that," said Kilgore stolidly. "I also realize something more. Bail or no bail, the prosecution has got to show some probable cause—some evidence—some scintilla, as we say—that the prisoner is guilty of the offense. Go ahead with your witnesses, and I'll show how empty of legality this outrage is. Call your witness!"

There was a moment of silence.

"Are you prepared, Mr. Beaudoin?" asked the justice of the peace.

"Um—" Beaudoin drew out the sound of doubt provocatively, wiped his mouth with a fine linen handkerchief, and turned to the bench. "Judge, I'd like an adjournment for about two weeks, while I give this matter some study. I need a chance to confer with my witnesses—"

"Adjournment?" Kilgore bellowed. "We're ready! The witnesses are here! My client is languishing! He wants an adjournment because he's got no case and he knows it! It's a political frame-up and that's the fact I'm going to demonstrate—"

A banging gavel finally brought the heated exchange to a conclusion. "Two weeks' adjournment!" Harrell said, and disappeared from the bench.

Throughout the tumult, Harry McCandless had waited quietly, regarding Kilgore's dramatic efforts with pale curiosity. He seemed detached, not concerned, appreciative of a performance in which he had no part. When the excitement had died, he responded to the nudge of the bailiff. "One moment." He came back to the lawyer. "I appreciate your efforts, Mr. Kilgore," he said. "I just don't know why you were so surprised when they pulled that dirty trick. I don't expect justice in any court run by Tilley's men."

Kilgore mopped his neck. "Nobody hands you justice on a platter, Harry McCandless. And it can't be bought for money, or it ain't justice. It's something you got to fight for damn hard. I wouldn't give up."

"I'm Dan McCandless' son," said Harry fatalistically, and was led away.

Kilgore paused and exchanged a troubled glance with Clem Erskine, whose own heart had been beating sympathetically with the effort of his chief to stand against the array of power represented in the final action of the court. It was a glance that seemed to indicate that the lawyer's chief problem would be the temperament of his client. Kilgore laughed harshly and turned to the crowd.

"Duer's scared stiff," he announced. "He didn't have the guts to expose himself to cross-examination. When the time comes, he'll regret this cowardly evasion of his responsibilities. Let's get back to the office, Erskine. There's nothing we can do here."

Stony silence followed them as they left the courtroom. Kilgore's mammoth appetite was protesting the lack of dinner. At his home, not far from the center of town, his elderly servant, Lupe, was probably boiling with impatience because he was not yet at the table. Well, he thought, dinner would have to wait awhile.

He crossed back to his office, at the far side of the plaza.

Erskine said, "Did you really expect to get him out on bail, Mr. Kilgore?"

Kilgore shook his head. "There was just an outside chance with Tom Harrell. He's semi-illiterate, and jelly-like when I fix him with my good eye, but with Beaudoin here there wasn't a chance. No, Tom's been talked to, and he's in the grip of fear. It was really just a bit of propaganda!" He grinned suddenly. "Pete Beaudoin never had the least intention of letting me get at his witnesses. But at least now there's a mite of public opinion working against him."

"Suppose you got him out on bail?" Erskine wondered, as the lesson sank in. "Wouldn't that have been irregular?"

Kilgore looked up at the towering young man. "The forms are there to guide us, not to bind us. My aim is to get Harry acquitted. Duer and Beaudoin will pull anything dirty to hang him, so I might as well try *my* tricks, too. Would have surprised me if Beaudoin had swallowed it, though. He's despicable, but that ain't to say he isn't smart." They entered the office. Sarah Hilleboe emerged, her arms full of typed papers, and inquired with a single raised eyebrow how the session had gone. Kilgore told her in three sentences.

"Drat!" she said. "Now what? I was getting all set to draft a bond for the sureties on that bail application. You can apply for bail to Judge Hazledine," she pointed out. "He's got those powers."

Kilgore rubbed a stubbled jaw. "Might as well drop that idea," he decided. "Once is enough to milk those possibilities. I don't want to be an actor that keeps repeating the same lines all night. No, I need quicker justice. Something real dramatic that can catch the imagination of these country jays. Something unusual! Erskine!" he said suddenly, "would you like a trip to Santa Fe?"

"Why yes, I suppose," said Erskine uncertainly. He was struck suddenly with panic at the idea of responsibility. "Doing what?"

Kilgore put a hand to his ear. "Nothing much," he said pleasantly, "I got this earache, so I can't travel in the cold. I got a simple task I'd like you to carry out. I want you to get

Judge Hazledine's signature to a writ of habeas corpus. I got to smoke out their evidence somehow."

"Habeas corpus?" Erskine echoed.

"Nothing to it," said Kilgore with amusement. "I'll dictate the application and you shove it under the judge's nose. He's got to sign it—and that's it. Or is that too much responsibility?"

"Oh, no, no!" said Erskine hastily. "It's just that it all sounds pretty feeble to me," he said. "A fraternity pin, a Navajo rug, a couple of unreliable native witnesses—"

"We don't know what they're holding back, boy. Duer can be full of little surprises. I keep telling you he wouldn't have dared to swear out that complaint unless he thought he had a chance of making it stick." Kilgore pulled out his pocket watch. "Getting late. Sarah, close up the office. Erskine, let's get over to my place and get some food. And then some relaxation. Sarah, why not come to the cantina with us? You like a nip of whisky as much as any of us. We can all get *borracho* together, eh?"

Sarah's expression was steely. "The day I start drinking with you, Jake Kilgore, is the day they make Mike Duer the Pope of Rome. Now get yourself home and put some hot compresses on that big ear of yours. We'll take care of that writ in the morning."

"Take Mr. Kilgore's things, Julian," said McCandless nervously. "We'll be in the library."

"Yes, Mr. McCandless."

Julian silently stood by as Kilgore slipped out of his sheepskin and unwound a woolen scarf from his ear and followed McCandless into the great library where a great log of piñon was ablaze in a giant hearth. An elk's head stared across a hall whose rafters seemed smoky and blue in the distance. The vast room had been decorated on a princely scale.

"Drink?"

"Always."

The McCandless party returning from New York had gotten off at the siding maintained on Wa-po-nah as a courtesy to the railroad magnate who owned the line. In consequence they had not entered San Carlos, and it was the telephone, relayed through Fred Hicks at the irrigation company that had summoned Kilgore to the conference. Kilgore felt in poor shape, but he could not resist the misery in Dan McCandless' humble message, begging him to visit Wa-po-nah. McCandless' hand shook as he poured brandy for two. His appearance shocked the lawyer. In his four months' absence in New York he had lost weight, and the skin of his face hung loosely. McCandless leaned forward and peered with bloodshot eyes.

"Tell me about the case," he said hoarsely.

Kilgore succinctly outlined the situation. McCandless listened carefully, digesting the circumstances with a sense of dreadful realism.

"What do you think?" he asked finally.

Kilgore shook his head. "Too soon to tell. I can't get much out of Harry. He just keeps reiterating that he's innocent—but he feels that there's a lot of prejudice against the family name. I don't like his fatalistic mood. Sorry, but I can't give you any kind of opinion."

McCandless waited. "There was a time when this would be unthinkable. You'd have an opinion."

"Times change," Kilgore said briefly. "There's a lot of feeling since you ran the irrigation company into a dry ditch. And the railroad! A lot of people have been wiped out."

McCandless nodded. "I'm worried about the boy's mother," he said, rising and standing by the crackling fire on the stone hearth. "It was a great shock to her, Kilgore. Dreadful, to find that boy charged with this crime. Harry's her son, you know! A Lucero! The coloring, the temperament! There's a bond between them, and sometimes I feel shut out of an understanding between them. Can you understand that, Kilgore?"

Kilgore nodded, staring at the brandy dancing in the goblet, lit by golden flames. The lawyer felt the appeal of one thinking man to another—and he had no taste for his usual raffish pose.

"I think so," he said seriously.

McCandless paused wearily at the flames. "I feel lonely for my son, Kilgore," he said wretchedly. "I've always felt lonely, but now I need him. I want this thing to end."

"I'll win the trial," said Kilgore thoughtfully. "I really will. If there's any balance to the issues, you can back the lawyer, not the case. I've met Pete Beaudoin, and I'll say this. He's tough, but I'm better."

McCandless considered his next remark. "I don't want it to come to trial," he said finally. "I don't want to let Harry get into that much jeopardy. I don't want the grand jury to vote an indictment."

"No indictment?" Kilgore smiled crookedly. "That's a tall order. I don't control the grand jury. That's up to Pete Beaudoin. He's just superseded all powers in this county, and he's proceeding *in camera*, as we say."

"Can't somebody be reached?"

"Maybe," said Kilgore shortly, "but not by me."

"Money?"

"It's not a question of money."

McCandless looked away. "I suppose not. You know what this is? It's some scheme of Tilley and the Territorial bunch to ruin me. The Chicago railroad men are out for my scalp, Jake, and Tilley's probably in with them." His hand shaking, McCandless refilled his brandy glass. "I'm on the edge of bankruptcy, Kilgore," he said in a shaking voice, "I'm overextended, and suddenly everyone's got an ax out for me."

"You haven't gone out of your way to build up friendships in the Territory, McCandless."

"I had no need of friendships. I had loyalties, instead. But they're all turning against me now. And this trial is the wedge designed to split me wide open." McCandless went on to describe the anxiety and misery of the months spent in the financial centers of the nation, the agonized waiting in the anterooms of bankers, the slow strangulation of his financial empire as the sources of money dried up at the behest of his formidable rivals. "It isn't only Harry!" he burst out. "It's the whole world. Kilgore, you've got to help the boy. You've got to help me." He turned suddenly and shook his fist against the unseen and powerful foe in the distance. "I'll smash 'em!" he shouted passionately. "I'll make 'em wish they'd never been born!"

Kilgore let the outburst pass. "That won't do any good, McCandless," he said quietly. "This didn't come out of a clear blue sky. A little girl was killed, or murdered, and justice has got to take its course. I'll see that it does. In my opinion, Harry's innocent, and I'll get him off."

McCandless shivered like an elk at bay. In a hoarse, tired voice he said, "Don't mind me, Kilgore. It's just that I feel—so helpless, for the first time in my life. It's a hard thing to feel yourself drowning in your own blood—with those you love. Kilgore, forget me, and help the boy."

"I'd like to see Mrs. McCandless."

"Not now, please. It's been a shock, and she's been taking some medicine. Another time?"

"Sure." Kilgore put his glass aside. "I'd like your help in one respect. I'm not satisfied by the way Harry has been acting. He's giving me no help, except for denials, and I have the feeling that he's keeping things back from me. Somebody's got to talk to him."

"I'll think about it," McCandless agreed.

Kilgore shook his head pityingly. It was a sad sight, watching the formidable Dan McCandless fumbling impotently for words in a welter of misery. He said in a quiet voice. "I'll do everything I can, McCandless. Not because he's your son, or because it's got some bearing on business, but because he's my client. I'd better go."

"I'm sorry I'm such a bad host," said Dan McCandless. He pulled a bellcord. "Julian!"

Julian DuVivier followed Kilgore out to a red-wheeled buggy that had been warmed in the McCandless stables behind the great house. He helped the lawyer into the seat and waited respectfully.

"If there's anything I can do, Mr. Kilgore," said Julian quietly, "anything at all, I wish you would remember that I love Mr. Harry. I would do anything in the world to help."

Kilgore exchanged a glance of understanding with the black man, and studying the mingling plumes of steaming breath, nodded, and drove off to his home on the road to San Carlos, nursing his ear against the cutting wind. The interview with McCandless had depressed him. He wished he had not been alone with McCandless, that Isabella or Carlotta had been there. He enjoyed Carlotta's company; she was a girl after his own heart, beautiful, stubbornly independent-minded—the sort of girl he'd be proud to have as a daughter, or, if he were younger and of a different frame of mind, a wife.

And Isabella, too. He remembered the Isabella of decades ago, and winced at the recollection. He had been a young lawyer then, and Isabella had just borne Harry. She was in the flower of her young motherhood, and Jake Kilgore had fallen under the spell of her loveliness.

Oh, there had been no romance. Kilgore was no wife-stealer, and in any case only a fool would have approached the wife of Dan McCandless. Kilgore had been retained to defend some Lucero servant on a minor charge, and Isabella had captivated him, and for weeks he had carried her image in his mind as he went about his professional duties. He had never really stopped loving that image of Isabella McCandless, he thought.

But the Isabella he recalled was the one of twenty years ago—not the cold, imperious creature of today. The old beauty still glinted in her, but now the cheekbones were unpleasingly harsh, the aristocratic nose perhaps a trifle beaklike. She had hardened. It had begun right after Harry's birth, Kilgore thought. And over the years she had grown bitter, had moved further away from her husband's love, had all but withdrawn from society.

A strange woman, Kilgore decided.

A strange family.

The buggy halted in front of the Kilgore house. His old Spanish servant scuttled out—Lupe, withered and dried, seventy years old and still stronger than any Anglo woman half her age. "The *joven* is here, Señor Kilgore. The tall, young one. He is in your study."

"*Gracias*, Lupe. Bring us some brandy and let me get warm."

Clem Erskine was prowling, as usual, through Kilgore's extensive library. Kilgore kept the lawbooks at his office, but he had many hundreds of books here.

"What are you reading?" Kilgore asked brusquely.

Erskine looked up. "Cicero, sir. *Against Catiline.*"

"You know Latin?"

"Only the legal phrases I've picked up. But I'm trying to puzzle it out all the same. It's a wonderful language, isn't it? Not a word wasted." Erskine closed the volume. "There's so much I'd like to learn, Mr. Kilgore. So much it frightens me. Besides the law, that is. I'd like to know Latin and geometry, and maybe something about the old philosophers and—oh, everything!"

The boy's eyes were gleaming. Kilgore gestured sweepingly at the rows of books. "Any time you want to borrow a book, help yourself. Just mind you treat them with respect. Handle a book like you'd handle a woman you love."

Clem smiled. "Thank you, Mr. Kilgore."

"But first learn the law. There's time for Plato when you're my age. Where's the petition?"

"Here, Mr. Kilgore."

"Have you checked it through thoroughly?"

"I assumed that you and Miss Hilleboe had used the proper form, sir. I've read it, though."

Kilgore's displeasure was monumental. "Is Sarah Hilleboe presenting the petition? Am I? What will you do if Hazledine finds irregularities and rips it up under your nose? Are you a messenger boy, or my representative to him?"

Erskine reddened. "I'm sorry, sir. I meant to have a look at it on the train."

Kilgore grunted sourly and called for hot soup to follow the brandy. "If I didn't have this ear, Erskine, I'd take the assignment from you. It's fundamental that a good lawyer takes nothing for granted. Not commas, not periods, not grammar, not law. Fortunately it's been checked by me." Lupe entered, bearing the brandy and two glasses. It was not the equal of McCandless' fine cognac, but it would have to do for now. "Drink hearty, Clem. In this weather you need fortification."

Kilgore's ear throbbed mercilessly. The nightmare-ridden face of Dan McCandless haunted him. Outside, a cold wind whistled. Kilgore downed the brandy, but somehow it made him feel little more cheerful.

8.

KILGORE was speaking earnestly in the cold morning air of the railroad platform.

"Take that worried look off your face, Erskine," he advised, rolling a cigar to the corner of his mouth. "When you're talking to a judge, there's nothing he dislikes so much as a fidgeting, worried lawyer. Just remember to look respectful, keep your counsel, and thank the judge, especially when he's hitting you with the book. Just remember that he makes the rulings."

Erskine said ruefully, "That's strong advice, Mr. Kilgore, especially coming from you."

"Kilgore's unique," the older man observed. "The mold was broken, the mold was broken," he added somberly. "Keep a smile on your face. It'll help loosen that nervous twist inside."

The first train to Santa Fe came through San Carlos shortly before nine on Monday mornings, and the two men were at the station early. Clem Erskine wore the new business clothes that he had bought at Ben Weingarten's Emporium with his poker winnings. He stood tall and straight in his crisp, somewhat somber new outfit. In the portfolio at his side, he carried a petition for a writ of habeas corpus, and the text of the writ itself, firmly commanding the sheriff of San Carlos County to produce the body of Harry McCandless before the court and to show the legality and cause of his imprisonment. Clem felt a twinge of nervousness. A week ago he had been threadbare and penniless; now he was en route to Santa Fe to present a petition before a judge of the supreme court of the Territory. And, though Jake Kilgore stood beside him now as they waited for the train, he would be all alone up there in the capital when he came before Judge Hazledine.

"What time is it, Mr. Kilgore?"

"Twenty past."

"Train's due, then."

"Give her another ten minutes, easy. Hello, look who's coming down to see us off!"

The tall, full-bodied girl in traveling clothes was Carlotta McCandless, descending from a McCandless buggy and striding briskly to the train platform. Clem Erskine stared at her in wonder as she approached.

"That's Harry McCandless' sister?" he murmured.

"None other. And quite some woman, won't you agree?"

Clem nodded. "Right fine. How come she's not married?"

"She's a stubborn filly, that's why. Headstrong. Too bright for her own good. She won't be just a bedwarmer for some man; she'll want an equal voice in family affairs, and it's a rare man willing to grant his wife that. So she goes without a husband. Doesn't seem to bother her yet."

Carlotta drew near. Even her brother's imprisonment had not completely dampened her buoyant spirits, and she favored Kilgore with a broad smile, reserving a curious stare of blunt appraisal for Clem as introductions were made.

" 'Morning, Mr. Kilgore. Off on a journey?"

Kilgore shook his head. "Not I. I'm just here to send my new clerk off to Santa Fe to see Judge Hazledine about your brother. Clem Erskine, Carlotta McCandless. How come you're here, Carlotta?"

The girl shrugged. "Off to Santa Fe myself. Looks like the train's slow today."

"Here it comes now," Clem said, using his great height to peer into the distance. A few minutes later, the chugging locomotive was coming to a halt, and the San Carlos passengers were getting aboard. Kilgore waved good-by to Clem and Carlotta and left the station before the train departed.

The car was practically empty. Carlotta seated herself at the nearest place. Clem hesitated, not knowing whether it would be ruder to sit down next to her or to move on elsewhere after they had been introduced. Carlotta put an end to his doubts by inviting him to sit beside her. He lowered his big frame into the cushioned seat, acutely aware of the warmth and desirability of the young woman at his side. It was the first time in his life he had ever managed to ride in a Pullman parlor car.

He glanced covertly at her as the train began to pull out. She was lovely, lovely. A high intelligent forehead, curly auburn hair, a finely made, thin-bridged nose, flashing eyes, gleaming white teeth. Her chin was strong and determined, her posture erect. She was a tall girl, too—at least five feet six, Clem had estimated. No wonder she was having trouble finding a husband. She was taller than a lot of men, after all. And only someone of Clem's own height—say, six-two or -three—could feel really comfortable with a girl so tall.

"How long have you been working for Mr. Kilgore?" Carlotta asked, as they pulled out into flat country.

"About a week. I came down from Colorado."

"He's a wonderful man, isn't he? A little crude, but he's got such tremendous vitality."

"I found that out the first time I ate breakfast with him," Clem said. "He ate like the government was going to call in all the food there was at noon."

"I think he's magnificent," Carlotta said. "And behind all the flamboyance and bluster, he's such a tender man. An idealist, almost. But he hides it well. It only slips through when he forgets to wear his cynic's mask. My father has always had the greatest respect for Jake Kilgore—and my father doesn't respect many men."

"They've known each other a long time, haven't they?"

Carlotta nodded. "Years and years. Kilgore was once a prospector for a mining company my father owned. He saved my father's life in a saloon brawl, and my father never forgot it. Later he got Kilgore out of some trouble with the law, and still later he helped him get admitted to the Territorial bar. So each owes the other debts. But of course they disagree on almost everything my father does."

"I imagine they would," said Clem seriously.

Carlotta turned an appraising glance. "Oh, why?"

Clem shrugged, wondering whether he was not getting onto dangerous ground. "Mr. Kilgore's a real lawyer," he said slowly. "I've just been with him a short time, but I get the feeling that he hates injustice. He's always on the side of the underdog and that's why—"

"Is my brother an underdog?" Carlotta asked. "It's hard to think of anyone in my family in those terms."

"Well, from what I hear, Miss McCandless, there's a great deal of antagonism to your brother. In that sense—why, yes, he'd be an underdog. Trouble is your father's been kind of ruthless." Clem paused. "I'm sorry," he said with embarrassment. "I didn't mean to let it slip out, only—"

Carlotta finished the thought. "Only you wonder what I think about it all?" Her laugh was short and hard. "You don't need to apologize to me. My father's an unusual man. He's gifted with limitless energy and a hunger for wealth and power that seems to be part of our times. This country is growing in wealth and population, but it's still the frontier—and nature is out there—" She paused. "He's my father, but that doesn't mean I haven't my own point of view. He's an enemy of the country."

"Strong language, Miss McCandless."

"I have strong feelings. Not only about my father, but about the way this whole country is going. A small bunch of rich men grabbing, grabbing, grabbing—and the ordinary people getting stepped on all the time. There's a new century starting in a few years, Mr. Erskine, and I'm afraid it's going to be a bloody one. Even bloodier than the last. A lot of capital is flowing into this country from Europe. Half the cattle business is financed in Antwerp and London and Paris. Our mining shares and other business are built on money flowing from Europe—and that's really what's going on in the West. You take that scandalous situation involving the Fallon Grant—"

As the clacking miles passed, Carlotta outlined earnestly and with precision a gigantic land steal engineered in the General Land Office and the Congress of the United States in which several million acres of land through fraud and chicanery had been transformed from free government land, made fruitful by settlers, into the private preserve of a group of financial manipulators who had fallen upon the virgin land like a plague of locusts. This tremendous operation, involving grazing lands and coal and silver and copper, had ultimately come into the ownership of a crowd of Antwerp financiers into whose hands the ownership of a substantial part of the West had passed. Clem sat with open mouth at the glimpse of manipulations which he could only dimly see.

"Somebody's got to own the land," he said feebly.

Carlotta paused abruptly. "I've been talking too much," she decided. "Trouble is that when people get despoiled and bitter, they take to violence. It isn't local. All over the world similar forces are at work. The European powers are getting prepared for a war that could destroy all civilization and involve this country. Dan McCandless isn't important—except as a symptom."

The train was chugging painfully up a rise now toward the north from which it would make the approach to their destination. He was surprised that so much time had passed.

"A war?" he said slowly. "That would involve the United States?"

"It would start in Europe, I'd say."

"Then why worry about it?"

"We'll be drawn in," Carlotta said vehemently. "Our whole way of life will be shattered."

Clem laughed. "We're not going to fight any wars in Europe, Miss McCandless. I agree that a lot of ugly stuff goes on in this country, but I can't foresee any wars or revolutions or stuff like that. Things are getting better all the time. Twenty years ago this country out here was lawless. Now we've got due process. America's growing up, Miss McCandless."

"Do you really think so? Do you believe that the country is getting more law-abiding of its own accord?"

"I do. I think another forty or fifty years and greed and selfishness will be overcome by force of law."

"How romantic," Carlotta said. "And I wish I could agree. But I'm more cynical. I think it'll take a panic and maybe a revolution before the corruption in this country is cleared up. As long as men like Joel Tilley and my father hold power, we won't have any utopias here."

"You're a pessimist, Miss McCandless."

"I'm a realist. When I was younger, I had your starry-eyed optimism. But I'm losing my faith in the human race, Mr. Erskine. I've come to foresee the worst." She smiled. "But we're talking so seriously, and my father keeps warning me not to get into deep discussions with interesting young men. May I call you Clem? And would you tell me exactly what you hope to do for my brother in Santa Fe?"

Clem reddened. He had left his innocence behind years ago, but sitting next to this dynamic young woman unnerved him and made him feel like a gawky sixteen-year-old all over again. He knew that there were two kinds of women in the world: the ones like Honey Morgan, whom you could have a good time with and maybe sleep with—and the respectable women, who stayed aloof and were chaperoned rigidly till their wedding day. But this Carlotta was in a class by herself—aristocratic and respectable enough, but yet bold, capable of taking train journeys by herself, capable of calling men she had just met by their first name and telling them they were "interesting."

She was different. She had probably had some affairs already, he thought. But even the idea that she had already given herself to some man didn't diminish the awe and respect he felt for her. He found himself powerfully attracted to her, almost uncomfortably so.

He said, "Call me Clem, sure. Is 'Miss Carlotta' all right?"

"If you like. Why to Santa Fe, Clem?"

"To apply for a writ of habeas corpus for your brother. Mr. Kilgore wants to get him up before the court and perhaps quash the whole indictment. You know what happened on the arraignment?"

She nodded. "It's been explained, but I'm not too sure what it all means. Or what you hope to accomplish now."

Clem paused to consider. "I'm not too sure myself," he admitted. "I only know I'm expected to present a petition for a writ of habeas corpus for your brother. It's got to be signed and then there's a hearing and Mr. Kilgore will have a chance to make an argument to show that your brother is being illegally detained."

"Illegally?" she asked curiously.

"If there's no basis for his arrest," Clem said, "then he's got to be turned loose. It's a way to test out the prosecution."

"I see," said Carlotta, and turned aside to study a snowy hillside covered with dark stretches of pine and darker stretches of fir.

"I'm on my way to see the governor," she said abruptly.

"Governor Tellegen? My gosh! You don't mean to say you can get him to help your brother?"

"I know Governor Tellegen," said Carlotta simply. "I met him in New York during the season and we chatted about his appointment to the Territory. He's been appointed by the President for the special purpose of dealing with Joel Tilley and the rest of his ring. I should think you'd know that."

"No, Miss Carlotta. I haven't been in the Territory that long." Clem paused. "Would you mind a delicate question? Why isn't your father seeing the governor himself?"

Carlotta considered her answer. "I don't know," she said slowly. "There's something strange about it. I know he'd cut off his arm to help Harry. No one ever loved a son more than my father. But there's something—"

She had been carried away by the recollection of a family

quarrel, a heated argument that had continued from the great library at Wa-po-nah into the bedroom and late into the night —a quarrel that had involved her mother and the distress of a family in agony. It was nothing she cared to disclose to the young man, she realized, and abruptly changed the subject.

"Governor Tellegen feels that it's his mission to clean out the corruption in the Territory. I'm afraid that he links my father with Tilley in some way. What I hope to do is to make a personal appeal not to let this trial be rigged by Tilley. I want the governor to remove Beaudoin as prosecutor and to replace him with somebody who isn't beholden to Tilley." She hesitated and added, "*Or* to my father."

"Do you think he'll do it?"

"I've got to try," she said. "I'm not asking for a McCandless man as prosecutor. I'm only asking for a fair trial."

A moment of silence passed.

Clem said, "You don't believe your brother killed this girl, do you?"

"No!" Carlotta was about to add something, then paused. "I don't think Harry could murder anyone. Certainly not that girl. I'm only afraid of surprises."

"Surprises? How?"

She shook her head. "I'm talking about the appearance of things. I don't want him railroaded in a rigged trial and by my father's enemies. I'm sure Harry's innocent."

"How can you be sure?" Clem asked curiously.

Carlotta turned and stared into Clem's face with level, grey eyes of deep certainty. "Harry's my brother," she said simply. "He could never, never be guilty of murder. I don't care what the evidence can be."

They talked for a while longer, then fell into silence. Carlotta opened her bag and produced two copies of *McClure's*, one of which she offered to him. He accepted—he was always hungry for reading matter of any sort—and was soon engrossed in the magazine. He was interested to find many of Carlotta's ideas echoed in the impassioned crusading articles.

They reached Santa Fe late that afternoon. The weather was cold there, too, thanks to the altitude, but the sun was shining and there was no wind, only the dry cold. Clem had been in Santa Fe before, but he never failed to respond to the old city's historic echoes. It was the oldest seat of government in the United States, after all. Spanish *gobernadores* had ruled here decades before the settlement of Jamestown. The ancient mission-style houses reeked of the past.

Both he and Carlotta were staying at the Manzanilla Hotel. But Clem so arranged it that they separated at the railroad station and drove to the hotel in different buggies.

Kilgore had wired ahead, making reservations for him. Clem walked into the ancient building, identified himself at the desk, and was shown by a desiccated old Indian to a room on the third floor. The room was large and spacious but rather drafty. Four dollars a night seemed like an incredible sum to be paying, Clem thought, but since Dan McCandless was underwriting all expenses he was willing to enjoy the extravagance.

It was too late in the afternoon to set about chasing Judge Hazledine. Clem settled down in his room and leafed through the papers he had brought with him.

There were five judges of the supreme court of the Territory, each one assigned to a specific district. Most of the year, they sat *en banc* at Santa Fe, considering appeals and acting collectively as a court. But part of the time they rode out as circuit judges to the various district courts to hold jury trials, consider motions, hear appeals from the inferior courts, and the like.

Hazledine was a Tilley appointee who had been on the supreme-court bench only about a year. But he was reputed to be a thorny individualist who did not always take dictation from Tilley. Kilgore hoped that Hazledine would rise to the occasion in this Harry McCandless trial, and show his independence. Otherwise the trial might become a mockery.

Clem tidied the papers and put them carefully away again. He had no particular fear of the assignment, merely awe at the gravity of it. Under the law, the judge was compelled to sign the writ upon application, provided the papers were in order. Kilgore had used some strong language here in protesting the detention of Harry McCandless, but Clem saw nothing in the petition that might cause its rejection. So Hazledine would sign it, and the writ would immediately take effect.

Frowning, Clem paced the room for a while, trying to foresee the course of the case as though he, and not Kilgore, were the lawyer. With dismay, he realized that for all his youthful energy he had no clear-cut idea of the strategy Kilgore would adopt. Clem consoled himself with the thought that perhaps at this early hour not even Kilgore himself knew the way he would steer things. Too many factors were unknown as yet.

Clem stripped down and gave himself a sponge bath to get rid of the dust of travel. Then, dressing again in his one good suit, he went downstairs to the lobby. A few well-dressed loungers were loafing about there. Clem took a seat, hoping to see Carlotta appear. He did not dare go to her room, nor even to ask the desk clerk where she was staying. For all he knew she was in the room next to his. The thought dizzied him. But it was a large hotel, he reminded himself. She was probably in another wing entirely.

He went into the hotel bar and treated himself to a glass of sherry, thriftily jotting down a fifteen-cent entry on the list of expenses Kilgore had instructed him to keep. "Don't stint yourself, boy," the lawyer had ordered. "Your mind won't function if you starve your body. You needn't order champagne for breakfast, but don't be niggardly while you're up there, either."

The sherry was good. He thought to have another, decided that it would be overly self-indulgent, and walked on through the bar into the restaurant. The hotel restaurant was reputed to be one of the finest in town, with nothing less than a French chef. Erskine was no connoisseur of food, but he liked good cooking nearly as much as Kilgore did.

He stood alone at the entrance to the big dining room, a tall and solitary figure. Even though it was still quite early in the afternoon, the dining room was crowded, and a steady hubbub of conversation arose. Most of the people eating there were middle-aged and wealthy-looking.

The head waiter appeared at his side. "One, *señor?*"

"Yes. One."

"Come this way, *por favor.*"

Clem followed him through the room, feeling awkward and out of place in such fancy surroundings. He made a stern inner effort to banish his self-consciousness. As a future lawyer, he'd be moving in a brand-new world, and he had better get used to it now.

"Here you are, *señor.*"

With a courtly bow, the man pulled out a chair for Erskine. He had been placed at a tiny table in the rear, against the wall. Well, no surprise, he told himself; he had neither looked important nor proffered a tip for a better table.

A waiter placed a menu in front of him. Erskine glanced at it cursorily, then looked up and around, hoping to catch a glimpse of Carlotta entering. He could invite her to his table— though it would be hollow, somehow, to treat her to dinner with her own father's money.

He did not see Carlotta. But he spied another familiar face only three tables away—a gaunt woman in black, talking animatedly to a sixtyish man of great strength and bearing.

Laurie Morgan. And though he had never laid eyes on him, Clem was willing to bet that her dinner partner was none other than Joel Tilley.

9.

LAURIE was signaling to him. Clem stared at her in surprise, realizing slowly that she was inviting him to come over and join her. She and her dining partner occupied a large table, one that could easily hold six. He rose, taking his menu with him, and walked over.

"Hello, Mrs. Morgan," he said with a forced smile.

Laurie stared petulantly. "What brings you to Santa Fe, young man? Some of Jake Kilgore's trickery?"

Clem felt uncomfortable standing there clutching his menu. Had she invited him over just to rail at him? He said as calmly as he could, "I'm here to take legal action in *Territory vs. McCandless.*"

"Just what I said. Legal trickery. Do you know Mr. Tilley?" Laurie asked, her voice loud and raucous in the genteel dining room.

Erskine shook his head. "I'm afraid we've never met."

"Well, now we have," the man boomed. He did not rise or offer his hand. He was short and stocky, with a barrel chest and a graying, spadelike beard. His complexion was dark, his skin leathery, his eyes deep-set and hooded. His mouth was a thin, cruel slash. "I'm Joel Tilley," he said. "I understand you're Jake Kilgore's new clerk?"

"Yes, sir."

Tilley seemed amused. "Join us, young feller?"

"All right." Clem hesitated and then sank into a chair facing the others. It was really no surprise, he reflected, to find Laurie Morgan in conference with the enemy, but it seemed unusual to receive a social invitation under the circumstances. Or was it? Was there anything in legal ethics to prohibit the conversation? Beneath the surface politeness ran an under-

84

current of menace and—what? Was it a note of warning? He waited quietly.

Joel Tilley swallowed a mouthful of local venison and wiped away gravy stains with a fat damask napkin. He seemed to be estimating the quality of the younger man. He said, "Been working long for Kilgore?"

Clem shrugged. "Little more than a week."

"Ornery, ain't he?"

"Not more than most," said Clem. "He's an individualist, I guess."

Tilley smiled grimly. "How come Kilgore's got you running errands so quick? Why ain't he here himself?"

"I think that's Mr. Kilgore's business," said Clem stiffly. "I don't mind telling you, he's just a bit under the weather."

Tilley grunted. "Drinking, more likely," he observed. "Kilgore's a boozer, and a chaser, and a reproach to the Territorial Bar. He's—"

"—a fighter!" said Clem quietly.

Tilley halted. "Yeah, I'll give him that," he conceded. "But only a disreputable fee-grabber would agree to defend Harry McCandless on this charge of murder."

Clem arose. "I don't want to hear this—" he began, when Laurie Morgan seized his wrist. "Erskine, you're new to the Territory," she said bitterly. "You don't know what kind of a man Harry McCandless is. Are you sure you want to start out on the wrong foot?"

"Wrong foot?" Clem was puzzled.

Tilley was toying with a knife. "I happen to know about your record back in Colorado, young feller," he advised. "I'm not too sure we'd admit a convicted thief to the Territorial Bar. Not unless he gave proof of good morals and improved character satisfactory to our courts." He smiled like a wolf. "It's just a thought."

Clem felt the blood drain from his cheeks. "I'm sorry you said that, Mr. Tilley. I'll have to report this conversation to Mr. Kilgore and he'll know what action to take. If you'll excuse me—"

"Oh, sit down!" said Tilley in a complaining voice. "I'm

only giving you a bit of advice. Dan McCandless is hated in the Territory. If you don't watch your step, you'll be marked and that can wreck you before you start out. I've got no personal ax."

Laurie Morgan had been sitting through this exchange between the men with a tight mouth of disapproval. "You haven't watched Harry McCandless grow up. We have," she said bitterly. "He should have been strangled in his crib. Eh, Joel?"

Tilley sat quietly in the hum and clatter of the dining room. A conversation in voluble Spanish arose and died in a corner of the room, and the banging of trays could be heard in the kitchen. His inward glance seemed to be on a distant scene.

"I knew him when he was a baby," he observed, almost to himself. "Knew the whole McCandless family then, especially Dan. Let me tell you something, young feller. A man can fool his friends, a man can fool his wife, but he can't fool his law partner—and we were partners. In those days, it was just after the big war, and there was a different spirit. We were all starting out and here was the Territory, with all this rich land and opportunities—and not too much law. A man had to depend on hisself and his friends. A partner—"

Tilley broke off a train of reminiscences and wiped his forehead with the napkin. He exchanged an enigmatic glance with Laurie Morgan and resumed the thread of conversation turning on the infancy of Harry McCandless. "There was always a devil in that boy," he observed. "He was a terrible baby. Smashed all his toys, wouldn't eat, wouldn't become housebroken. He wasn't weaned till he was close on five. Had Spanish wet nurses to give him the breast, until the day he took a grudge on his nurse. Bit her till blood flowed, and then nobody would nurse him any longer, so he was weaned. At *five!*"

Laurie said, "We could tell you plenty about him. How Dan gave him a puppy and Harry flayed it. He was ten, I think. We could tell you about the women Harry had—he'd take a *ranchero's* wife practically in front of the man's eyes, and nobody dared say otherwise." Laurie shook her head. "I warned Honey not to take up with him, but she said he had calmed down some since going to college."

"Since getting expelled from college," Tilley said. "Dan's bribed schoolmasters all his life to keep Harry enrolled."

"Kilgore is defending a monster," Laurie burst out vindictively. "Don't think I'm taking it personal because my own girl was brutally murdered. Harry ought to be exterminated for the good of all mankind, that's what."

Clem moistened his lips, not certain how to take the extravagant description of Harry McCandless. In his own mind was the recollection of a graceful youth whose eyes were alert with intelligence and whose manner was cultivated to a degree unusual to the Territory.

"I don't believe any of this," he said decidedly. "It's easy enough for stories to get around. It's all part of the smokescreen that's affecting this trial. In any case, Mrs. Morgan, much as I sympathize with your position, it's a matter for the courts. We don't hang a man just because he's got a mean reputation."

"We hang murderers," said Laurie grimly.

Clem shook his head. "Mrs. Morgan, I'm terribly moved by your grief, but there has got to be proof of guilt. With all respect, Mr. Tilley," he added, "the case so far is just inference piled on inference. Finding a fraternity pin on the body don't establish that the owner of the pin put it there. It only shows that he gave her a pin sometime during her life. It looks suspicious, but there's no motive—"

"No motive?" Laurie echoed.

"Quiet, Laurie," said Tilley.

"No motive?" Laurie repeated, rising and knocking over a glass, spilling wine on the fine cloth. "There's all the motive in the world, young man! I'll tell you—"

"Shush!" said Tilley peremptorily. Laurie rounded on her companion. "Don't you shush me, Joel Tilley!" She said strongly. There was a stir in the restaurant, and faces began to turn toward the rising disturbance. "I'm not giving away anything. This is one fact Jake Kilgore won't be able to laugh off."

She turned to Clem again. "Harry McCandless was going to marry my daughter."

Clem frowned. "Marry? I don't see—"

"He proposed to her on a hayride last month," Laurie added. "He gave her a diamond ring worth two thousand dollars."

Clem's eyes widened. "He—he did?"

Laurie nodded triumphantly. "Oh, he promised her the sun and the moon. I saw that ring myself last time I saw Honey in San Carlos. Diamond as big as a five-dollar goldpiece, maybe. Prettiest stone I ever saw. But then the next week Harry McCandless snatched the ring back from her."

"Laurie, stop it!" Tilley warned.

"I'll stop when I want to!" she shot back at him. She continued, "Harry could be expected to do that—give the ring, then change his mind. I just about was ready to get her to institute civil action to get that ring away from him again. And sue for breach of promise. Well, Harry must have got wind from Honey that I was going to get her to take him into court."

"Suppose he did?"

Laurie paused. "I think Harry would do anything before he'd admit any of this to his father."

Tilley said shrewdly, "Didn't Harry tell any of this to Kilgore? No, I can see he didn't! Scared stiff!"

Laurie said, "I'm still going to bring that action against McCandless. That ring belonged to Honey, and now it belongs to me!"

"And how much do you expect for that piece of blackmail?" asked a new voice suddenly.

Clem turned in surprise, as did the others. It was Carlotta! There was a moment of silence.

"How long have you been standing behind our backs?" Laurie demanded finally.

Carlotta's hands were shaking. "A minute, perhaps. Long enough to hear your dirty scheme to extort money from my father."

The two women exchanged glances, and it was the older woman whose eyes finally were lowered.

"It's not blackmail," said Laurie grimly. "I only want justice. Justice for my little girl, my poor dead little girl. It's something I'll get if I have to die for it."

"Justice—and two thousand dollars," said Carlotta with contempt. "You'll get the one, but not the other. Not at our expense!"

"You fancy bitch—!" Laurie began with rising fury.

Joel Tilley said in his ominous voice, "Calm yourself, Laurie. This is a public restaurant, and you're making the management uncomfortable. We shouldn't have invited this young man over."

"That's all right," Clem said. "I'm going back to my own table now."

Tilley leaned back and ran his fingers through the stiff wires of his beard. "A word of free advice, son. You're a well-turned-out boy, and I'd hate to see you get yourself into any trouble."

"Sir?"

"What I mean is simple. You're putting your life in danger by siding with Dan McCandless. If you ever want to practice law, get away from San Carlos and from Kilgore. What you're doing now isn't healthy. Go East, maybe. Out here you may not find it safe, understand?"

"Are you threatening me, Mr. Tilley?"

"I'm advising you in a friendly way. There are a lot of lawyers in this Territory who may not live to see that new century dawn in a few years."

Clem nodded frostily. "I'll take my chances. Good day, Mr. Tilley, Mrs. Morgan. Miss Carlotta, care to join me for dinner?"

They withdrew to the small table Clem had originally occupied. A few moments later, Laurie and Tilley rose and left the dining room. Clem and Carlotta consulted the menu and ordered—garlic soup and *arroz con pollo* for Clem, the same soup and *cordero asado,* roast lamb, for Carlotta. A few moments passed as they collected their thoughts. When the attentive and overly curious waiter had left, Carlotta looked up with a lurking smile.

"So you've met Joel Tilley?" she remarked. "I imagine he had a few things to say about my father?"

"Oh, yes."

"Not complimentary?"

"No. He seemed to be giving me a warning," Clem said slowly. "Telling me to clear out of this case if I wanted to live out a natural lifetime."

"You're not frightened?"

"For a wonder, no!" Clem replied. "I'm not sure why I'm not. He seemed to be in earnest."

"Oh, he is!" Carlotta replied. "Joel Tilley is always in earnest. There's no chivalry in the West, you know. It's a land of violent feelings. Sometimes embittered litigants have been known to take out their feelings in an ambush. Read the back files of our newspapers. A Territorial lawyer doesn't always have a good life expectancy."

"Kilgore—"

"Kilgore's been lucky. He's been in practice twenty years and only got shot at a couple of times. But others haven't been as lucky. I don't mean Tilley goes around murdering lawyers who oppose him, though they say that's happened. But a disgruntled client who loses a civil suit might just let some shotgun pellets off in the direction of the opposing lawyer."

"That stuff happened years ago. The West isn't like that any more!"

"You're still an optimist, Clem!"

"Well, never mind my life expectancy," he said, looking steadily at her. She had changed dresses, and now looked lovelier than ever in a clinging gown that molded the full curves of her bosom excitingly. "What's this story about a diamond ring your brother's supposed to have given Honey Morgan?"

Carlotta lowered her eyes. "It's true."

"Why wasn't Kilgore told?"

She said unhappily, "I would have told him before the trial started, if Harry didn't. But I hoped it wouldn't come up. It'll upset my parents terribly."

"You knew about it, then?"

"Harry wrote me while I was in New York with my parents. He said he'd had too much to drink one night, and made a sort of mock proposal to Honey, and gave her the ring. All as a joke. It was my great-great-grandmother's betrothal ring. It's been in our family since—oh, since 1790 or so. My mother used to wear it all the time, but in the last few years hardly ever. Naturally, Harry had no business giving it to anyone. Least of all to a—a prostitute," she said, naming the word boldly.

"A funny sort of joke," Clem said.

"Harry's like that. Well, I was horrified when he wrote me that he'd given the Lucero ring away. I wrote back immediately ordering him to get the ring back. Why, if my father and mother found out—"

"Did he get the ring back?"

"I don't know. He promised faithfully he would. If Laurie says he demanded the ring back, he probably did. I wish I knew." Her voice was toneless. "I haven't been alone with him to ask him about the ring. I don't know where it is now. This is serious, isn't it?"

Clem hesitated. "It might be," he said slowly. "If Harry knew that Laurie was contemplating an action against him, the prosecution could claim a valid motive for the murder."

"Nonsense!" she protested. "Just to avoid a lawsuit? It sounds far-fetched!"

They sat in silence while the first course was brought and placed before them. Clem made a pretense of interest in the steaming and hearty garlic soup for which suddenly he had little appetite.

"Carlotta—" he began, and considered his approach. She was holding herself in good control, he saw, but her distress was marked. "Of course it's far-fetched," he agreed without conviction. "But that's not the point. I haven't got any experience in the criminal law, not yet, but certain things stand to reason. The prosecution seems mighty confident they can make out a case. I guess they've got no eyewitness, or we'd know about it by now. So it's got to rest on the circumstances of the case—"

"Circumstantial evidence?"

Clem nodded. "Exactly. Sometimes circumstantial evidence is far more persuasive than direct evidence. An eyewitness can lie—but circumstances speak for themselves. If Mr. Beaudoin can show motive as well as all the rest, it can carry him a long way to a guilty verdict. But I wish," he added with distress, "that I had more experience under my belt. I'd be more sure of what I'm saying." An unhappy moment passed before he went on. "Mrs. Morgan and Mr. Tilley were telling me some of your brother's childhood escapades. A puppy your father gave him—"

Carlotta shuddered. "Don't remind me. Harry is—well, unusual. He's a brilliant boy, you know. But somewhat off balance. As though the burden of his intelligence had deranged him somehow."

"They'll throw out an insanity plea, I'm sure."

"I'm sure, too. But he's not completely normal. Whatever that woman was telling you should have proved that. But so brilliant! His marks in school were always terrible—but he got interested in languages and started teaching himself, and almost overnight learned Dutch and Portuguese and I don't know what else. Chinese, maybe. Or Turkish."

Clem was silent, torn by confusion and doubt as to the significance of the revelations brought by the hour. Had Kilgore sent him out on his own in the hope of evoking such information? He could not be sure. "I wish I knew what Mr. Kilgore will think about this ring business," he said finally. "A trial can turn on the smallest thing. But at least we have a better idea of what we'll have to fight. When are you going to see Governor Tellegen?"

"Tomorrow, I hope."

"And I'll try to see Hazledine then."

"Good luck."

Clem nodded seriously. "Oh, I'm not worried about Hazledine. The law says he has to approve the petition for the writ. But the important thing is getting the governor to supersede Beaudoin. I hope you manage it."

"I hope so, too."

After dinner they strolled around the gracious city, while Carlotta explained its ancient sites. Clem struggled with the temptation to offer his arm, and decided against it. He was still conscious of the gulf between himself and this beautiful, intelligent, and wealthy young woman who had been to school in the East and in Europe. Although she showed no condescension, and was perfectly eager to treat him as her intellectual and social equal, he shrank back from capitalizing on the opportunities she provided.

They returned early to the hotel. Clem saw her to her room—it was in the other wing, as he had feared—and then went to his own. He took off his coat and sat on the brass bed and considered the position. Kilgore had suggested a round of cantinas and houses where the sporting element could be expected to gather. "Shoe leather, Erskine!" Kilgore had said heavily. "You won't learn a thing raising calluses in your office. When a big trial is on, keep in motion and get the feel of the community. It's the atmosphere that influences the court and jury, and you never know where the tidbits lie!" It had seemed good advice but at the moment, with Carlotta McCandless lying sleepless in another wing of the hotel, Clem was not sure that he cared to encounter the cheap and furtive. Now why, he wondered, was the image of Carlotta so large in his thoughts?

It was many hours before he fell asleep.

He was up at dawn. By seven, he was dressed and downstairs to breakfast. An hour later, he was on his way to the offices of Judge Hazledine, portfolio in hand.

A pale, thin-lipped clerk greeted him at the judge's offices. "I'm Ariel Donovan," he announced. "Have you business with Judge Hazledine?"

"That I do," Clem said. "I'm up from San Carlos to apply for a writ in the matter of *Territory vs. McCandless.*"

"Oh, yes! Oh, yes!" Donovan said with a show of interest. "Kilgore's case, ain't it? Why ain't he here himself?"

"I just want the judge to sign the writ," said Clem. "Mr. Kilgore will make the argument on the return day."

Donovan stared with interest at the younger man's pale face of determination and turned aside to squirt a stream of tobacco juice into a sandbox.

"Judge is out of town," he said curtly.

"When will he be back?"

"Tonight. Tomorrow. Wednesday, maybe."

"Can't you be sure?"

Donovan said, "Or maybe not for another week." The tone was insolent. "I'm not responsible for Judge Hazledine's comings and goings."

"I'll be back this afternoon," Clem said, wondering if the clerk were lying to him.

"No use that. The judge wouldn't possibly deal with any legal matters the moment he returned. And I'm not saying he'll be back today, anyway."

"All right, then. I'll come again tomorrow."

"Why not just telephone? Call here around this time tomorrow, and I'll let you know if the judge is available. What's the name?"

Clem stared into a hard face and slowly shook his head. "Never mind about my name," he said slowly. "You just tell Judge Hazledine that Mr. Kilgore's law clerk was here to present this application. If he won't sign it, I'll find who will. What's more, I'm sure Mr. Kilgore will have something to say on the record when the time comes!" He turned on his heel and left.

The telegram advising Kilgore of the turn of events cost two dollars. Carlotta was not at the hotel, nor could he find any trace of her all that day. When night came, fretful and impatient, he went in search of amusement and information. He found it, cheaply enough, in a cantina not far from the old Santa Fe Trail where the talk was very much about the murder in San Carlos that was agitating the Territory.

"McCandless is guilty!" a bartender named Garcia advised. "Stands to reason."

Clem paid for a whisky. "How can you tell? You haven't heard any evidence?"

"Don't have to," said the bartender, biting a silver dollar.

"Kilgore's defending him! Stands to reason he's guilty." There was a burst of laughter. "I'm only giving out the general opinion."

For a second night Clem Erskine found it impossible to sleep against the sense of impending doom.

In the morning he met Carlotta at breakfast and learned that she had had no luck seeing the governor. At Judge Hazledine's offices, he was told bluntly by Donovan that the judge was not yet back from his "trip."

Another day of idleness went by. Too cold for sightseeing, it was, and Clem and Carlotta remained in the hotel lobby and argued politics while the dreary hours passed. Toward evening came a wire from Kilgore, expressing impatience and urging Clem to get a fast signature from the evasive Hazledine.

Wednesday morning. A telephone call to Donovan brought advice that the judge was back and would receive him.

10.

"PLEASE come in," said Donovan.

There was a subtle smile of amusement on the clerk's face as he opened the door of the antechamber. Clem entered uncertainly, followed by Carlotta. A rail divided the room, which held shelves of books. A door of varnished oak was painted with the name of Judge Abraham Hazledine.

"Can Miss McCandless attend?" asked Clem.

"I'm sure it's all right," Donovan replied with a sly grin. "We've had a lot of San Carlos people coming through this morning. One more or less can't make any difference. It's nothing formal."

"San Carlos people? Who?" Clem asked.

"You'll see. They're still here, talking to the judge. It might interest you to meet them." Donovan turned and rapped on the inner door and stood back on a command given by a deep voice of authority. The judge's chambers were filled with cigar smoke—a haze of fragrance to which Mike Duer and Pete Beaudoin were adding their contribution. A man of middle years with a hard face and a full jet Vandyke beard came forward.

"Miss McCandless? I'm sorry about this business," he said abruptly, and turned to Clem. "I'm Judge Hazledine. I'm told Kilgore sent you up here with an application for a writ in that Morgan case?"

"Yes, Your Honor," said Clem.

"Well, sit down," the judge said, waving Clem and Carlotta to a pair of deep leather chairs. "Can I offer refreshments?" Clem shook his head. "Let's see your papers."

Clem said, "This isn't a public hearing, Your Honor. Do we need these spectators?"

Judge Hazledine glanced up with surprise at the clear, hard voice of the younger man. "There's no rule about it, Mr. Erskine," he replied harshly. "If your papers are in order, you'll have my signature. I'm here to protect all rights guaranteed by the laws of the Territory and the United States— even those of murderers."

"I'm sure you will, Your Honor!" said Clem with an edge of antagonism. He was somewhat taken aback to feel the trembling of his hands as he reached into the portfolio for the sheaf of documents he had brought from San Carlos. The resounding language of the writ of habeas corpus was committed to memory. He handed over the petition drafted by Kilgore in support of his application.

"Verbose!" said Judge Hazledine grimly. "Full of words! Typical Kilgore—never can make his point without going around Cape Horn. What's the basis of this application, Mr. Erskine?"

Clem glanced at Carlotta in dismay. He had not expected verbal interrogation. She nodded encouragingly and he wet his dry lips.

"Why, uh—" he began weakly, and resumed, "Mr. Kilgore explains all that in his affidavit—"

"I want you to explain!" Judge Hazledine lit a cigar and sat back, testing the springs of a deep leather chair. "Give me the nubbin."

Clem drew a breath. "Just as simple as this, Judge," he said haltingly. "Seems to be no question that a crime was committed in San Carlos County. Ordinarily Sheriff Duer here would be justified in making an arrest, provided he's got some basis in evidence to go by. Mr. Kilgore's point is that our client—his client, that is—is being detained by the sheriff without any evidence at all. It's an illegal arrest. There's been no indictment, no warrant, no probable cause to think our client committed this crime. On top of that, the justice of the peace wouldn't, or couldn't, fix bail. I guess that's about it," he concluded, drawing a breath, and faced a fixed stare.

"All Mr. Kilgore wants is a hearing," he added. "It'll be up to this court to discharge the prisoner or to fix bail."

Judge Hazledine nodded appreciatively. "Unless Sheriff Duer's got something to say about it?" He turned inquiringly to the other side of the room, where the sheriff and the attorney general were following the discussion with every appearance of interest.

"Not at this moment," said Beaudoin, touching the sheriff's wrist lightly to cut off discussion. Judge Hazledine stroked his beard thoughtfully and invited further comment. "Yes, Miss McCandless?"

"May I have a moment with Mr. Erskine?" Carlotta asked. She took Clem aside into the corner of the room. "I'm worried, Clem," she said in a low voice. "I have a feeling there's something wrong here."

"He's got to sign," said Clem reassuringly. "It's all a bit of stageplay for the benefit of the others."

"Yes, but why should he stageplay? Why are they here at all? I don't like it, Clem. I think you ought to telegraph for instructions."

"I can't," he replied. "The judge has my application. If I don't get him to sign now, he might leave the county and we'd be losing time. Gee, I wish Mr. Kilgore hadn't put me in this spot."

The two glanced at each other, troubled by the weight of their responsibility, and finally Carlotta sighed and released his hand and they returned to the judge's desk where the scratch of a steel pen was loud.

"All signed," said the judge. "Now, since this writ is directed to the sheriff of San Carlos County, commanding that he bring up before me the body of the prisoner to inquire into the manner and legality of his detention, I direct that service of this writ be made here and now." He sat back, tranquillity itself, drawing on a rank cigar, staring with cold eyes at Kilgore's messenger.

"I—I don't know if I'm prepared to make service," said Clem. He was afflicted with a cold feeling of disaster. On the judge's command, he handed over the writ and petition to the peace officer, who glanced at the document perfunctorily. "It's for you, Mr. Beaudoin," Mike Duer drawled, handing on the document, and a disagreeable grin split his face. "It seems legal on its face. I reckon we'll have to answer."

"Yes, we will," Beaudoin agreed.

"I don't see any reason to waste time," Duer added with amusement. "Young feller, if Judge Hazledine will forgive me, I think you made a fine presentation. Real fine. Kilgore ought to be proud of you. And when you get back to San Carlos, you can tell that talkative windbag that I'll meet this petition with an affidavit and testimony that I've got an eyewitness who can fill in all the facts I need regarding the night that poor little girl was murdered."

Clem heard the gasp of dismay from Carlotta. "An eyewitness? Who?" he asked, stupidly.

Beaudoin said, "I'd keep quiet, Mike—"

Duer brushed this aside. "This is one time I don't mind letting Kilgore know what he's up against. The witness is Eli Weingarten. The one that's working at the Emporium in San Carlos for his daddy, Ben Weingarten. Since he's Harry McCandless' closest, and maybe only, friend, there can be no question. Tell Kilgore I'll meet him in court."

"There'll be a sworn affidavit in Judge Hazledine's hands on the return day of the writ," Beaudoin interposed. "It's no joking matter. Eli Weingarten's in custody of the United States marshal right here in Santa Fe. I wouldn't advise any attempt to get at him." He added with a polite flourish, "I'm sorry about this, Miss McCandless. It wasn't my idea that you be present."

Carlotta was pale. "It's quite all right, Mr. Beaudoin. I'm sure my father will have something to say about all this when the time comes." She turned to the judge. "Thank you for your courtesy, Judge. I'm a bit shocked that you permitted this deception to be played on Mr. Erskine."

"Deception?" the judge asked stiffly.

"You permitted him to submit that application, knowing the circumstances—"

Clem held out a restraining hand. "I believe there must be a draft affidavit here," he said in a shaking voice. "Might I look at the statement?"

In the moment of silence, the others exchanged glances, and a slight shrug from the judge acted as a release. Beaudoin handed a statement to Clem, who took it with nerveless fingers and passed it on to Carlotta.

It was a bombshell.

Eli had declared that he was prepared to testify that on the fatal night he had driven Honey Morgan out to Wa-po-nah, using a McCandless buggy and picking the girl up on Harry McCandless' specific request. He would, furthermore, testify that during the course of the evening there had been drinking and that both he and Harry had had relations with the girl. Further, Eli would testify that as the evening continued, Honey had grown violent and ugly as a result of consuming large quantities of cognac. She had become a general nuisance, fighting and kicking them, and finally it had become necessary to get rid of her before she caused serious damage. She was subdued after something of a scuffle, and Harry had left with her. Eli had gone to sleep, and in the morning the girl was not on the premises. Harry told him in explanation that he had driven her back from Wa-po-nah to

Dade Rawlins' place, leaving the ranch at 11:00 P.M. and returning at 1:00 A.M.

Clem looked up from his reading. "Well, so you've got yourselves a witness. But this doesn't add anything to your case. Two hours isn't long enough for Harry to have raped and killed the girl, driven out twenty miles into the mountains with her, and returned."

Duer smiled. "Harry's the one who said he came back within two hours. Eli went to sleep, remember? Harry may have been out till dawn doing just those very things, and then come back and lied to Eli."

Beaudoin said, "You don't seem to get the point, young feller. Harry McCandless swore he never saw the girl at all that week. We can prove he did. That shows he was conscious of guilt."

Clem exchanged a stricken look with Carlotta. "It has no bearing," he said stubbornly. "I'm not even sure your witness is telling the truth."

Beaudoin laughed unpleasantly. "That's just what Kilgore's going to say. It's up to the jury, isn't it?" With a leisurely gesture, he restored a cigar to his mouth and winked.

Clem felt his face turn red. The trap was sprung. He realized his blunder fully. He started to speak, but Hazledine sat back with a cold glance and folded his hands across a heavy cloth waistcoat.

"The writ has been served," he said coldly. "The prisoner, Sheriff Duer, will be brought up before me on the first day of the next term of the district court of San Carlos County. You are instructed accordingly."

"Yes, Your Honor," Duer said, with deliberate obsequiousness.

"Is there anything further, Mr. Erskine? Mr. Beaudoin?"
Clem shook his head. Beaudoin shrugged.
They were dismissed.

In front of the courthouse, after Duer and Beaudoin had taken their leave, Clem turned to Carlotta in anguish.
"I'm sorry," he muttered.
"For what?"

"For the mess I made of things in there. Any experienced lawyer would have withdrawn that petition the moment he smelled out the situation. The writ is an empty formality now. When Hazledine dismisses it next week, it'll score a nice juicy point for the prosecution, and all my fault. I should have listened."

"Clem, nobody expects you to make no mistakes. You're up against the slickest prosecutor in the Territory. Anyway, it isn't very serious, really."

"It is," he said bitterly. "Hazledine would probably have dismissed the writ anyway, but now he'll do it with fanfare. I should never have presented the petition and now allowed the prosecution to draw first blood."

"Well, maybe we'll have some luck with the governor. I finally got an appointment with him, for one o'clock this afternoon. You come along with me."

At one sharp, Carlotta and Clem were shown into the office of Charles Tellegen, the newly appointed governor of the Territory of New Mexico. A dignified, imposing man in his early fifties, he smiled graciously at Carlotta and listened with evident sympathy as she unfolded her story. But the smile vanished as she concluded.

"You see, Governor Tellegen, I'm not asking for a prosecutor who's in my father's pay. I know McCartney is my father's puppet, and I can't blame anyone for superseding him. But not with Beaudoin! Everyone knows he's a Tilley man, and Tilley hates my father! Can't it be arranged that a neutral prosecutor be appointed?"

"I'm afraid it can't, Miss McCandless."

"But—"

Tellegen seemed to droop. "Since taking office, Miss Mc-Candless, I've discovered that there are certain harsh realities to be faced in this Territory. I don't like Joel Tilley's activities, and I confess a lot of things your father has done have made me unhappy, too. But I can't supersede Beaudoin. He's the attorney general of the Territory, and so long as he's in office he'll decide who prosecutes which cases."

"But he's obviously prejudiced," Clem blurted.

"Not so obviously, my friend," Tellegen said quietly. "You forget that the prosecutor is *supposed* to achieve the conviction of the guilty. Prejudice is irrelevant. If he believes the defendant to be guilty, his task is to devote his strength to obtaining a conviction."

"Suppose the defendant isn't guilty, but Tilley and his friends are trying to make him look that way?" Clem asked.

Tellegen shook his head. "No, no, and no. I don't like to see the innocent punished, and assuredly I don't care for Pierre Beaudoin. But he's been duly elected, and there are no visible grounds for removing him from office. I'm unable to replace him, and unable to help you in any way. Believe me, I'm sorry."

Further argument was futile. Discouraged, Carlotta and Clem left the governor's mansion.

"I feel sorry for that man," Carlotta said outside. "His hands are tied by Tilley. He wants to accomplish good, but he can't act." She laughed bitterly. "Where's your optimism now? Things are getting better all the time, are they! We elect a reform governor—and can he act? Score one for the cynics, my idealistic friend."

Clem nodded. "We might as well go back to San Carlos immediately. We haven't accomplished very much here."

During the three days of Clem Erskine's absence, Jake Kilgore had been busy in San Carlos. He had viewed the body of Honey Morgan. He had talked to Doc Hewlitt, to Julian DuVivier, to Charlie Bear. He had learned little from any of them.

He had also talked three times with Harry McCandless. Getting information from him had not been easy. Harry took a detached attitude toward the whole affair, as though he did not understand or did not care that his life was at stake. Sweating, cursing, Kilgore managed to extract the grudging and reluctant admission that he *had* seen Honey Morgan on the night of her death, and that Eli Weingarten had been with him at the time.

"You sniveling fool!" Kilgore raged. "Why did you make those denials to Duer? Are you out to hang yourself?"

Harry smiled. "They say you're a good lawyer, Kilgore. I have faith that you'll be able to get me off."

"If I do," Kilgore vowed, "I'll double my fee. If you weren't my client, I'd cheer at your execution."

"How unfriendly, counselor."

"Don't give me that college-boy snideness!" Kilgore roared. "Just answer my questions."

Harry had answered them, after a fashion. And it became evident to Kilgore that Eli Weingarten was going to be a key witness at the trial.

On whose side, though? A grave danger existed that Beaudoin would make capital out of Eli's testimony, would perhaps even use him as a witness for the prosecution if he knew the extent of Eli's involvement.

Eli had to be spoken to.

But where was Eli? Kilgore inquired. Eli was "out of town." Ben Weingarten did not know where, and did not seem to care.

Kilgore fidgeted uncomfortably. From one hour to the next, the pain in his ear grew in intensity. The continuing cold weather, the uncooperative attitude of Harry, and the delay in the return of Clem all added to Kilgore's general miseries. He took advantage of the delay in proceedings to fill himself thoroughly with alcohol, and to make use of the accessibility of Tia Anna's. Tia Anna's social resources weren't a patch on those of Laurie Morgan's house, but circumstances didn't permit a visit to Santa Fe.

Kilgore's discouragement waxed. And on Wednesday afternoon, when Clem Erskine walked through the door of Kilgore's office, the lawyer knew the instant he saw Clem's facial expression that things had gone wrong.

"Welcome back, boy."

Clem shook his head. "I've got terrible news, Mr. Kilgore. So many different kinds of bad news that I don't know where to begin."

"At the beginning, then. Hazledine granted the writ?"

"Yes, of course. But—oh Lord, you'll roast me for this! Duer and Beaudoin were there. They presented an affidavit to the effect that Eli Weingarten would testify for the prosecution."

Briefly Clem summed up Eli's testimony. Kilgore uttered five astonishingly obscene words. Then he said, "I'm cursing myself out, not you. I've got no right to expect you to outfox Pete Beaudoin. All right, we have a writ. And they've got a witness. What else?"

Clem described the circumstances under which Laurie Morgan had told him of the diamond ring given to Honey.

"Lord Jesus Everlasting," Kilgore muttered. "Go on, then. What other calamities can you relate?"

"Just one more, sir. Carlotta—Miss McCandless—went to Santa Fe with me, you know. She petitioned Governor Tellegen to supersede Beaudoin with someone less beholden to Tilley. But the governor refused. Said his hands were tied. That was this afternoon. We got right on the train and came back."

For a long moment, Kilgore was silent.

Blow upon blow upon blow. A motive for the murder provided—a damning witness in the prosecution's hands—and the door closed to any hope of fair treatment from the prosecutor.

His head ached mercilessly. He felt the cold in the marrow of his bones.

"I suppose Duer has placed Eli Weingarten in custody, Clem?"

"Yes, sir. The U.S. Marshal at Santa Fe has him."

"That explains why I couldn't find him to question him." Kilgore looked up, his heavy-featured face racked with pain. "Well, I never seriously thought Beaudoin would be superseded. And I was pretty sure Laurie would produce something amounting to a motive. And I even thought that Beaudoin would make good use of Eli under cross-examination. But one thing puzzles the deuce out of me."

"That is, Mr. Kilgore?"

"How did Duer and Beaudoin find out about Eli Weingarten? Eli certainly wouldn't have gone to the authorities on his own. And I don't think Ben Weingarten would have told Duer, either. But *someone* tipped Duer off. Someone gave him this vital information. Who could it have been?"

"Maybe it was Dade Rawlins. Eli went to his place to get Honey."

Kilgore shook his head. "Dade told me he didn't see who was driving the buggy, and I believe him. No, I doubt it was Dade. Or Eli, or Ben. And nobody else knows—except the servants at Wa-po-nah, who saw Eli out there that night."

"Would *they* inform against their own master?"

Kilgore frowned quizzically. "I doubt it, but you never can tell. Some old grudge, maybe. There's got to be a traitor at Wa-po-nah, Clem. Either that or Beaudoin can read minds. There's no other way he could have gotten that statement out of Eli Weingarten."

11.

ANOTHER TALK with Harry McCandless was called for. Kilgore bundled himself up warmly, and he and Clem went out. The lawyer was deep in thought. It was, he thought, as though a curse had descended on the House of McCandless—a curse as potent as that which had shriveled the House of Atreus. The now almost inevitable collapse of the McCandless financial empire. The transformation of the gay Isabella Lucero whom Kilgore had known decades ago into the frigid matron of today. The foppishness of Harry, culminating in this Honey Morgan incident. Even the spinsterhood of Carlotta, a definite possibility now despite all her charm and beauty. One by one, the important things in Dan McCandless' life were being destroyed.

Atreus, though, had brought the vengeance of the gods

upon himself and his seed by committing an unspeakable crime against his brother Thyestes. What hideous deed lay in Dan McCandless' past? What had he done that was causing this grim expiation?

Kilgore liked the image of the family curse. He suggested it to Clem, embellishing it with details out of Aeschylus and Sophocles. A dreadful act, leading to the destruction of a powerful man. "You're seeing a Greek tragedy unfold, boy," Kilgore said resonantly. "Every ingredient is present. Only for Kilgore's sake, let it not end the way most of the old stories did."

"But what could Dan McCandless have done?" Clem said. "What could have brought all this upon him?"

Kilgore shrugged. "I can't rightfully say that. But I might as well let you in on some conjectures of mine. You know, some twenty years back all this land around here was part of the Lucero Grant. Don Alfredo Lucero—Isabella's father—owned it. Then came Dan McCandless, and his partner Joel Tilley. Dan courted Isabella and married her. The old don obviously didn't care much for his new son-in-law, but he recognized that McCandless had strength and was a worthy heir, even if he was an Anglo. For a few years everything went well. Then—not long after Harry was born—old Don Alfredo was murdered, out in the malpais, the badlands. Remind me someday to show you the place where the body was found. It's marked by a single white oak in a treeless plain."

"And they never found out who did it?"

Kilgore shook his massive head slowly from side to side. "No. Dan McCandless inherited the Lucero Grant. And right afterward, he and Tilley had their quarrel. Nobody knows over what. But Tilley lit out for Santa Fe, where he became a big man in the Territorial government, with lots of connections in Washington."

Clem said, "You think McCandless might have—might have murdered the old don?"

Kilgore shrugged. "I'd rather not say what I think. But if there's an old-fashioned Greek curse on the House of Mc-

Candless, it's got to have a cause. You can draw your own conclusions. And meanwhile be good enough to change the subject, because here's McCandless himself."

They had walked all the way across the plaza by this time, and were outside the sheriff's office. Dan McCandless approached on foot from the opposite side, his face bleak, his huge shoulders slumped wearily. Only the blazing intensity of his eyes hinted at the powerful man who once had been.

He greeted Kilgore with a nod. Kilgore introduced Clem; it developed that Carlotta had already told her father something about Kilgore's new clerk.

McCandless said, "Carlotta's told me everything that happened in Santa Fe."

"Including the fact that Eli Weingarten will testify for the prosecution?" Kilgore asked.

"Including that. I've just been for a talk with Eli's father."

In alarm Kilgore said, "You didn't get violent, Dan!"

McCandless shook his head. "I just talked to him. I asked him if he had been the instigator of Eli's visit to the sheriff. He said he wasn't. He *swore* he wasn't. He's pretty disgusted with Eli." McCandless smiled faintly. "When Ben Weingarten takes an oath, he means it. So somebody else tipped Duer off about Eli. Who, Jake?"

"I'm sure I don't know." Kilgore shivered. "Will you keep me out here in the cold all day, Dan? I'm on my way to talk to your son."

"I'll accompany you, if you don't mind."

"Suit yourself," Kilgore said.

As they entered the lockup, McCandless said, "I'd like to know who tipped off Duer. It might be someone at Wa-po-nah. And if it is, I'll smash him!"

One of Duer's deputies led the three men to Harry McCandless' cell. Harry was sprawled out on his cot, reading a selection from a crate of books brought down from Wa-po-nah by Julian DuVivier. His look now was one of indifference and cool reserve as the lawyer and his assistant entered, but as his father appeared, his expression changed. He closed his book and arose.

"Hello, Father," he said quietly.

"Hello, Harry," said Dan McCandless. "Are they treating you all right?" His glance took in a scrubbed cell, a warm Franklin stove blazing in the corridor, a neatly made cot covered with rough blankets, and a devotional picture drawn in charcoal on the cell wall by a previous prisoner—or so it seemed, until the father, taking a closer glance at the macabre scene of a Crucifixion, indicated it apparently was the work of the current occupant of the cell. "I wish you wouldn't do those drawings, Harry," McCandless murmured unhappily. In the lengthened, twisted body of the Man in torment, something Byzantine could be seen.

"I'm sorry, Father," said Harry. "I'm being well treated. After all, royalty is royalty—even in captivity. I'll be well fed until the moment I'm hanged."

"Oh, Harry, Harry," murmured Dan McCandless, twisting his face with pain. "Don't take that line. You'll be acquitted. You listen to Kilgore—"

"If you say so, Father," said Harry. "I just don't think they mean to give me a chance. It looks hopeless. Well, gentlemen, I can't offer chairs, but you can sit on this couch—"

Dan McCandless looked uncertainly at the lawyer. "I'm sorry, Kilgore," he said apologetically. "I guess you'd better take over. I don't trust myself to talk." He turned aside and gripped the bars and let his shoulders sag with weary frustration as the interview went on. Kilgore covered a few preliminaries before he came to the main point. Crouching in the narrow space, he put his questions in a low voice.

"What made you deny you saw Honey during that week?" the lawyer asked.

The youth shrugged. "I told him I didn't murder that girl," he said coolly. "Isn't that what you're working so hard to prove?"

Kilgore searched the level, intelligent eyes of the youth, so close to his own, looking for a trace of fear—but saw— what? He could not be sure.

"I don't object to a denial of guilt," he said slowly. "What bothers me, Harry, is something else. What made you deny that you saw the girl at Wa-po-nah the entire week of her death? It was bound to come out, that lie."

Harry looked aside. "I didn't think—" he muttered. "Is it important?"

"Yes, it's important," said Kilgore quietly. "But I'm puzzled, Harry. You're the most intelligent man I ever met. You've got a penetrating understanding of these things a grown man would envy. But you must have known that Eli Weingarten was roaming around outside. What made you sure he wouldn't fall into the hands of the other side?" Harry Mc-Candless was silent. "A lie is one thing. A lie that can come out in court is another. *Falsus in uno, falsus in omnibus!* Once you're caught in one lie, the jury can disbelieve all the rest."

There was silence in the cell, broken only by the heavy breathing of Dan McCandless.

The youth finally raised a twisted face of cynicism. "They wouldn't believe me anyhow," he muttered. "What difference would it make? You're the expert on courtroom lying, Kilgore. Can't you figure out some smart tactic?"

"Oh, Harry!" Dan McCandless burst out.

Kilgore raised a hand for silence, touching the stabbing pain in his ear. His deep eyes searched the pale, desperate face of the youth. "I ain't a miracle man," he said quietly. "I got that reputation because of my unusual talents and my persuasive, golden tongue, but I can't work against stupidity. Unless you want to hang, you'll change that smartalecky attitude and listen to your lawyer. We got the whole Territory against us. Your only hope is with the jury."

Dan McCandless' voice was choked. "How could you do this to your mother?" he burst out. "It's my fault, Kilgore! My fault! When he gets out, he'll live on five dollars a month. Fifty cents, maybe! If I've still got fifty cents to my name—"

"McCandless—please," Kilgore said.

McCandless subsided. Kilgore hesitated, mastering his anger at this worthless boy, mastering the pain in his skull. He said quietly after a moment, "You've made a lot of trouble for me now, Harry. The prosecution can fasten on evidence of a guilty conscience. It's a rule of evidence in criminal law that flight, and denials, and lies that point to guilty conscience, are in themselves some evidence of guilt. You should have realized that."

Harry remained silent.

Kilgore said, "You're intelligent. Too damned intelligent for your own good. And you're calculating. How could you have possibly committed an act so out of character as that stupid denial? It was unworthy of you, Harry!"

"Is that a compliment or an insult?" Harry asked thinly.

"Take it as you like. But it throws an element of confusion into this case that I could have done without. It leads me to wonder what other nasty surprises lie ahead. Eli Weingarten is going to testify against you."

Harry's glance was unwavering. "I rather expected that Eli would do that."

"And still you lied to Duer?" Kilgore said. "All right, then. I want you to tell us exactly what happened the night you and Eli had Honey Morgan up at Wa-po-nah. And no more lies, damnit! Erskine," he added, "make notes."

Harry sighed. "Well," he began, with a sidelong glance at his father, "Eli and I decided to have some fun, and Honey had been begging the longest time to come out to Wa-po-nah. It was a pathetic dream of hers to see the big house. I guess she imagined it to be something out of this world—a sort of palace, not the place it truly is in reality. Rather ordinary, rather drab, really—" Harry begged for a cigarette and went on. "I had arranged for Eli to pick her up on the quiet when he drove into town. He brought her back to the house and we had some fun, all right—"

Kilgore interrupted. "Did you get her to bed? The two of you?"

Harry hesitated. "What would be the better version?" he asked. "I mean, what would make a better impression on the jury?"

"Harry!" Dan McCandless burst out.

Kilgore put up a hand. "The only thing that can help you now is the solemn, unvarnished truth," he said grimly. "I get the impression both of you had that little girl. Suppose Eli were to say that?"

Harry looked about at implacable eyes. "I couldn't deny it."

"You both had her in bed?"

Harry nodded, turning his glance from his father to the overcast winter sky seen through the prison bars. "Around half past ten she started getting wild on cognac. By this time Eli was drunk and ready to fall asleep in the guestroom. I knew I had to get her out of the place before she started to smash some of Mother's fine Wedgwood china—which she was threatening to do."

"Go on."

"Go on about what?"

"How did she get all bruised up?"

"Oh, that!" Harry closed his eyes. "I had her one last time—with force. Oh, it wasn't exactly rape, Kilgore. Honey was wild and we wrestled around a bit, but she was inviting it. It was all part of the drinking. At any rate, when it was over I dressed her and I helped her out to the carriage. I told Eli I was taking her home and I left. That was about eleven o'clock at night."

Dan McCandless was staring with glassy eyes. "Why the hell did this have to be at Wa-po-nah?" he groaned. "Why in your mother's house? Why not at the girl's own place? Or in some barn? Or out in the fields? This will kill your mother."

"I don't know why," Harry muttered. "It just happened."

Kilgore said, "Never mind that now. The point is, that Harry is beginning to give some reasonable explanation of the facts. It's a hell of a lot better than some fool lying that wouldn't deceive a cow." He turned back to the prisoner. "How drunk was she? Could she walk on her own power?"

"Yes, she could," Harry said emphatically. "But she was plenty drunk, and pretty sore at me. I got her into the carriage, and—"

"A carriage, not a wagon?" Kilgore suggested.

"Right!" Harry paused and went on. "Ask Julian, and he'll back me up. He was watching when I left."

"And the girl was alive?"

"Alive," Harry agreed. "I got her almost to San Carlos, and I guess somebody must have seen the lights of the carriage—but when we were almost in town she grabbed the reins and started flogging the mare. It was a fine, spirited animal, and not used to that sort of treatment. We damned near had a runaway. Honey was thrashing around pretty wildly, and I was afraid we'd get wrecked if I kept her with me. Besides, I was pretty tired myself, and bored with her. So I stopped the carriage and dumped her out on the road."

"Where did you do this?" Kilgore asked.

"It was practically in town. I could show you the spot."

"Did you dump her physically? I mean, did you hurl her to the ground?"

Harry shook his head. "I grabbed her by the waist and set her down on her feet. She was drunk, but sober enough to stand up. She cursed me out and shook her fist at me, but I turned around and drove back to Wa-po-nah."

"Then she was alive and well when you last saw her?" the lawyer asked.

"Definitely," Harry said.

"You aren't talking to Duer now. I want the truth, even if it's not so nice."

"The truth," Harry said, "is that I left her alive on the road. I figured she'd walk the rest of the way home. In her state, the fresh air would have done her good."

"What time did you get back to Wa-po-nah?"

"Around one. Eli was asleep. I went to bed, and in the morning I told him what had happened. Next thing I knew, it was a few days later and Duer was arresting me for a murder. You know what happened, of course. Somebody else found Honey and raped and killed her on the road after I left her. It's that simple."

Kilgore snorted. "Is it, now? Suppose *you* try to make a jury believe that, with all the other evidence that's piled up against you!"

"The other evidence?" Harry said.

"Your fraternity pin was found by her body," Kilgore said.

"What of it?" Harry said. "I gave it to her months ago. She

wanted some kind of token from me. And since I'd been expelled from college, I gave her the silly pin."

"Was she wearing it the night you last saw her?"

"She wore it all the time. It must have been ripped off her in the struggle with her killer."

"All right," Kilgore said. "I might be able to find someone reliable who remembers having seen her wearing the pin before her death. That would be sufficient refutation. But what about the Navajo blanket she was wrapped in? Might it not be proved that it was your blanket?"

"I have several blankets. They all look alike, anyway."

"And the *campesino* who saw the body being lowered from a buckboard with the Wa-po-nah insignia?"

"He might have been lying," Harry said. "Or dreaming. Or perhaps someone else from the ranch picked her up after I left her, murdered her, and took her out into the hills. I don't see any link to me. Wa-po-nah has a lot of wagons."

Kilgore arose and began to comb his hair, pulling the comb through grease with a thoughtful expression. A pattern of hope was beginning to emerge, but incredible difficulties lay ahead.

"The girl was found with her mouth full of plaster," he said. "You have any ideas about that, Harry?"

"Not one, except that maybe it's some Indian custom and an Indian killed her. I don't have the faintest notion what it could signify. And I don't see how that can rightly be held as evidence against me."

Kilgore paused. There was only one item left to discuss with Harry, but it was an explosive one. "When my assistant, Mr. Erskine, was in Santa Fe the other day, he learned from Laurie Morgan that you had given her daughter a diamond ring, an heirloom valued at some two thousand dollars. Is this true?"

Dan McCandless was on his feet and roaring, "What? You gave that trollop your mother's ring?"

"Quiet!" Kilgore said commandingly, brushing the big man into his seat before he could do violence to his son. Harry had turned quite pale. His upper lip was trembling. For the first time since his arrest, he looked genuinely frightened.

Kilgore said again, "Is it true, Harry?"

"N-no. I didn't give her any diamond rings. Only the fraternity pin, and that wasn't worth much."

"Laurie said you had," Kilgore went on. Dan McCandless made a strangled sound as Kilgore added, "Laurie also said that you had subsequently taken the ring back. In fact, she had been threatening to start an action in replevin against you to recover the ring. Do you know anything about this?"

Harry shook his head. "Small wonder that Laurie would think up such an idea. She probably thought I was going to marry her little tart of a daughter. But I didn't give her that diamond ring. It's been in our family for generations, you know."

Kilgore was silent. Harry was lying—either that, or Carlotta had lied when she corroborated Laurie's accusations to Clem—which was unthinkable.

He said heavily, "Where is the ring now, Harry?"

"I'm sure I don't know," Harry said. "With all the other family valuables, I suppose."

Kilgore glanced at McCandless. "McCandless, when you get back to the ranch, check and see that the ring is still where it ought to be. Let me know." To Harry he said, "Very well. That's all I have to say to you, Harry."

"But not all I have to say," McCandless burst out. He crossed the cell and Harry shrank back at the unexpected gesture of sorrow and anger. "It was bad enough that you brought that girl out to Wa-po-nah," he cried. "I guess something in you has got to come out—but to give her your mother's ring! The Lucero ring! Harry, why? Why? The Lucero blood goes back three hundred years in this land. Is this what it comes down to? This cell and the gallows out in the yard? Is this the end for the McCandless line? Oh, my God, my God!" He groaned and turned with fierce eyes of hatred to the lawyer. "Stop 'em, Kilgore! Stop 'em—or I will! If they touch one hair of the boy's head, I'll kill 'em! Joe Tilley, Pete Beaudoin, Mike Duer, the whole pack! There was blood once in the land. Blood will run again! I swear it, on my soul—on my hope for redemption!" His massive hands opened and closed in a convulsion of grief.

Kilgore took the big man's arm. "The boy's not going to the gallows, Dan," he said quietly. "And you'll have plenty of time to upbraid him after he's acquitted. Let's go now. Get back to Wa-po-nah and try to relax. Don't let the boy's mother see you like this."

McCandless nodded. He did not speak to or look at his son. Bowing his head, he stalked out of the cell.

12.

THEY RETURNED to Kilgore's office. The lawyer asked Sarah to fix up some hot compresses for his ear; now, instead of spasmodic needles of pain, he was starting to feel an almost constant throbbing ache.

Sarah did as she was asked, though not without muttering that Kilgore ought to get himself to a doctor instead of going through agonies to save Harry McCandless. Kilgore shrugged off her argument. His ear could wait, he said stubbornly. The case came first.

Clem said, "He was lying about the ring, wasn't he?"

"I imagine he was, Clem. Well, it's sometimes necessary for a lawyer not to press his client too far. We'll just have to hope that any testimony concerning the ring will be ruled out at my objection. Anyway," he said, applying the hot compress to his ear and wincing at the not altogether unpleasant sensation of heat, "the rest of Harry's story is a damned clever one. I feel encouraged for the first time since you came back this afternoon."

"Why do you say it's clever, Mr. Kilgore?"

"Because it makes no denials of Eli's story. If it did, the jury could presuppose that Harry was lying, since he's already demonstrated a tendency to lie when it suits him to. But Harry doesn't contradict Eli's story. He simply cuts the ground out from under it. He puts the fatal events into a convenient limbo of time and space."

Clem nodded. "That's what I told Duer and Beaudoin when they confronted me at Judge Hazledine's. I told them then that Eli's story wouldn't give them a case. Of course," he added with a grin, "I was bluffing, but it seems to have worked out."

"And Harry now has backed it up properly. If Honey left Wa-po-nah alive and kicking, as Harry will declare under oath, then the prosecution will have no way of pinning the actual murder on him." Kilgore removed the compress and rubbed his jaw thoughtfully. "What we need now, Clem, is a witness to the fact that Harry actually did leave the ranch at eleven and return two hours later. If we can demonstrate that he left with a living Honey at eleven, and was back without her by one, then it'll put Harry in the clear, since he couldn't possibly have assaulted and raped her and taken the body all the way out to the mountains in that short a time."

"Suppose the jury doesn't believe our witness?"

"We'll face that when we come to it. The important thing, Clem, is to find the witness. Which will be your job. Tomorrow."

"Me, sir? How?"

"You, sir. You'll go up to Wa-po-nah without me and interview the house servants. *Habla usted español?*"

Clem smiled. *"Solamente un poco."*

"How little?"

"Very little, Mr. Kilgore. *Muy poco.*"

"Well, Carlotta can translate for you. I'm sure you won't mind being near her. Eh, Clem?"

The younger man blushed and grinned, but said nothing.

Kilgore grunted sourly and rolled a cigar. His assistant's romantic turn of mind was no concern of his own, and at least he was big enough not to look ridiculous beside a tall girl like Carlotta McCandless. Now there was a thought! he reflected, grimly amused. Dan McCandless probably planned to marry his daughter off to some young member of the alleged Territorial aristocracy—if the term, outside the Spanish element, were not self-contradictory. More likely he had his goal set on the rich and powerful elements of Eastern and European families—or marrying into royalty, which seemed the fashion in New York and Philadelphia and Boston. A lot of ridiculous stories kept drifting back from the great metropolitan centers—and the mere thought of Clem Erskine, raw-boned, unlicked, penniless, not even yet a lawyer—aspiring to Carlotta McCandless would be enough to raise a head of steam and set McCandless screaming with rage.

Or so it would seem at any other time. Just now, the McCandless household lay in the shadow of tragedy. All this was pure daydreaming. Kilgore had another reason to send Clem alone to Wa-po-nah. It was a matter of finding, not creating witnesses. The day would come, Kilgore foresaw, when Pete Beaudoin would get a crack at some future witness for the defense. It was possible to foresee the stabbing forefinger, the voice of icy scorn, the howl of ridicule. "Aha! Mr. Witness! And what else did Mr. Kilgore tell you to say?" No, it was milder strategy, and more effective, to send an emissary with smooth cheeks and an ingenuous manner.

Kilgore grunted. "Clem, I'm placing no obstacle in your way to the development of a romantic interest. But I want you to handle yourself with legal acumen. You can go at it in two ways. One way is to ask that pack of house servants what they know. Being dumb, they won't know a thing. Or you can make a little preliminary speech. Present the pathetic circumstances of the young master of the household. Toss out the time element and the other significant factors. Stress what it might be advisable or useful for the defense to establish in court. Savvy?"

"Oh, yes!" said Clem.

Kilgore raised a finger of admonition. "However, Clem!

Bear in mind a cardinal principle of this law firm. *You will not put words in the witnesses's mouth.* Is that clearly understood?"

Clem nodded. "I wouldn't dream of it," he said seriously. "It's one thing to draw out the spontaneous narrative of the illiterate and barbarous witnesses we've got to use in the courts, Mr. Kilgore. It would be entirely another thing to coach a witness. I'm sure I've got that straight. The witness has got to find his own words."

"Hum," Kilgore said suspiciously. He could not be sure whether or not a smile lurked in the corner of his assistant's mouth—and then a mighty belch shook his frame. "Time for dinner!" he announced. "*Ipse dixit!* The inner man is talking. Let's attend to it. But I'll tell you one thing that would make me easier in my mind . . ." he added.

"Yes, sir?"

Kilgore paused, shaking his head in thoughtful wonder. "Some show of natural remorse!" he murmured, his eyes on a distant scene in the icy hills. "Some feeling for that pretty little girl whose life was cut short. I'm defending Harry Mc-Candless, but it would sit better if I could see some human feeling for that girl he once had.

"I guess he's human," Kilgore added gloomily, stretching his frame, "and I can't think of a thing worse to say for him. Let's see about that food."

The following morning, after breakfast, Clem Erskine was picked up by a Wa-po-nah buggy and taken to the ranch. The cold had abated, slightly; the sun was strong and bright, the sky cloudless, the air so clear that the purple mountains far to the west jutted up, clearly visible, like discolored fangs stabbing the sky.

He found Dan McCandless and Carlotta waiting for him in the library room.

Dan McCandless did not seem to have slept all night. He and his suit both had a rumpled look. His hair was unkempt; cigar ashes flecked his vest; even at half past nine in the morning, he had a brandy smell. Nervous and jumpy as a cat, he paced back and forth in the big room.

Carlotta, too, was showing the effects of the family troubles; there were dark rings under her eyes, and her cheeks looked hollow and pale. She was dressed informally, in a plaid flannel shirt and a suede riding skirt which clung to the firm contours of her body.

"I'll get the servants," Carlotta said. "Do you want to speak to them all?"

"Please, yes," Clem said. "Are there many?"

"About a dozen in the immediate household. Plus many more who live on the grounds."

"How close to the main house?"

"Oh, anywhere from half a mile farther out."

Clem shook his head. "I won't bother with them. Let's talk to the household servants. I'm told most of them don't speak English."

"Only a few," Carlotta said. "But none of them really *understands* English. It would be better if you questioned them through me, in Spanish."

She walked to the door and tinkled a bell. Julian DuViviér, who stood just outside, nodded and glided away. A few moments later, the first of the servants filed in.

Clem pointed to one, a man of about fifty. "Who's he?"

"Hermano Perez. The groom," Carlotta said.

"All right. Ask him if he gave any horses to anyone the night Honey Morgan was supposedly brought here."

Carlotta looked at the groom. "*¿Diste algunos caballos a cualquiera cuando la señorita Morgan fué traída aquí en la semana pasada?*"

Perez answered briskly, and Carlotta translated. Yes, Perez remembered the night. Young Eli Weingarten had been here, and Perez had given him a horse. Weingarten had driven a buggy to town and had returned with the Morgan girl.

"How about later on that evening?" Clem asked. "Did he see Harry leave the ranch?"

No, Perez had seen nothing. He had gone to bed about ten

o'clock that night. Harry had stabled the horse himself upon returning to Wa-po-nah.

"Try the next one," Clem said.

"Juana Garcia, cook," Carlotta said.

"Ask her what she remembers of that night."

Juana Garcia remembered little. She had prepared food for the two boys and their guest, and Julian had brought it to them. She had gone to sleep early, too, about ten or ten thirty. She remembered hearing laughter before she fell asleep. She knew nothing else.

Clem called the next servant, and the next, and the next. None of them knew anything. Every single one of them claimed to have been asleep from ten or ten thirty on, the fatal night. Some of them remembered having seen Honey and Eli earlier in the evening, but none could offer any testimony about the hours between eleven and one.

Clem had deliberately questioned the lesser servants first, hoping to learn something unexpected. Now, only Julian DuVivier remained. Clem glanced at Carlotta and the brooding, despondent McCandless, then at the ageless Negro.

Julian said coolly. "I will be glad to answer your questions, Mr. Erskine. I may tell you that I have a fair idea of what Mr. Harry told Mr. Kilgore and Mr. McCandless in the lock-up."

A flicker of intelligence passed between McCandless and his servant, and this was interrupted by Carlotta and Clem Erskine. The young lawyer felt a measure of relief. If there were a problem in the legal ethics of coaching witnesses, it had solved itself.

"Suppose you tell me what you know, Julian," he said quietly. "And pretend this is a courtroom and you're testifying before a jury."

Julian nodded. "Yes. That evening Eli Weingarten was here for dinner. Afterward Mr. Harry sent Eli into town to get the Morgan girl. She arrived here about nine o'clock, I would say. I served drinks to them. If Miss Carlotta will forgive me, I must tell you that the Morgan girl was quite naked at one time when I entered the room, but displayed no embarrassment. It was rather disgraceful, and I told Harry so, but he commanded me to mind my own business, which I did."

"Was that the first time you ever saw the girl in that condition?"

"Yes, sir."

Carlotta had reddened slightly. McCandless' scowl of gloom deepened. Clem said, "Go on, Julian."

"During the latter part of the evening there was the sound of a struggle. I went to the room and was told by Mr. Harry that the girl was drunk and unmanageable. Mr. Weingarten had gone to sleep, he told me, and he was going to drive the girl back to town. I helped Mr. Harry take her down to the wagon, since the rest of the staff was asleep. I watched Mr. Harry drive off. Then I returned to my room."

"What time did he leave?" Clem asked.

"Just about eleven, I'd say."

"And then what?"

Julian shrugged. "About two hours later, I heard the sound of a buggy approaching. I glanced out my window and saw that Mr. Harry had returned. I helped him stable the horse. He had come back alone."

"How come you were up so late?"

"I sleep only a few hours a night," Julian said softly. "I rarely close my eyes before two in the morning."

Clem hesitated. "Will you tell the same story to the court that you've told me?"

"Of course, sir."

"All right, then. Keep out of town and if Mike Duer comes to question you, don't give him any concrete information. For instance, if he asks you whether you—"

"I don't think Julian needs any further advice," Carlotta interrupted. "I'm sure he knows how to talk to the sheriff."

Clem paused. "Very well, Julian. Mr. Kilgore would like to see you at your earliest convenience. At the office, if you don't mind."

"Not at all," said Julian, and disappeared into the kitchen.

"Oh, my God, my God!" said McCandless despondently. "That the boy's life should depend on things like that—"

"Dad!" said Carlotta warningly.

There was a moment of constraint, and then Clem asked for leave to telephone. Kilgore took the news without surprise and suggested that his assistant might spend the rest of the day at Wa-po-nah if invited. It was important to get the feel of the place—the concrete sense of the land and its people. That painstaking attention to atmosphere and detail, he advised, was the difference between the legal hack and the artist. Abruptly he rang off.

When Clem returned, McCandless was nowhere to be seen. "He'll be up in his study," said Carlotta, clutching her throat with an expression of distress. "Since this case began, he does nothing but wander around the house. I think he's blaming himself—"

With an effort, she composed her face and invited Clem to remain. "We'd be very happy to have you stay the morning with us, Clem. And to stay for lunch. I'd like to show you the grounds. Can you mount a horse?"

Clem was pleased to accept the invitation. Carlotta was abstracted and troubled, but polite, and after coffee showed her guest through the big house. For the first time, Clem appreciated the vast scale of building—the princely magnificence with which McCandless had expanded the original *hacienda* of the Lucero family that he had acquired at the time of his marriage to Isabella. Wa-po-nah was a showplace of the West, and the exploration of its resources covered the bulk of the morning and magically came to a halt with all its areas yet unvisited.

"Perhaps we can see the rest some other time," Carlotta said. "My mother's rooms have some interesting furnishings. Castilian. That's her wing, over there."

"She keeps to herself a lot, doesn't she?" Clem asked.

Carlotta's smile vanished. "Yes. She's an unhappy person, Clem. There's tension between her and my father. I don't really understand why. But they're miles apart, and have been for years."

She changed the subject quickly by taking Clem down to the wine cellar. Case upon case of fine vintages were stored there. Carlotta handled the dusty bottles with confidence, showing ports and sherries and champagnes, Château d' Yquems and Mouton-Rothschilds, Johannisberger Kabinets and Clos-Vougeots.

They emerged from the wine cellar, Clem taking the lead. As he reached the top step, he heard a little cry and turned, just as Carlotta tripped and began to fall forward. His big hands caught her wrists and pulled her to her feet. For a moment they stood that way, their bodies close, his hands on her wrists, their lips only inches away. But the moment passed as Clem, surprised and caught off guard, released her. They smiled self-consciously at each other, and Clem knew that he had missed an opportunity. He might have kissed her. But, he thought, she might have slapped him, too. Regretfully, he resolved to have his wits more about him the next time Carlotta stumbled into his arms.

The tour of the ranch went on until finally it was lunch time, and Clem, ravenously hungry, sat down to a meal of a kind he had never had before. A slab of steak the size of his head, blood-red and tender, a bottle of wine, elaborately sauced salads and vegetables. Isabella McCandless did not come to the table; her husband muttered in explanation that she was ill and was remaining in her rooms at least for the next few days.

There was brandy after the meal, and then Dan McCandless excused himself, saying it was time he went into town and to oversee the office work. Again Clem was left alone with Carlotta.

"I hope you'll come again," she said.

"I'd love to. And I hope it doesn't have to be a professional call."

"You could come out here to see me, I suppose. That is, if you wanted to."

"I'd guess I would," he said. She gave him her hand, and he held it a moment, feeling the strong, cool fingers, and then, succumbing to the impulse, he bent and kissed it. She touched his hair.

"Thank you, Clem. And do come again. Julian will show you out."

The Wa-po-nah buggy clattered rapidly down from the ranch into the town. Clem sat back, his eyes closed, dreaming of Carlotta. A kiss on the hand—then, perhaps, the lips—and then what?

Mrs. Carlotta Erskine, he thought, trying the name out for size. He invented an imaginary newspaper report: *Mr. and Mrs. Clem Erskine arrived in London today for the first stop on their three-month grand tour of Europe. After a week here, the Erskines will depart for Calais. Mr. Erskine is a well-known American barrister.*

He grinned and told himself to stop building castles in Spain. Dreaming like this would only set himself up for ultimate disillusionment. Carlotta wouldn't have a country oaf like himself. She had only been politely friendly today, nothing more.

He said nothing to Kilgore of the events at Wa-po-nah after the telephone call. But Kilgore did not care to know the state of romance between his assistant and Carlotta. He had other news.

The grand jury had convened and had handed down its expected indictment: murder in the first degree. On Monday next, Judge Hazledine was prepared to deal with the writ of habeas corpus.

The legal process was under way. Before long, Harry McCandless would be on trial for his life.

13.

JUDGE ABRAHAM HAZLEDINE adjusted his glasses and drew a sheet of paper closer as he prepared to enter a notation in his minute books. The courtroom was crowded on the return day of the writ. The stove was blazing and hot to his right near the window and the stink of wet wool was strong in the press of humanity. Without raising his glance, he could visualize the array of humanity who had turned out to see the opening skirmish. Laurie Morgan, mother of the dead girl, was seated in the front row, garbed in black, flanked by a pair of private detectives hired by Tilley. This was not his concern. It was merely an indication of the struggle of forces yet to come. A stout, bald man was surely Ben Weingarten—father of the key witness, and this relationship might be deduced from the expression of uneasiness and shame of a man whose son was about to betray a friend to the law.

A stir in the rear heralded the arrival of Jake Kilgore, whose progress through the crowded benches was like that of a Roman emperor on a triumphal march. Kilgore swaggered through the press, cheeks ruddy under a close shave, his flaunting mane of jet hair gleaming with brilliantine. He was in the courtroom regalia of the period—Windsor collar, black four-in-hand ornamented with a pearl stickpin, black coat, and linen handkerchief. A pair of gold cuff links clanked with the authority of affluence as he shook the hands of well-wishers and exuded the gusto of a gladiator assured of victory in the arena. Close on his heels, slightly embarrassed and self-conscious, swayed the lanky, tall young apprentice whom the judge recalled with respect and appreciation. Erksine was young, the judge thought, but a strong mouth showed the makings of a trial lawyer.

"Order, order!"

Judge Hazledine tapped the bench in warning as Kilgore reached the oak rail that divided the divinity of the bar from the mortality of the populace.

"Kilgore!"

"Beaudoin!"

The rival lawyers shook hands with mutual respect. Pete Beaudoin was resplendent in his Prince Albert—a courtly affectation that put Kilgore slightly in the shade. Like two fighting cocks, thought Judge Hazledine acidly, putting out colorful plumage to dazzle the fair sex and overawe their rivals. Champions of the right! He smiled grimly and nodded to Sheriff Mike Duer who had been waiting glumly for the signal to begin.

"Bring in the prisoner!" the judge ordered. "Are you gentlemen ready?"

"For the Territory!" Beaudoin's voice cut like a knife, and the subdued murmur of voices making side bets in the rear subsided.

"For the defense!"

Kilgore sank heavily into his chair and tightened his mouth with pain. Clem Erskine busied himself with a valise of lawbooks. He had noted the play of jaw muscles as the fire darted through his senior, but he was silent. He was worried about Kilgore. Earlier that morning, while crossing the plaza, Kilgore had staggered, supporting himself with an effort against a dizzy spell. Clem had tried to support the older man, only to draw a blast of indignation. But the fact remained that Kilgore was a sick man.

A hush swept the room as the rear door opened and there appeared the white, intelligent face of the prisoner. Harry McCandless glanced at the wall of hostility, noting Anglo faces, Spanish faces, a multitude of strangers—and the absence of McCandless faces was an immediate blow. Julian DuVivier was seated in the rear—cool, reserved, his eyes cast on a pattern in the splintered pine flooring.

"Stand there!" Duer said.

Harry obediently took a position before the bench and assumed an air of disdain as Kilgore came to his side. Toying thoughtfully, Beaudoin came forward and requested certain papers from the sheriff. Kilgore turned a murderous glance toward his young client.

"Stop staring at the people like they're sheep," Kilgore hissed. "Can't you show that you're seriously affected by this charge? I'll have to draw a jury from those people. You need their sympathy. Look worried. Anything but indifferent."

"Sorry, Mr. Kilgore," Harry said casually. "I'm depending on you to show my innocence."

"Jesus!" Kilgore groaned.

The judge tapped the bench. "Mr. Kilgore? I'd like to dispose of your writ. Would you like to withdraw your petition?"

Kilgore shook his head. "I'd like to argue, Judge. I can see that the sheriff has produced the prisoner. I've got a copy of his answering papers that show some lame attempt to repair the illegality of the arrest by scraping up some worthless and misleading testimony from an incompetent and jealous rival of the prisoner's—but this transparent effort can hardly repair the deficiency of the original arrest."

When Kilgore had concluded his peroration, the judge turned to the attorney general. "Mr. Beaudoin?" The prosecutor patted his mouth with fine linen and retorted with an air of complacency, "The only question before the court is the legality of the arrest." Clearly, economically, he marshaled the case against Harry McCandless. The fraternity pin. The testimony of Eli Weingarten. The Wa-po-nah insignia on the buckboard seen by the *campesino*.

When he was finished, Hazledine looked down from the bench. "Mr. Beaudoin, unless you show me something more, I'm inclined to sustain the writ and discharge the prisoner. So far as I can see, you have no sufficient grounds to make this arrest merely on the circumstances described. They point to guilt, but they are far short of being conclusive."

A murmur of disbelief followed the calm statement of law, uttered in the hard tones of a judge accustomed to authority. Kilgore showed no change of expression. Judge Hazledine went on, "I presume you have something more to show, Mr. Beaudoin?"

"Indeed I have, Judge!"

Smoothly, pleasantly, almost in the manner of drawing-room conversation, Beaudoin advised the court that the grand jury had returned an indictment based on other, secret information and that the prisoner was now in the hands of the sheriff on a warrant of arrest. The arrest therefore was now completely legal and an attack against the indictment would await the outcome of the trial. The judge nodded thoughtfully.

"Anything wrong with that, Mr. Kilgore?"

Kilgore shrugged. "Grand-jury proceedings are ex parte and *in camera.* Those words are Latin, Judge. For the benefit of the ignorant, they mean that there's where the prosecution can practice its unfair and prejudicial tactics safe from Kilgore. But a day of judgment is coming! It's coming—and I'll expose the worthlessness of those star-chamber proceedings!"

Hazledine tapped the bench. "Petition is denied. The writ is dismissed. The prisoner is continued in custody of the sheriff. This case will be set down for early trial." The words rang out peremptorily. "Are you ready to plead to the indictment, Mr. Kilgore?"

Kilgore nodded, closing his eyes.

Harry McCandless' tone was cool and indifferent, somewhat high pitched, but clear and earnest.

"Not guilty!"

Hazledine nodded. "I'll set this case down for trial one month from this date. Anything else, Mr. Kilgore?"

Kilgore hesitated.

"Your Honor, I ask that the defendant be admitted to bail until the trial. I'll accept custody."

"Bail?"

An air of grim amusement touched the judge's mouth at the effrontery of the request. "Bail?" he echoed, incredulously. "Oh, Mr. Kilgore! Even you, even you must admit that the indulgence of the court is being strained to the limit in a hanging case!"

Kilgore said doggedly, "This court has inherent power to

admit to bail anyone, even Judas Iscariot, where there is so little evidence that a verdict of acquittal is a foregone conclusion. I'm asking for bail. I'm asking for the son of Dan McCandless."

"Are you, indeed?" Judge Hazledine's air of amusement was unpleasant indeed as he made ruling. "Denied!" he said harshly.

Kilgore scowled. He took his seat. There was nothing further to say. The entire proceeding had been ludicrously fast. He had made only token attempts at obstructing the serene progress of the steamroller.

Hazledine rapped with his gavel.

"The court stands adjourned."

The onlookers filed out. They were disappointed, for they had come to see legal fireworks and instead had seen nothing but dull routine.

Kilgore heard someone mutter, "Jake didn't even put up a fight today, did he?"

Kilgore thumbed his eyes wearily. He felt one of his rare moments of doubt. Had he let things slide by too easily? Was the damnable infection in his ear affecting his conduct of the case?

He shook his head. There had been no roadblock he could have used. Beaudoin had a case, and the dismissal of the writ was scarcely surprising. This morning, Pete had held all aces, and there was no sense fighting that fact. Kilgore had already resigned himself to the fact that Harry McCandless would have to come to trial.

But maybe I could have done more this morning, he thought. *It's still not too late for me to resign from the case. Dan McCandless can get a new lawyer, maybe some sharp Easterner. There's none better in the country than Kilgore, but if Kilgore is not up to form, why, I'd be doing a disservice by continuing to take the case. And I should really get this damn ear looked at before the infection gets to my brain and kills me.*

Kilgore blotted all thoughts of giving up from his mind. It

would look bad, he knew, if he withdrew now. Nobody would believe that he was sick. They would simply think that Jake Kilgore had run out on a losing battle.

Besides, Kilgore reassured himself, *that infection can't hurt my brain. The old cerebellum is so thoroughly preserved in alcohol that it's proof against all decay.*

He smiled. Rising, he followed Clem out of the courtroom, walking erectly though a trifle unsteadily.

A joyous Sunday feast was the rule at Wa-po-nah. Fine thick steaks, the best wines and liqueurs, and a mighty array of tempting vegetables. But the Sunday before the opening of the trial, there was no joy at the McCandless table. Dan Mc-Candless sat in his position at the head of the table, his eyes veiled in sorrow. To his right sat Isabella, to his left, Carlotta. The fourth seat at the big table, the one facing Dan, was empty.

Julian DuVivier stood by, a decanter of brandy at his elbow. McCandless needed only to signal by flicking his finger, and the amber fluid would appear as though by magic in his glass when Julian glided noiselessly to the table.

McCandless had begun his drinking at eleven in the morning. It was now half past two, and he had consumed close to a fifth of brandy. He was a big man, and burned the liquor rapidly. Yet there was a residue of fog in his mind at all times, now. It was as though only by drinking heavily could he lift the burden of fear and guilt from his brain.

Tomorrow, he thought, *Harry goes on trial.*

My only son. On trial for his life.

He did not look at his wife, or at his daughter. He lifted the glass to his lips and let the brandy pour down his gullet. He no longer tasted it now. He simply tossed it down. It might have been dime-a-quart rotgut, and not expensive cognac shipped from Paris.

They say my boy killed that girl, McCandless thought broodingly. *Well, maybe he did. But this isn't just a murder trial. They're trying Harry's whole past. And worse. They have me on trial, too. They've always hated me, and they know they can stab me in the heart by hanging Harry.*

Sheep, that's what they are, he thought contemptuously. *The honored citizens of San Carlos are a bunch of sheep. Only suddenly they've grown fangs and claws.*

I would have made them all rich, if they had had faith in me. Sure, I would have been richer. I would have deserved to be! But they'd have prospered. Instead they grew jealous of me. Hated me. And here's their chance to bring me down, and they're delighted. Little people always hate big ones. Pygmies have to cut the legs off giants. And I was a giant, dammit! I carved an empire out here. Could Joe Valdez have done that? Dade Rawlins? Doc Hewlitt? Of course not. But I did! I! That's why they hate me, because I had the strength to do what they didn't dare to do.

And now they've got me caught, and they'll be able to take out their petty little hates against me. And crush me.

He stared off into nowhere in particular. Everything was falling apart at once. His wife had not addressed a direct statement to him in days. His daughter was distant and cool, his son a stranger.

And this trial was not helping his financial woes. Instead of going to the office, instead of spending hours fighting the Eastern vultures, he was letting Hicks handle everything, letting things slide. McCandless spent his time nervously pacing the long halls. It was too cold to go out, too harsh.

And while he lurked at home, neglecting matters of importance, trouble brewed. The McCandless railroad line—the Denver, San Carlos, and Galveston—had never extended its lines to Galveston, and this was widely regarded as his fault, his bad management. But, he asked himself bitterly, was it his fault that financial panic gripped the country, that investment funds had dried up?

The railroad faced bankruptcy. That would mean ruin not only for the investors but for the homesteaders who had put down roots in the expectation of the railroad. They had hated Dan McCandless because of his tactics as an empire builder;

now they hated him because his empire was not strong enough.

The railroad had failed to meet its obligations at the first of the year. The trip to Wall Street, cut short by the news of Harry's arrest, had been a failure. The Chicago railroad crowd stood by, ready to take over, to pick up the crumbs of his empire. They had blocked his quest for funds. And he was certain that they and Joel Tilley had conspired to arrange this trial in such a way as to engage him fully and thus leave him open for destruction.

The wolves were baying already. In New York they were applying for a Federal receiver to take over the railroad. He had knowledge of this, but he had no way to fight it. He could not go to New York now. His influence in Washington was less than Tilley's. He could only remain here, paralyzed and impotent for the first time in his life, and watch his empire collapse and his son go to the gallows.

He drained his glass.

"Julian, serve the meat," he muttered.

They were the first words anyone had spoken since the McCandless family had come to the table for Sunday dinner.

To her husband's right, Isabella Lucero McCandless sat quietly, eating only a bit of her food. She rarely ate much, rarely said much these days. She lived in a shadow world of renunciation, aware that her life had gone off the tracks but unwilling to face the situation.

She was not surprised at this murder business. There was murder in the family, Isabella knew. Harry had inherited her feminine instability and his father's rapacity, and the combination was an unhealthy one.

And now, she thought, old crimes were arising to haunt the family and bring down retribution.

She thought of her father, Don Alfredo Lucero, six feet one, a giant by Spanish standards, with his skin like Cordovan leather and his eyes like eagle's eyes, and his stiff gray beard and stiffer back. His only child, child of his old age, Isabella, had loved him fiercely. Then along had come an even bigger man, perhaps a stronger man, and he had won her love—for a while.

She could date exactly the day when she had stopped loving Dan McCandless. It had been on that day, a month after Harry's birth, when her father was murdered by the white oak in the desert. That night, when he had come into her bedroom to say good night, she had seen something in his eye, a look of guilt, perhaps, and that had killed her love for him forever. It was a month before she permitted him to take her in his arms again, and she had pretended mourning as her excuse. How could she have told him she no longer loved him?

She had never again taken pleasure from his embrace. He knew that now, and did not come to her.

Isabella had no certainty that her husband had been involved in her father's murder. The question had been raised; men said that McCandless and his friend Tilley had lured the old don to the malpais and murdered him there. McCandless had angrily denied such stories.

She could not be sure who had committed the murder, then. It had been a time of murder. How the land had run with blood in those days when the Tejanos came! When the Anglos came!

She did know that, through her, Dan McCandless had inherited the Lucero Grant. And not long after the estate had been settled, her husband and his partner Tilley had quarreled bitterly.

Why?

Isabella thought she knew. The suspicion, dark though it was, had grown with the years. Either they had murdered her father themselves, or they had caused his death, or they knew who was responsible. She suspected that the quarrel had come because, after acquiring the Lucero Grant, McCandless had dissolved the partnership with Tilley, shutting his old companion out of the newly acquired fortune.

So they hated one another. By their violent code, they kept their own counsel, neither having recourse to the law. Isabella sighed. She knew she had passed into darkness. There were long hours when she thought she was out of her mind. The priest was little help. And she could not, like her husband, use alcohol to wash away the gnawing silent voices. She had to live with her fears and her hatreds.

If he wanted to, Joel Tilley could easily squelch the trial, Isabella thought. A word to Beaudoin, another to Hazledine, and the trial would be ended, the Territory would yield its case.

But Tilley hated her husband.

This was Tilley's revenge. Harry would die.

Blood would end in blood, Isabella thought. For his violent deeds, Dan McCandless would suffer. Isabella scarcely considered that it would be her own son, flesh of her flesh, mounting the gallows. Harry had always been close to her, had been her son more than his father's. But she felt no pang of regret that his life was in jeopardy now. To her racked mind, she could only see Harry's death as an event in the humbling of Dan McCandless, in the ruin of that proud, lawless man to whom she had so foolishly given her heart a quarter of a century before.

"Aren't you hungry, Isabella?" McCandless said loudly.

Isabella McCandless looked into her husband's face. What she saw pleased her. It was a face of despair. Drunk as he was, not even a vat of brandy could give him peace now. She smiled quietly, and nodded in satisfaction. He was suffering. That was good, Isabella thought.

14.

KILGORE in *Territory v. Harry McCandless* was Kilgore the frontier lawyer at his best. The invasion of manners from the East which had lifted the raw Territorial Bar from its minor beginnings of ridicule and contempt at the regular conventions of the American Bar

Association to a position of respect and eminence—an eminence shared by fewer than fourscore contentious advocates who roamed the vast expanse—that elevation of manners was to be seen in the elegance of his attire. Catlike on his feet and animal-like in his instincts, with the looming bulk of his gleaming black mane radiating splendor in the blazing electric lights of the courtroom—with the attention of the national press nurturing his natural vanity, and with a fabulous fee scraped from the dwindling treasury of his client's father, a fee already celebrated in the ballads circulating in broadsides composed in Kansas City, he was the exemplar of the Western bar, the cynosure of reporters gathered from the four corners of the nation. All this was on the surface.

His heavy coat of blue serge, buttoned to the throat to conceal the resplendent silver and black four-in-hand, added bulk to his fleshy chest. This looming effect was accentuated by the tapering pants legs which disappeared into the tops of his boots. As he grasped his lapels and exhorted the courtroom, a student of legal history might have detected the faint voices of the ghosts of Calhoun and Henry Clay and Daniel Webster echoing in the entranced chamber of rough-clad men.

Kilgore played for time. The selection of the jury took a week and exhausted the entire panel of citizens presented by the clerk of the court. Kilgore's preparation had been thorough—and his own intimate knowledge of the county was supplemented by the efforts of detectives hired at great expense in Dallas to comb the history of every prospective juror for each nuance that might reflect upon his qualifications for the great trial. Spanish, Anglos, neutrals, and indifferent—a fine-tooth comb had gone through hundreds of lives to determine the element of favor or prejudice that might lie behind hostile eyes. On the *voir dire*, the examination of the jurors, Kilgore spoke, quietly, effectively, vehemently, probing the responses with instinctive skill.

Could justice be done to the son of Dan McCandless?

In a score of ways, he put the question—for he defined the issue early in the trial. It was not the visible prosecutor he feared, he charged, but the invisible effect of hatred and resentment against the great figure who had dominated the Territory for decades—Dan McCandless. Was the hatred too great? Was the prejudice beyond control? Could a fair and square trial be given a youth against whom no cogent evidence had yet been presented? Could the jurors weigh the issues solely on the evidence? Would they realize that they alone were judges of the facts and the judge relegated alone to issues of the law?

At the end of five days, panting and exhausted, Kilgore threw up his hands and announced that the jury was satisfactory to the defense. More than three hundred prospective jurors had been excused for prejudice by one side or the other or at the direction of the court.

"Satisfactory!" Pete Beaudoin groaned, glancing in fatigue and disgust at the ceiling.

By and large, it was a neutral jury—a jury that might have been selected from a hat; nobody wealthy, nobody poor, nobody who would concede prejudice either against Harry McCandless or against capital punishment. It was as satisfactory as a jury could get—hard men, but ready to listen to the defense.

Kilgore waited as calmly as possible in the recess, considering the throbbing in his ear and the general feeling of dull fatigue that weighed him down. Anxious faces crowded in at him—Dan McCandless, Carlotta, even Isabella, making her first public appearance in San Carlos in years. Clem Erskine sat at Kilgore's side. The lawyer was glad to have the boy there; Clem's strength and determination were assets he would need.

Dan McCandless was not susceptible to cheer at the moment. His voice was husky as he asked, "What chance do you think there really is, Kilgore? Don't spare us, now. We'd rather not have false hopes to live by."

Kilgore said solemnly, "Dan, there's every chance in the world for your boy."

"You're just saying that," Carlotta put in.

"I mean it," Kilgore insisted. "It's at least fifty-fifty as it stands. Assuming Beaudoin's got nothing up his sleeve, and I doubt that he does, all the evidence against Harry is purely circumstantial. As a matter of law it's insufficient to prove his guilt beyond a reasonable doubt."

"It's not his guilt they're trying to prove," Dan McCandless said bitterly. "It's mine!"

"Guilt for what?" Kilgore asked curiously. Dan McCandless failed to answer. The lawyer turned to his assistant. "Clem, when the trial starts, I want you to sit in the back and get the feel of the courtroom," he said in a low voice. "When I play to the onlookers, I expect to raise a bit of feeling—and that's got to come across the rail and influence the jury. Keep your ears open and your eyes peeled." When Clem Erskine had left the group, Kilgore returned to Dan McCandless. "There's ten Spanish names on that jury," he said quietly, "and your boy is Alfredo Lucero's grandson. That'll count in his favor. And I'll have to attack the virtue and chastity of that little Morgan girl, poor thing, and that's bound to have an effect—at least on the Spanish jurors. It won't endear me to Laurie Morgan"—he shot a glance at the tense, white face of the dead girl's mother, a face that had become a mask of hatred—"but that's a small price, all things considered. You mustn't assume the jury's against you to that extent. Kilgore's speaking for you."

"I'm the one who's really on trial," McCandless said miserably. "Those jurors hate me."

"Even if there's a conviction, we can appeal to Santa Fe. Unless Beaudoin makes out a legal case, any verdict can be set aside," Kilgore replied.

"By four other Tilley men? Never!" McCandless groaned.

"Then we'll appeal to the Supreme Court at Washington," Kilgore retorted impatiently. He was weary and annoyed at the hopeless tone. "Or are they in Tilley's pay, too? Get a grip on yourself, McCandless. The whole damn court is watching!"

"Order, order!" chanted the bailiff.

Looking refreshed, Judge Hazledine returned to the bench wiping the corners of his gleaming Vandyke beard. He tapped the bench and announced that all demonstrations would be met with jail sentences for contempt and ordered that the trial proceed.

Pete Beaudoin's opening to the jury was brief, no more than twelve or thirteen minutes, and it was brilliantly organized. It touched on the alleged unsavory character of the defendant, the circumstances of the victim's death, the intention to prove that the defendant was the last person to see the victim, and the various items of proof that would be adduced to show that the defendant had committed the crime for which he had been indicted. Beaudoin stressed Harry's denials of guilt, setting them up as straw men for afterward.

Kilgore listened, taking no notes. Beaudoin had offered no surprises thus far.

Beaudoin finished his speech and turned to Judge Hazledine. "If Your Honor please, the Territory will call Dr. Spencer Hewlitt to the stand."

Kilgore arose. "Your Honor! I think it's been the custom for about a thousand years to let the defense get a crack at the jury before the frame-up actually starts."

Judge Hazledine's tapping pencil cut into the prosecutor's objections. "The observation is uncalled for, Mr. Kilgore. You may address the jury."

"Well, good!"

Kilgore stepped forward, conscious of the agony of his infected ear, and faced the jury. Twelve men, two Anglos and ten Spanish. The youngest thirty, the oldest sixty. Their faces were like stone images now.

Kilgore said, "Gentlemen of the jury, I'd like to address one brief plea to you before the action of this trial begins. I wish to remind you that the defendant is Harry McCandless, and no other member of his family. Don't let old hatreds, old prejudices sway you. You are here today to serve the interests of justice, not to take revenge on a man whom perhaps you have come to hate." He saw Beaudoin fidgeting, getting ready to object, and decided to cut his words short before being forced to. He faced the foreman of the jury, a swarthy farmer of mixed stock named Thomas Martinez, and said, "I have no further words for you now. I ask only that you remember the sacred quality of justice. Thank you."

He resumed his seat and put his hand to his ear as the official translator put his brief address into Spanish. Pete Beaudoin now rose before the court to present the case for the Territory and called his first witness.

Marty Leach, the court clerk, rose to swear the witness. Doc Hewlitt looked as though he had made a special effort to look respectable today. He walked to the witness stand with a definite swing of sobriety; his cadaverous cheeks were shaved, his clothes neatly arranged.

Beaudoin said, "How long have you been a resident of San Carlos, Dr. Hewlitt?"

"Eight years."

"And during that time what has been your profession here?"

"Doctor, sir."

"Are there many doctors in San Carlos?"

"There were a couple when I came. I'm the only one in town right now."

"I will ask you if about December seventh of the last year you made a post-mortem examination of the body of Mary Margaret Morgan, otherwise known as Honey Morgan?"

"Yes, sir. I first examined the body at the Sanchez place, about twenty miles out of town."

Beaudoin nodded. "At whose request were you present there?"

"Why, the sheriff told me to come out. Someone had told him a corpse had been found out there, and I came along to examine it."

"In other words, the body was not brought to you. You went to the site of the corpse."

"That's right."

"Would you describe the condition of the body?"

Hewlitt hitched up his trouser legs. "Well, sir, it had been exposed for around three days, but on account of the cold weather there was no deterioration at all. The girl was wrapped up in a bloody Navajo blanket."

"Is the blanket present in this courtroom?"

"Yes, sir. It's right over there on that table, marked Exhibit A."

"That's the same blanket the girl was wrapped in?"

"Yes, sir."

"All right. Continue. What else was the girl wearing?"

"A silk dress. No undergarments."

"And what was her position?"

Kilgore rose like a buffalo from a mud wallow and a meaty hand went aloft. "Hold it!" he said wearily. "Your Honor, may it appear on the record that our good doctor is evidently refreshing his memory from a paper, which I would like to have marked for identification?"

Beaudoin said, "I object to the interruption unless the witness is first asked if he is refreshing his memory."

Judge Hazledine turned about. "Are you using that paper, Doctor?"

"Certainly," the doctor retorted irritably. "I got to keep the facts straight. Anything wrong?"

"Only this," Kilgore said. "This whole procedure is unfair and prejudicial. I've been begging the attorney general for a glimpse of that paper since this ridiculous information was handed down. I've been trying to get the minutes of the so-called proceedings before the coroner. I've been unable to prepare for this cross-examination because of the ferocious disregard of the defendant's right to know exactly what he's up against."

"Come to the point!"

"Point is, I want a copy of that paper and a day's recess to study its alleged findings. This whole procedure is unfair!"

"Denied!" Judge Hazledine flushed darkly and directed that the testimony continue. Kilgore sat with an air of outward anger, secretly pleased at the minor points established. The prior question as to the position of the body was repeated.

"Lying on her back," Hewlitt said. "Legs spread, one arm across her breast, the other one thrown back."

"How would you describe the condition of her body?"

"She'd been in a fight. She was bruised and scratched up, and there were bits of skin under the fingernails like she'd scratched someone else. Her face was swollen, and there were contusions on the body. Her nose was bloody, like she'd had a nosebleed before she died."

"Anything unusual about her?"

"Yes, sir. Her mouth was stuffed full of builder's plaster. Completely crammed. Like the man who murdered her had stuffed up her mouth, first, and—"

Kilgore rose. "Your Honor, I move that that be stricken. It has not yet been demonstrated that the deceased was murdered, and any assumptions to that effect can't be considered as testimony."

Judge Hazledine nodded. "Very well. Let it be stricken."

Beaudoin's only reaction was a smile. Doc Hewlitt seemed nettled by the interruption, but the attorney general swiftly regained control. "Let us go on, Doctor. You examined the body *in situ*. What did you do then?"

"I assisted in removing it to town for a further examination."

"What was the purpose of that further examination?"

"To find the cause of death."

"Well, you may go on and describe your examination, what you found and what was the cause of the poor girl's death."

Hewlitt looked at Kilgore, who stared at the ceiling without change of expression.

"The girl had sustained a fracture of the skull with damage to the brain."

"Would those injuries be sufficient in your judgment to cause death?"

"Yes, sir." The doctor hesitated and added, "And there was rape."

A sigh went through the courtroom.

"Why do you conjecture rape, Doctor?"

Hewlitt shifted in the chair. "Well, I examined her and I could tell she'd had sexual relations shortly before her death. And coupled with all the bruises and such, I'd be inclined to think she was forced."

"Would you elaborate on the cause of death?"

"Sure. She was hit on the head, hard. Skull fracture caused a rupture of the dura mater. That's the tough lining around the brain. Compression of the brain by effusion of blood caused death. I found blood clots."

"Did you know the deceased during her lifetime, Dr. Hewlitt?"

"Yes, sir."

"Would you say she was in a good state of health?"

"Why, yes. I mean, she was slightly anemic and had an enlarged heart, but nothing really serious. I examined her a few months ago. Her teeth were sort of decayed, too."

"Very well, Dr. Hewlitt. Thank you." Beaudoin glanced at the judge. "Your Honor, I have no further questions at this time."

Judge Hazledine nodded. "Mr. Kilgore?"

Kilgore rose ponderously for his cross-examination. He came slowly toward the stand and stared at the watery-eyed doctor. After a long moment he said, "Are you a graduate of an accredited medical school, Dr. Hewlitt?"

"Yes, I am. St. Louis Medical School. Class of Seventy-seven."

"That's in Missouri?"

"Now, Jake," said Hewlitt in a whining voice, "you know damn well that St. Louis is in Missouri. I don't see any call for that sarcastic tone of voice."

"You might be right," Kilgore agreed amiably, and a glint came to his smoldering eyes. "Does the year 1885 mean anything to you in connection with the magnificent state of Missouri?"

Hewlitt licked his lips. "Not especially."

Beaudoin sensed a dangerous question. "Now what kind of a thing is that to ask?"

"It doesn't register, Doctor?" Kilgore said.

"Not at the moment," Hewlitt replied.

Kilgore nodded sardonically. "Would it refresh your recollection if I were to suggest that it was not the year of Halley's Comet? That it was the year your license to practice medicine in that state was withdrawn? Oh, now, don't look to Mr. Beaudoin! This is one signal he can't give you."

"Your Honor!" Beaudoin began.

"The witness will answer!" Hazledine said curtly.

Hewlitt tugged his collar uneasily. "They only suspended my license. They didn't revoke it."

"Might I ask why this action was taken?"

"Your Honor, I respectfully object!" Pete Beaudoin declared. "This attempt to smear my witness is unwarranted!"

"Overruled," Hazledine said crisply. "Proceed, Mr. Kilgore."

Kilgore turned stolidly. "Will you answer my question, Dr. Hewlitt?"

"All right, yes," Hewlitt said uncomfortably. "They lifted my license. They had no right, none at all—"

"Now that interests me," Kilgore said indulgently. "For what reason did they lift your license?"

"Objection!" Beaudoin arose. "It's been established that the license was suspended. There's no need to go behind the record."

"Sustained," the Judge ruled.

Kilgore shrugged. "Very well. If the court feels that the witness's past career as an abortionist is inadmissible, then I withdraw my question."

"I move that be stricken!" Beaudoin howled.

"The jury will disregard Mr. Kilgore's remark," Judge Hazledine said. "And Mr. Kilgore will refrain from similar tactics in the future."

Kilgore said equably, "I apologize to the court. Dr. Hewlitt, after the suspension of your license in Missouri *for abortion*, you came to this Territory?"

"I went to Colorado first. I've been in New Mexico eight years."

"Practicing medicine?"

"That's right. I'm medically trained. My disagreement with the Missouri authorities doesn't disqualify me from practicing here."

"Where such matters are conducted more informally," Kilgore said. "Very well. You testified that you had examined the late Honey Morgan and found her to be in good health. Would you consider the presence of an enlarged heart a sign of good health?"

"I said it wasn't a serious matter. Nothing requiring treatment."

"Mmm. Would you mind telling the court how you came to examine Honey Morgan?"

"Well, she just came to me for a checkup."

"Is that all? Are you sure you're not being too vague?"

"She was worried about her health. I checked her out."

"Specifically, what was worrying her?"

"She was run down and tired."

"Nothing beside that."

"Well—"

"Could it be, Doctor, that she suspected that she had contracted a venereal disease? To be precise, a syphilitic infection?"

A murmur went through the spectators at Kilgore's statement. Pete Beaudoin said, "Your Honor, I don't see what this has to do with—"

"One of the intentions of the defense," Kilgore said strongly, "will be to demonstrate the promiscuous character of the deceased. In view of the gratuitous insinuations as to rape, I think the question is admissible."

"You are directed to answer," Hazledine told Hewlitt.

Hewlitt paused. "She thought she might have syphilis, and wanted me to look at her."

"Your Honor, the counsel for defense is guessing! Just because he's lucky doesn't mean we can let hearsay and speculation stand!" Beaudoin declared.

Hazledine shrugged. Kilgore said, "If you mean that I have no first-hand knowledge of the girl's condition, you're right. I may be the only man in San Carlos who can make that statement, but it's true. However, the girl's mother confided to me—"

"Objection! Objection!"

Hazledine looked angry. "Mr. Kilgore, this is despicable. You are directed to drop the subject of such diseases."

Kilgore bowed graciously and went on. "Since you were willing to conceal one illness the girl had, perhaps you are concealing others, Doctor. You now admit she had syphilis, an enlarged heart, dental caries, and anemia. Does her history include any other little ailments you may be keeping from us?"

"It does not," Hewlitt said.

"Very well. Now, you conjecture she was raped. I presume you made a thorough examination of the vaginal tract?"

"Well, yes—"

"Including tests for the presence of semen?"

"I tested, yes."

"Microscopic examination?"

"Yes. I also used chemical tests."

"Which proved positive."

"That's right."

"So the girl had sexual relations before her death. She also had bruises on her body. You link these two unrelated factors and conclude she was raped."

"I do, indeed," Hewlitt said.

"You admit you're merely guessing."

"Well, yes. I've already said that three or four times. Seems to stand to reason."

"Murder itself does not stand to reason, Dr. Hewlitt. I am through with questioning you, sir."

"You may step down," Judge Hazledine said. "Does the Territory have its next witness ready?"

"Yes, Your Honor," Beaudoin said. "We intend to call Sheriff Duer to the stand."

"I request a recess, Your Honor," Kilgore said.

Hazledine nodded. "Request granted. It's now ten past noon. The court will recess until one thirty." The judge arose, went along the bench and out back into his chambers. Kilgore turned about wearily and suggested that the defense take refuge in the clerk's private office, a room set aside as a courtesy for his use. The hammering in his ear was remorseless.

There was a better mood as the group gathered to consider the position. Even Dan McCandless looked more cheerful. Battle was joined, and it did not look hopeless.

Kilgore said, "Somebody's got to get up to Denver right away."

"Denver?" Carlotta asked.

Kilgore lit a cigar and waited for his thoughts to clear. It was the autopsy protocol, he explained, and the testimony given by Dr. Hewlitt. His own claim of surprise had been a stage effect for the benefit of the jury—known to be such by Hazledine and Beaudoin and not too seriously intended. The issue would not turn on the medical issue—but on the identity of the criminal. However, a line of cuttlefish tactics had suddenly opened up.

"I wasn't expecting that enlarged-heart testimony," he said, "but it gives me ideas. If I can talk about heart failure, I might confuse the jury. More justice, more *substantial* justice, that is, has been reached by confused juries than they get credit for. It's the clear-minded jury I mistrust. They use their heads, not their hearts, and that's dangerous. I want those twelve men to give me an answer based on instinct—because instinct is sound. It's like a jackass out in the hills. He ain't got the brains of a desert rat, but his instinct can bring you to water. Who wants to improve on that?"

Dan McCandless broke in on Kilgore's prolix ruminations. "Jesus, Kilgore! Will you get down to it? What's to be gained in Denver?" he cried out in torment.

Kilgore looked hurt. "There's a pathologist in Denver," he said slowly. "Connected with that new free hospital they've got there. One of the most eminent pathologists in the world. Knows almost as much forensic medicine as Kilgore. Name is Arthur Vance, and I'd like to get him down here for a consultation. I've got total recall, and if I get a glimpse of that autopsy protocol, I'll commit it to memory—and give it to Vance. Who knows? There's a wild chance a big fee can get Vance to muddy the issues."

"You mean he might testify that the girl died of heart failure?"

Kilgore said stolidly. "Let me talk to Vance first, fix an adequate fee, and then we'll know. I never yet saw a case where a monetary consideration couldn't get one expert to call another expert a liar. And Hewlitt's qualifications are about as low as medical science can get. Heart failure? Who knows?

Who knows? Trouble is," he added slowly, "I need Clem to stick with me. I'm having a little trouble in that courtroom."

"I'll go!" Dan McCandless cried.

Kilgore shook his head. "You'll mess it up, McCandless! And besides, Beaudoin will raise a howl about bribery and the McCandless millions—"

"The McCandless millions!" McCandless said bitterly.

Carlotta said quietly, "Let me go, Mr. Kilgore. I don't think Mr. Beaudoin would make any such accusations against me. It would make a very bad impression for him."

Kilgore paused to consider the matter. Carlotta had called attention to a principle of importance—the good name of a decent woman. In a swiftly evolving society, that principle, like all other principles, was vanishing, but it still prevailed in the West. He nodded slowly and it was a decision.

"It's worth a try," he agreed. "And I know Vance is a top-flight man. If you leave right away, you can be back here by Saturday. I don't think you'll miss much. I'll hammer that enlarged-heart idea until we know definitely that it can be ruled out. And don't say a word to anyone about where or why you're going. Hear?"

As they returned to the courtroom, hope seemed to dawn for the first time on the face of Dan McCandless.

15.

MIKE DUER took the stand after the recess. Kilgore sat back, relaxing now, starting to forget his private pain as he involved himself in the dialectical interplay going on between the sheriff and the attorney general. Efficiently, briskly, the series of questions and answers brought out the details of the discovery of the body: Father Crespin's visit, the ride to the hills, the finding of the corpse. Kilgore did not interrupt until Duer came to the part about the fraternity pin.

"And then Charlie Bear bent down and picked up the pin," Duer said.

"Is this it? Do you recognize it?" Beaudoin said.

"Yes, that's the one. Harry McCandless' fraternity pin. It was lying right next to—"

"Objection!" Kilgore said. "What's the materiality? We've got nothing to connect that bauble to the defendant!"

"Yes," Hazledine said. "Sustained. Mr. Beaudoin, you'll have the pin tagged for identification. It can then be admitted merely as a pin found on the body of the deceased girl."

A moment of formalities passed.

Beaudoin came back to the same line of questions. "Did you question the defendant about this pin?"

"I did."

"Did he say anything about the pin?"

Duer said grimly, "He said it was an Amherst fraternity pin. I asked how he could be sure. He said he was briefly a student at Amherst before he was kicked out for some prank—"

"Objection!" Kilgore said.

Duer amended his answer. "Before he was kicked out. I asked if it was his pin. He said he couldn't be sure."

Kilgore arose. "In that case I move that this entire line of testimony be stricken."

Hazledine turned to the witness. "What did he say about ownership of the pin?"

Duer turned a cold glance to the white-faced defendant. "First he entirely denied it was his pin. Then he admitted it was identical with a pin he once gave the little girl. Finally he admitted that nobody else in the Territory had such a pin except himself. For all practical purposes, he admitted it was his pin."

Beaudoin glanced significantly at the jury. "After first *denying* ownership?"

"Exactly."

"Did you ever see Harry McCandless wear such a pin?"

Duer said stolidly, "I guess everybody in this room, one time or another, saw Harry McCandless sporting that pin—or its twin."

Beaudoin sat down with a flourish. "Your witness, Mr. Kilgore."

Kilgore put one question. "Mike, I'll ask this question, fair and square. After two days and two nights of fiendish torture, all you got from this boy was the information that he gave the pin to that young woman—" He paused and repeated the word "woman" as though it were an ultimate term of opprobrium—"at least two months before her unfortunate demise. So it don't prove a thing."

"Objection!" Beaudoin shouted. "If there's any fiend in this case, it's Harry McCandless! Not this peace officer—"

"Order, order!" Judge Hazledine warned.

Kilgore's flourish of disdain was magnificent. "No further questions for this witness!" he said with contempt and loathing. With an air of disgust, he began to trim his nails with a gold-handled pen knife. Duer's testimony had been strictly factual, and there was nothing to be gained by giving it further emphasis.

Charlie Bear now came to the stand. The Indian corroborated all that Duer had said, dwelling at some length on the condition of the ground, the tracks, and other technical matters. He mentioned the plaster stuffing the girl's mouth.

Beaudoin said, "Do you happen to know if this is a custom among your people, to stuff a dead body's mouth with plaster or any such substance?"

"No, sir. Apaches don't do such things."

"What about other Indian tribes?"

Charlie Bear shrugged. "Not that I know of."

"So it's fair to say, then, that no Indian would have done such a thing."

"Objection!" Kilgore said wearily. "The witness is not an expert on the customs of every Indian tribe."

"Overruled," said the judge. "The witness is an Indian. Let it be understood that he's answering to the best of his knowledge."

Beaudoin said, "Answer on those terms, Charlie."

"As far as I know, no Indian tribe around here has any kind of custom of stuffing the mouth."

Kilgore could not object to the statement so phrased, nor did he wish to cross-examine. The Territory's next witness was Father Crespin, who described his discovery of the body and his colloquy with the *campesino*. Kilgore was crisp enough as he said, "Father Crespin, you made your discovery of the body on the night of December third, correct?"

"*Es verdad.*"

"But the girl disappeared on November thirtieth, so the body had been exposed for three days before you found it. However, you were not the first to find it?"

"I have said not. Sanchez found it first."

"When, *Padre?*"

"He said he had found it the third day before. Which would be November thirtieth."

"Objection, Your Honor," Beaudoin said. "This will all be brought out by the next witness."

"One moment more," Kilgore pleaded. "I'm trying to establish something."

"Overruled," Hazledine sighed. "But establish it quickly, Mr. Kilgore. It grows later."

Kilgore said, "Do you happen to know, *Padre*, why Sanchez waited three days after discovering the body and did not report it to anyone?"

"Yes. He was afraid to report it. He is a simple man."

"Your Honor," Beaudoin objected, "why should we waste time on this line of inquiry when Sanchez himself is our next witness?"

Kilgore turned with a grin. "You're slipping, Pete. You've got a better objection than that! Why not object on the ground that he ain't qualified to testify to the operation of another man's mind? That would be a legal objection. For you that would be making history."

A titter of laughter went around the courtroom. Kilgore's chest swelled with gratification, and he bowed to his discomfited opponent.

"I withdraw the question," he said handsomely. "Nobody can be expected to figure out what goes on in the mind of another man—"

"That includes your client," Beaudoin said nastily. "What was in his mind that night?"

Harry McCandless half-rose and sank back, white and staring, as the barb went home. And then the gavel restored order to the noisy courtroom.

Beaudoin said, "Mr. Kilgore is a privileged clown, Your Honor. I don't think these taunts are appropriate where murder is the issue."

"Proceed!"

Kilgore turned back to the witness soberly. "One more point, *Padre*. Did you move the body at all after discovering it?"

"I pulled down the skirt to cover the nakedness. Otherwise I left the body exactly as I found it, and ordered Sanchez to do the same."

"No further questions," Kilgore announced.

Manuel Sanchez was next to the stand, and a court interpreter came forward. Sanchez was plainly terrified of being in court, the Anglo court. Beaudoin was alternately suave and peremptory as he extracted the *campesino's* testimony. Sanchez declared, in many fits and starts, that on the night of November 30, after midnight, he had seen a buckboard bearing the *crux ansata* insignia drive up, had seen a man wrapped in sheepskins carry out a bulky, blanket-wrapped object, deposit it in the thicket, and drive away. He further testified that he had known that there was a dead body in the blanket, but that he had not gone to look at it until the third day, shortly before the priest's arrival on the scene.

"You recognized the insignia on the buckboard?" Beaudoin asked.

"Yes. It was the mark of the Wa-po-nah ranch."

Cross-examining the *campesino* was difficult, since the man was so frightened he could hardly speak at times. But Kilgore managed to ram home to the court and to the jury the point that the insignia on the buckboard, though it indicated

Wa-po-nah if the *campesino's* eyesight in the dark were to be trusted, still did not provide any necessary connection to Harry McCandless. Beaudoin made no concession. But Kilgore began to feel that he was making headway.

Joe Valdez and Sam Dodge now testified, supporting the stories of Duer and Charlie Bear. Kilgore's objections were few and largely procedural; he was overruled more often than he was sustained, but he regarded that as of no moment. The case was moving along. It was nearly four in the afternoon. Beaudoin would be saving his heavy artillery for the next day, when everyone would be fresh.

"The Territory now calls Dade Rawlins."

Rawlins took the stand. With much vagueness of recall, he traced his relationship with the dead girl up to the night of her disappearance, stressing the point that he had never slept with her but simply offered her the use of his shack as a residence.

"How long had she been living with you?" Beaudoin asked.

"Oh, about three-four months. Maybe five. Since the warm weather, anyway."

"Where did she live before then?"

"With her mother, in Santa Fe."

"Will you tell us when you last saw the deceased alive, Mr. Rawlins?"

"That week, you know, I guess the end of November. She told me she was going up to Wa-po-nah to spend the night. Buckboard come down to get her."

"Did you see the buckboard?"

"Yes, sir."

"Did it have the Wa-po-nah insignia on it?"

"Uh-huh, it did."

"And did you see who was driving it?"

Rawlins shook his head. "I couldn't see him. Honey went outside without me and got in and they drove away."

"Would you say it could have been Eli Weingarten driving the buckboard?"

"Objection," Kilgore said. "It could have been Weingarten

or it could have been the Queen of England. Witness has no way of offering anything but a speculation."

"Sustained," Hazledine said.

Beaudoin was unruffled. He asked half a dozen more questions relating to Honey's disappearance, then yielded to Kilgore.

Kilgore was in no mood to be gentle with the old drifter. He glowered ferociously at the witness and said, "Rawlins, you said Honey told you she was going to Wa-po-nah to spend the night."

"That's right."

"Did you understand this to mean that she was going there for the purpose of having sexual relations with someone?"

"Why, yes. I figgered if she was going to be there overnight she'd be sleeping with somebody."

"I'm trying to establish, Rawlins, that you were aware of the immoral purpose of the visit."

"Your Honor, this is really too much," Beaudoin expostulated. "To defame a dead person—"

"Honey Morgan's character or lack of it is material!" Kilgore replied, catching a glimpse of Laurie's hate-filled face in front of him.

"Overruled. You may continue, Mr. Kilgore."

"I thank the court humbly. Mr. Rawlins, were you aware that Honey Morgan engaged in sexual acts with a number of men in San Carlos?"

"Well, yes. I guess I knew that."

"In fact, she was a prostitute, wasn't she? She accepted money and gifts in return for her body?"

"I wouldn't call the child a *prostitute!*" Rawlins said, fidgeting. "She was a sweet girl and real religious. She—"

"Just answer the questions, please. When she did not return from Wa-po-nah the next day, were you worried?"

"A little."

"But you didn't notify the police?"

"Didn't see any reason to. She'd been away overnight before."

"At Wa-po-nah?"

"I didn't know where. But she'd been. Only never two nights. So when she didn't come back the second night, and Mrs. Morgan stopped in town the day after, I told her, and Mrs. Morgan went to report that the girl was missing."

"How long had you known Honey Morgan?"

"Since she was a baby, I guess."

"And when did you become aware that she engaged in acts of sexual intercourse with men?"

Rawlins shrugged. "Gosh, I don't know. I guess she did practically as soon as she filled out."

There was laughter in the courtroom, and the hammer of a gavel from the bench. Kilgore turned slowly, a figure of sorrow and compassion, and when the laughter had subsided he returned to the bench.

"May the court please," he said solemnly, "I find no cause for merriment in the tragic death of the young woman whose physical loveliness is known to us all. This young woman met her death—for what cause we know not! through whose agency we dare not guess! but if through some criminal agency, surely it was not to be laid at the doorstep of our client. In pursuing this painful line of questioning, conscious as we are of the presence of the bereaved mother, whose grief is not greater than ours, we are moved only by our solemn duty to serve the cause of justice—a cause that transcends grief, that leaps over the pain in the heart of fathers and mothers. It would be regrettable and unseemly not to remain aware that there is grief in more than one heart—in the mother of my client, the former Isabella Lucero"—he glanced at Martinez, the foreman, and noted the effect of dropping the beloved name—"and his father. The sole purpose, the only purpose, as God judges our hearts and motives, is merely to show the jury that the unfortunate sexual weakness of this deceased young woman was such as to make her a prey to any one of several thousand unknown assailants. We forgive her promiscuity. She was what God made her. But what God made her was common prey to all men. This is the unfortunate truth that hovers over this inquiry—that the young woman was alone on the road on that icy night and anyone—anyone at all might have been her assailant, and might have disposed of her body. If indeed her death was caused by a criminal agency—for which we have only the worthless testimony of a discredited abortionist who has taken refuge in our midst.

"I rebuke this unseemly laughter!" Kilgore added handsomely, turning an expression of disdain to the silent, abashed spectators. "I call on the court to remind us all that we stand in the face of tragedy. I call on the court to proceed to justice."

Glancing briefly at the array of newspapermen in the first bench, Kilgore sank back into his chair and began to comb his hair. It was, he felt with satisfaction, an admirable note of pity and compassion and could only help the defense. At his side, he could hear the breath whistle in the compressed nostrils of his client.

"Court's adjourned! We'll resume tomorrow at nine."

Judge Hazledine's face was a study of respect mixed with irritation as he strode off the bench and into chambers.

"Call Eli Weingarten!"

Kilgore advanced to the cross-examination toward noon and noted with satisfaction that the witness's eye wavered and sank to the pine flooring. Like Harry McCandless, the youth had spent time in Eastern colleges, and like Harry, he had been expelled and now lived off his wealthy father's substance in San Carlos.

Kilgore began, "You have seen the blanket in which the dead girl was wrapped, and you have testified that you had seen the same blanket in Harry McCandless' room at Wa-po-nah."

"Yes, Mr. Kilgore. Harry had several blankets."

"Suppose you describe the one we have here, without looking at the exhibit table."

"Well—uh—it's kind of red, and green, and it's got some brown in it, and the design is sort of bars and zigzags and curlicues—"

"Isn't there a predominant area of white, too?"

"Yes, come to think of it."

"And four large triangles in the corner?"

"Yes, that too."

"So your description was none too accurate. How about describing in detail the other blankets you've seen at Wa-po-nah, then?"

Eli squirmed uncomfortably. "Well, I guess I couldn't do that in detail. What I mean to say is, they all look pretty much alike."

"Try, Mr. Weingarten."

Eli tried. But from his fumbling attempts, it was evident that he had no clear visualization of the blankets he had seen.

Kilgore nodded to Clem Erskine who left the courtroom and returned with a package wrapped in heavy paper. It was, Kilgore announced, a blanket brought that day from Harry McCandless' room at Wa-po-nah.

"Will the attorney general concede that I hold here a Navajo blanket which is the subject of the testimony given by the witness?"

Beaudoin arose warily. "I'm afraid I'd like to have some foundation laid for the introduction of this exhibit. Unless Mr. Kilgore wants to testify to that blanket from personal knowledge?"

Kilgore turned to the court and asked that the blanket be marked for identification. "Mr. Witness! Do you recognize this blanket marked 'Defendant's Exhibit for Identification A'?"

Eli Weingarten said feebly, "All those blankets look alike. I couldn't say whether it is or isn't."

"You can't exclude it?"

"No."

"You can't include it?"

"No."

"Let me now show you the Territory's Exhibit in Evidence Seventeen. It's the twin of Exhibit A, ain't it?"

"It is."

Kilgore turned to the bench. "If the blankets are twins, and the witness can't identify one twin, I submit that he can't identify the other. I move that the exhibit be stricken from evidence and that the jury be instructed to disregard all testimony taken in that connection."

"I only said it looked like one of Harry's blankets—" Eli Weingarten muttered.

Judge Hazledine finally restored order and waited as Sam Dodge left the room for the telegraph office to get the latest development on the wire for Santa Fe.

"Motion granted!" he said grimly. "The jury is instructed to disregard any testimony regarding the Territory's exhibit. It's just a blanket in which the deceased girl's body was found."

Kilgore balanced his thick body lightly on the balls of his feet. So far, so good. The rest of Eli's testimony, the details of the final night, would need no refutation, since Harry's own story would serve to cancel it out.

"I have no further questions," Kilgore announced.

Beaudoin looked displeased with the course of events, though nothing he could have done would have saved Eli from Kilgore's trap. Scowling blackly, he said, "Call Mrs. Morgan."

16.

BEAUDOIN said, "Mrs. Morgan, how was the deceased related to you?"

Kilgore broke in, "Just a minute. Is it *Mrs.* Morgan or *Miss* Morgan?"

Laurie said stolidly. "Miss Morgan. I'm not married."

Kilgore said, "Missus is a courtesy title?"

"Yes."

Kilgore bowed. "I am enlightened!"

Beaudoin repeated his question, and the answer was given

with a dry stare. "Honey was my daughter. Her true name is Mary Margaret but we all called her Honey."

"And she lived with you until when?"

"June. We had a little quarrel then, and she moved out of my place in Santa Fe and came here to San Carlos."

"Did you know where she was staying?"

"Yes. With Dade Rawlins. He could be trusted to look after her some."

"And did you hear from your daughter at all after she left your household, Miss Morgan?"

"Oh, yes," Laurie said. "She wrote to me practically every week. Mostly about how she was spending time with Harry McCandless. In November she wrote me that Harry McCandless had asked her to marry him."

Hubbub in the courtroom. Gasps of disbelief and surprise. At the defense table, Kilgore grasped Clem's arm and squeezed it tight, as though trying to squeeze off the words Laurie was about to speak.

"A promise of marriage?" Beaudoin said, savoring the words. "Was there anything but a verbal promise?"

"Yes, there was," Laurie said, her voice loud and clear. "Honey told me that Harry had given her a diamond ring worth two thousand dollars. Then, she said, Harry wrote his sister in New York, and his sister advised him to get the ring back from Honey, and so Harry took it back—"

Kilgore was instantly on his feet in the midst of the general murmur that went about the room. But as he gathered his breath, Beaudoin shouted, "A promise of marriage? Was there anything more than a verbal promise?"

Everyone then seemed to be shouting at once, and Clem Erskine, to his own amazement, found himself protesting and forward in the well of the court with a scuffle of lawyers at the bench. Judge Hazledine was banging for order. Kilgore's voice arose like the bugling of an elk in rutting time.

"Objection! Objection! Objection!" Kilgore howled. "The Territory knows this is hearsay thrice confounded! The Territory knows this is not admissible! How can I cross-examine a letter from a dead girl? Objection! I move for a mistrial! I ask the withdrawal of a juror! I ask for a directed verdict!"

"Order! Order!"

And Laurie Morgan was shouting from the witness chair directly at the defense lawyer. "The girl told me in that letter that Harry McCandless had given her a diamond ring worth two thousand dollars. He told her he wrote his sister in New York, that stuck-up bitch, Carlotta McCandless, about the ring, and Carlotta advised him to get the ring back one way or another. He grabbed that ring and I was going to sue—"

And so on and on the enraged woman shouted the damning facts across the well of the court.

Beaudoin finally managed to be heard. "Mrs. Morgan," he said in tones of soft reproof, "you really shouldn't volunteer testimony. When a lawyer objects, you really should wait for the ruling of the court. Mrs. Morgan!" he said helplessly, "Mrs. Morgan! Please—"

"He killed her for that ring!" Laurie Morgan screamed. "He told her he'd kill her unless she gave back that ring—"

"Order! Order!"

Order was finally restored, and Beaudoin's head hung meekly in shame. "The Territory apologizes to the court," he said humbly. "The Territory had no idea the witness would develop this line of testimony. The Territory consents to strike her testimony."

"Counsel will step to the bench."

Judge Hazledine stared at the circle of lawyers. "Mr. Kilgore, it's your move," he said grimly. "I'll grant a motion to strike the woman's testimony. Is that satisfactory?"

Kilgore shook his head. "That was a fast one that Pete pulled," he said grimly. "I don't mind hard blows, but this was right to the groin. He knew damn well Laurie was set to make that outburst. There's complicity here!"

Beaudoin looked pained. "Jake, I swear I don't know where you got these ideas. I put her on in good faith. She's ignorant, and she's a mother, and she got out of control. I'll join in your motion."

"The hell you will!" Kilgore said. "The cat's out of the bag.

The jury heard all that prejudicial and illegal testimony. I'll make that motion to strike, but without your help."

Hazledine turned to the attorney general. "Mr. Beaudoin, if this happens once more, I'll cite you to the governor to institute removal proceedings. If you get a conviction, I don't want any reversal because you can't keep a straight record. Get back to your places!"

Judge Hazledine said, "Miss Morgan, can you produce those letters from your daughter?"

"No. No, I didn't keep the letters."

"Mr. Beaudoin," Hazledine went on, "is it your intention to produce a witness who can testify that the diamond ring was actually in the deceased's possession?"

Beaudoin looked distressed. "Not at the moment, Your Honor. It seems the girl kept the ring hidden away and showed it to nobody during the few weeks it was in her possession, for fear it would be stolen."

Judge Hazledine turned to Kilgore and said, "It would seem, Mr. Kilgore, that your point about hearsay is a telling one. Since the prosecution is not prepared to prove that the ring ever was in the deceased's possession, I'm inclined to sustain your objection and order the entire matter of the ring stricken from the record."

"Thank you, Your Honor," Kilgore said.

"However," Hazledine went on grimly, "the witness claimed that the defendant wrote to his sister informing her of his gift of the ring, and that he took the gift back upon her advice. Mr. Beaudoin is at liberty to adduce testimony from the sister on the matter of this letter. If no letter existed, then I'll sustain your objection. On the other hand, if she confirms the claim of the present witness, I'm afraid I'll have to allow all statements to stand, but subject to connection. Letters by the defendant himself are of course admissible evidence to show motive. Mr. Beaudoin, Mr. Kilgore—either of you is at liberty to call Miss McCandless as a witness."

Kilgore winced. He had hoped no one would bring Carlotta into this. The important ring testimony had been on the verge of going into the discard, but now all was altered. He returned to his seat. Clem whispered, "Carlotta will never perjure herself! She'll admit that she received the letter!"

Kilgore nodded. "We're in trouble. Harry denies giving the ring—but I'm afraid Carlotta will back up Laurie's story, I'm sure. Beaudoin will make us sweat over this!" He pounded his fist into his palm. "I was too slow objecting. I should have cut Laurie off before she dragged Harry's letter to Carlotta into this! But I didn't even know she had heard about the letter!"

Kilgore shook a little as he confronted Laurie for the cross-examination. He said, "You're a resident of Santa Fe, are you not?"

"Correct."

"May I ask your profession?"

"I'm a sporting-house proprietor."

"Might I ask you to be more specific about the nature of such a house?"

"Oh, stop pussyfooting, Jake Kilgore! You know damn well—"

"Let's remember we're in a courtroom," Kilgore said. "Answer the question."

"I serve drinks and food there, and offer entertainment for men!"

"Would it be unfair to describe your establishment as a brothel, Miss Morgan?"

"This man is impossible, Your Honor!" Pete Beaudoin said. "He's out to demean every witness!"

"How can anyone demean the owner of a brothel?" Kilgore asked wearily. "We all know Miss Morgan. It's an ancient maxim of law that owners of brothels are notoriously unreliable as witnesses. *Res ipsa loquitur,*" he quoted learnedly. "Says so in Magna Carta."

He was allowed to continue. Forcing Laurie to admit that her house was indeed a brothel, he went on to ask, "And while your daughter lived with you, did she live on the premises of your house?"

"Yes."

"Was she ever employed by you as a prostitute?"

Laurie flamed. "No. Never in my house!"

"What about outside? Were you aware that she had affairs with other men from an unusually early age?"

"I never pried into her private life. She was a good girl, Jake Kilgore!" she said bleakly.

Kilgore's bushy eyebrows rose in tolerant indulgence of a mother's heart. "Do you seriously ask this jury of twelve intelligent men to believe that the son of one of the wealthiest men in the Territory would marry the illegitimate daughter of the keeper of a bawdy house?"

The look in Laurie's eyes was deadly. Kilgore faced her complacently, benignly, compassionately, sweetness gleaming from his scalp—and wishing he were called upon for any job but this. He felt like apologizing to the woman. But there was no turning back.

Laurie finally said in a low voice, "I don't believe he ever meant to marry the child. I don't know what kind of a game he was playing. But he made her a promise and she believed that promise. He gave her a diamond ring and then he killed her and robbed her when he got scared of what Dan Mc-Candless would say."

Kilgore glanced at the bench. "I ask that the last remark be stricken."

The judge agreed. Kilgore returned slowly to his chair. Beaudoin had produced all his witnesses now, and not one had emerged unscathed, he reflected. He should be pleased with the state of the record. Only the bothersome matter of the ring flawed Kilgore's defense. Otherwise, he had scored off each of the items of evidence as proving nothing, and he had thoroughly pegged Honey Morgan for the worthless trollop she was.

"I have no further questions," Kilgore declared.

Beaudoin arose. "The Territory rests, Your Honor."

The judge said, "Is the defense ready to go ahead? Or shall I declare a recess?"

Kilgore replied, "Your Honor, I respectfully move to dismiss the indictment on the ground that the Territory has failed completely to show that Honey Morgan was not attacked *after* Harry McCandless had left her on the outskirts of town. They have failed to make out a case."

Beaudoin's face was ugly. "No one can prove that Honey was *not* killed *before* Harry McCandless got rid of the body, Mr. Kilgore."

Kilgore said grimly, "In this Territory, Mr. Beaudoin, we have an old-fashioned belief that the burden is on the prosecution to prove guilt, not on the defense to prove innocence." He turned to the court. "Your Honor, I move the indictment be dismissed."

For a moment Hazledine's eyes were veiled in thought. Then he said, "Motion denied. Call your first witness."

"In that case, Your Honor, I request a recess of fifteen minutes."

"Granted."

Kilgore and Clem drew Harry McCandless aside. He would be the first witness in his own defense. In a low, threatening voice, Kilgore said, "I want the truth about that diamond ring, Harry."

Harry had remained impassive, smiling enigmatically, throughout the entire trial. He had said nothing. His smile vanished now. "What truth?"

"*The* truth," Kilgore glowered. "We're in a bad spot. You might have been freed five minutes ago if it weren't for this business of the ring. When Carlotta comes back from Denver, she'll testify. She's already told Clem she received a letter from you concerning the gift of the ring. She'll testify that way, if I know her at all."

Harry said, "Suppose Carlotta disappears? From what the judge said, that means that all of Laurie's raving about the ring will be stricken?"

Kilgore groaned. "Harry, Harry! That's not the point," he said desperately. "You're too intelligent not to understand the trap that Beaudoin dug for us. Sure it's hearsay—and he'll get the judge to strike it from the record. Point is, the whole damn courtroom heard that woman screaming like a catamount. The point is indelible in the public mind. Even if we got a mistrial, that ring will always stick in our craw.

"No," he went on gloomily, "we're out on a limb. I'm putting you up now to testify, and you can bet that Beaudoin will ask you about the ring. I don't mind a little perjury when a man is desperate and about to be hung. But if you deny giving that ring to the girl, Beaudoin will call Carlotta to ask her about your letters. Will Carlotta lie for you?"

The thin, intelligent face was a study in distress. "I—I don't know, Mr. Kilgore," Harry McCandless admitted. "I think she'd do anything for me, but I don't know if she has the capacity."

"That means you *did* give her the ring?"

"Y-yes."

"Why did you lie to me the other time we discussed this?"

"My father was in the cell. I was afraid of him."

"Will you lie on the stand?"

"No. I'll answer truthfully."

"You'd better," Kilgore said. "Or else I won't give the Territory a chance to hang you. I'll pull your head off myself."

The recess was at its end. Kilgore conferred with Clem for a few moments, trying out on Clem the various points he wanted to raise in his introductory words to the jury. Then, as Hazledine reconvened the court, Kilgore took his position before the jurors, thrust his fingers through his galluses, and looked at each man individually before beginning.

He said, "Gentlemen of this jury, you have just heard our esteemed attorney general present the case for the Territory. I submit to you the fact that his case was insufficient to prove an act of murder committed by the defendant, and I propose to show this through questioning of witnesses.

"Now, none of you here are philosophers, so I won't go into any learned babble of causality and necessary relationships. I'll use simple language in stating a simple fact: that we can't always be sure that A, B, and C prove D. We can only make assumptions.

"For instance. I rub a match along the floor, and it bursts

into flame. You can thus conclude that cause and effect is at work. Given a match and given a floor, the friction of one against the other necessarily produces flame. And—if the match isn't wet or badly made—it *will* produce flame. Cause and effect. We can be pretty sure of the relationship, can't we, between the striking of the match and the appearance of the flame. To get one, you have to have the other. And in a specific order. You can't have the flame first and strike the match afterward. So we say that the striking—the friction— is the *cause* of the *effect,* flame.

"How about here? Mr. Beaudoin has presented certain factors. A fraternity pin, a Navajo rug, a rumor of a romantic relationship, an identifying mark on a buckboard. Out of these factors, he expects you to conclude that this man here murdered a girl.

"I submit to you that the chain of evidence is incomplete. It does not prove anything. A girl is dead; this is undeniable. A man is accused of the crime. But the Territory has not shown with any clarity that this man is guilty.

"One further point, please. You will remember my words to you yesterday, at the opening of this trial. I cautioned you not to let emotional feelings enter into your framing of judgment. You are not here to pass judgment on the character of Harry McCandless. You are not here to express your resentment for real or fancied injustices committed by his father. You are not here to punish a person you may have come to dislike. I know that the defendant is not a well-loved person in San Carlos. He makes no apologies for his past behavior, and neither do I.

"You are here for one purpose, and one only. You are here to weigh the evidence presented, and to conclude, *solely on the basis of that evidence,* whether the prisoner before you did or did not commit the crime for which he has been indicted. I say to you that the Territory has not shown any chain of guilt. I call upon you to clear your minds of anything but the matter at hand—to narrow the focus of your perceptions—to examine critically what the Territory has shown you in the past two days.

"But this is not the summation of the defense, merely its opening speech. I won't belabor my point any further, but will proceed to show you just how flimsy the case against Harry McCandless really is.

"The defense calls its first witness: Harry McCandless."

17.

THE COURTROOM was terribly quiet. This was the moment everyone had been waiting for, the moment when the mercurial, unpredictable McCandless boy would take the stand. Harry looked very pale, and he crossed and uncrossed his legs uncomfortably. But his eyes were steady, unfrightened. They looked out at the assembled onlookers with calm, contemptuous appraisal—the eyes of a self-appointed Nietzschean *Übermensch*.

Kilgore, his back to the spectators, looked almost pleadingly at the boy, appealing to his instincts of self-defense. Silently, Kilgore begged him to cooperate. Harry did not seem to feel fear at this trial. Perhaps he was sublimely confident of his own ultimate vindication. Perhaps he did not fear hanging. Or, perhaps, he was mad.

Kilgore thrust one hand into his pocket, fondling the knife he always carried. He warmed Harry up with a few preliminary questions: his age, his full name, his educational background. Harry answered with no trace of sullenness or contempt. The jury seemed to drowse.

Suddenly Kilgore changed tack. "Where were you at dinnertime on the night of November thirtieth, Mr. McCandless?"

"At home. The Wa-po-nah ranch."

"Did you have a guest there?"

"Yes. Eli Weingarten."

"But your parents and sister were not present?"

"No. They were in New York."

"What did you say to Mr. Weingarten after dinner?"

Harry rolled his eyes to the ceiling. "I said something like 'Let's get the Morgan girl and have some fun.' "

"And what reply did Mr. Weingarten make?"

"He said it was a good idea. He agreed to take one of our buggies and go to town to fetch her from Dade Rawlins' place, where she lived."

"How long was he gone?"

"About an hour and a half."

"Is that exceptionally slow time to make the round trip from Wa-po-nah to Dade Rawlins' place?"

Harry shook his head. "No, it's pretty good time. Eli drives fast. It usually takes fifty minutes or so each way."

"What time did he return?"

"Around nine."

"With the girl?"

"Yes."

Kilgore paused. "Now, we have all heard Mr. Weingarten's testimony concerning the events of the two hours that followed. Are you in agreement with his account of these events?"

"Yes. Yes, that's what happened."

"Mr. Weingarten went on to state that it became necessary to subdue the girl violently and remove her from the premises. He said furthermore that he went to bed before you subdued the girl. Would you relate the events that took place after Mr. Weingarten went to bed?"

Harry stroked his smooth cheeks thoughtfully. "Well, I got the girl's clothes on her. She was kicking and fighting, and it was pretty rough going. While we were thrashing around, Julian, our steward, came to the room. He helped me take the girl down to the wagon. This was around eleven. I started to drive back to San Carlos. On the way, Honey began acting up. She grabbed the reins and started mistreating the mare. I realized that if I kept her aboard we'd have a runaway or a wreck, so I halted the wagon and ejected her from it."

"How did you accomplish that?"

"I put my arm about her waist and set her down on her feet. She was drunk, but able to stand. She yelled at me, and she was very angry. I turned around and drove back to Wa-po-nah."

"She was alive and well when you last set eyes on her?" Kilgore asked.

"Definitely. I left her on the outskirts of town, a short distance from her home. I figured she'd walk the rest of the way herself."

"When did you return to Wa-po-nah?"

"It was around one in the morning."

"So the round trip took you two hours. This would be about average time, figuring in the difficulties you had with Honey en route."

"Yes, sir."

"Was anyone awake when you returned?"

"Julian was. He helped me stable the horse, and I went to bed."

"In the morning what happened?"

"Eli—Mr. Weingarten—awoke and asked about Honey. I told him I had taken her home and had returned at one."

Kilgore nodded. "You would say, then, that someone else might have attacked and murdered the girl on the road after you left her at approximately midnight?"

He had expected response from Beaudoin, and he got it. "I object to that question, Your Honor! Witness's conjectures are hardly admissible as testimony!"

"Sustained," Judge Hazledine said wearily. "Mr. Kilgore, I have asked you before to spare us these little tricks. Examination of the witness does not mean making rhetorical statements to the jury."

Kilgore smiled. "I beg the court's pardon."

Kilgore said, "You see this fraternity pin that the prosecution has introduced as evidence. Do you recognize it?"

"Yes, sir. It's mine. Or was."

"What do you mean, *was?*"

"I gave it to Honey Morgan last August. She wanted some

sort of souvenir. And since I was no longer going to college, I didn't have any value for the pin, so I gave it to her."

"Did she wear it often?"

"Quite often."

"Was she wearing it the night you last saw her?"

"Yes, sir. It was pinned to her dress. I noticed it when she came in."

Kilgore nodded. "She wore the pin often. So its presence near her body would not imply your presence, because you had not had possession of the pin for some months."

"That's correct."

Kilgore looked at Beaudoin. "Cross-examine."

Beaudoin came forward with a vengeful smile on his sharp-featured face. Harry stared at him without interest.

Beaudoin said, "May I ask, Mr. McCandless, why you sent your guest to town to pick up the deceased on the fatal night, and not one of your servants or yourself?"

"I don't believe in sending our servants on two-hour drives for my pleasure," Harry said. "It was after dinner and they were supposedly free for the evening. Besides, Eli had eaten too much at dinner and said he wanted the fresh air of a drive."

"This expression of concern for your servants' welfare is very touching, Mr. McCandless. But is it not true that several years ago you showed so little regard for one of your servants as to beat him senseless—a man some three times your age? A man named Diego Barca? And was there not a maid in your household named Maria Vasquez who charged you with fathering her illegitimate child and—"

"Your Honor, I object strongly!" Kilgore said. "Defendant is on trial for murder, not for past offenses."

Beaudoin retorted, "I'm trying to demonstrate the wholly amoral character of the defendant. This is cross-examination as to character. I didn't ask the man to take the witness stand. That was strictly Kilgore's idea."

Kilgore said, "I object to that, too!"

Judge Hazledine tapped the bench. "Now, Mr. Kilgore," he said wearily, "you know the rules too well to take any objection. When the defendant elected to take the witness stand, he opened the door to cross-examination as to his credibility *as a witness*. It's got nothing to do with his rights as a defendant. Objection overruled!"

Beaudoin went exhaustively into the story of Harry Mc-Candless, in which fact and legend were blended. The youth sat at ease, discussing in detail each alleged misdemeanor with an air of deprecation, as though the peccadilloes of youth were absurdly blown up out of all proportion to their value. He was a bit wild as a boy, he conceded readily enough. The privileged life of wealth had perhaps given him a touch of conceit and arrogance. It was true that the resources of a brilliant mind had given him an evaluation of his own worth beyond that of ordinary men. But this was merely the ordinary reaction of a boy to a set of circumstances not of his own creation. The shocking events of the past few months, he suggested, had sobered him up. Kilgore sat with folded arms, glancing occasionally about the courtroom, marking the pallor of Dan McCandless' cheeks, the deep anxiety in his eyes, sensing a tension between father and son that he could not fathom. Harry McCandless was doing well—surprisingly well —parrying the hammer blows of the prosecutor with deft and modest disclaimers and wearing an air of candor and humility for which the lawyer was not prepared.

I'm damned! thought Kilgore. *I think he's going to make it! I really do!*

Beaudoin finally gave up an unprofitable line of interrogation and walked back to the rail, where he turned and put his next question with folded arms. The windows were shut tight against the cold, and the blazing stove was heating up a fetid atmosphere.

"McCandless! I'd like to ask a few questions about your past relationship with the deceased. How long did you know her?"

"About six or eight months."

"Was she living in San Carlos when you met her?"

"No. She came down on a visit. She didn't move here for a month or two after that."

"I see. And you first became intimate with her—ah—when?"

"The day I met her."

There was a murmur in the courtroom. Beaudoin himself looked upset; nothing Kilgore had said against Honey damned her so effectively as what Beaudoin's own cross-examination had revealed, just now.

Recovering, Beaudoin went on, "These intimacies continued regularly after she moved to San Carlos?"

"That's right. But she was sleeping with other men, too."

"Just answer my questions!" Beaudoin said coldly. "You needn't interpolate any thoughts of your own!"

Harry said seriously, "I'll try not to think, Mr. Beaudoin."

"May I remind you that you're on trial here, as well as on the witness stand?" Beaudoin asked. "Did you, at any time, intend to marry the deceased?"

"Never," Harry said.

"But did you tell her you had such intentions?"

Harry paused. "I might have," he said slowly. "For a joke, that is. The way I gave her that fraternity pin. But I certainly didn't mean what I said. I might have been drunk."

"You were trifling with her, is that it?"

"I suppose you'd have to call it that. But I didn't think she was taking me seriously."

"Did you," Beaudoin asked slowly, "give her any other tokens besides the fraternity pin? Such as a diamond ring of considerable value?"

Harry was silent a long moment. Kilgore looked up at him, his eyes menacing. Harry said finally, "Yes. Yes, I gave her a diamond ring."

There was a loud, involuntary groan of despair in the courtroom; Dan McCandless' face was contorted in anguish and humiliation as he buried his face in his hands.

Beaudoin said, "When did you give her this ring?"

"Early in October."

"And you subsequently took it back from her?"

"No," Harry said, and Kilgore looked up in surprise. "No, I never saw the ring again after I gave it to her. For all I know, it's still hidden somewhere in Dade Rawlins' shack."

"He's lying!" Laurie Morgan burst out. "He took the ring away from her! He's got it!"

She was silenced. Beaudoin said, frowning, "Did you send a letter to your sister Carlotta informing her that you had given the ring to Honey Morgan?"

"Yes, I did."

"And what reply did your sister make?"

"She said I should get the ring back immediately."

"But you did not do this?"

"No," Harry said, "I didn't take it back. And I don't have any notion where it might be now."

Kilgore put his hands to his pounding head. A client who changed stories under cross-examination, a client who lied up and down to his lawyer—this was too much! But the sudden turn of events, confusing though it was, nevertheless helped Harry's case, Kilgore realized. If Harry had *not* taken back the ring, then his major motive for the murder, fear of Laurie's civil suit, was wiped out.

Beaudoin realized this, too. For five minutes he hammered relentlessly away at Harry. But the youth stoutly maintained his story. He had given the ring, yes, in a drunken moment. But he had disregarded his sister's advice about getting it back. And he had no idea of its whereabouts now.

Throwing up his hands, Beaudoin dropped the matter of the ring and said, "You have heard the coroner and Dr. Hewlitt testify that the dead girl was found with her mouth stuffed full of building plaster."

"Yes, I have."

"How would you interpret that?"

"I'm sure I don't know," Harry said.

"Would you care to guess?"

Harry said, "Well, it might be that some renegade Indian had killed her and stuffed the plaster in her mouth following some superstition to prevent the girl from speaking ill of her murderer in the hereafter."

"Very ingenious." Beaudoin stared at the ceiling. "Unfortunately, none of the Indians of this region have such a superstition. An Apache has testified to that effect already."

"Well, perhaps."

"Would you concede the possibility," Beaudoin went on, "that some non-Indian committed the crime and stuffed the girl's mouth to give the impression that it was a murder according to some Indian ritual—thus laying a false trail away from any white man?"

Harry shrugged. "It's far-fetched, but I suppose it's possible."

"I suppose it might be," Beaudoin agreed. He signaled to Duer, who handed up a large brown volume. "Mr. McCandless, are you familiar with this book?"

"I've read it, yes."

"Would you tell the court what it is?"

"It's an anthropology text published in Berlin in 1889."

"You own a copy of this book, do you not?"

"Yes, I do."

"And you have a reading knowledge of the German language?"

"Yes," Harry admitted.

"Furthermore, you are known to have an interest in such subjects as anthropology?"

"That's true."

Beaudoin paused dramatically. "Your Honor, I'd like permission to read a few paragraphs of this book and have them entered in the record in their original language."

"Go ahead," Hazledine said.

Opening to a marked page, Beaudoin read resonantly in a somewhat Americanized German. When he had finished, he recited a translation. The passage dealt with customs of Bantu tribesmen of Africa—in particular, an alleged custom of stuffing the mouth of a dead person with earth to prevent the spirit from naming the murderer.

Kilgore sat stunned. Where had Beaudoin obtained this obscure book? How did he know Harry had read it? Who at Wa-po-nah had informed the prosecutor of its existence, Kilgore wondered. The courtroom was quiet.

Kilgore rose. "Let's see that exhibit!"

It was a work of more than one thousand pages printed in

small Germanic type and bound in calf and boards. His eye caught the name of a publishing house in Leipzig and the word *Naturwissenschaft*. He said thickly, "I'd like to ask Mr. Beaudoin how he happened to get hold of a book belonging to my client. Maybe somebody ought to be on trial here for book stealing."

Judge Hazledine tapped for order. "What's that got to do with the issues, Mr. Kilgore?"

Beaudoin seemed amused. "May it please the court, I'm not embarrassed by Mr. Kilgore's insinuation. I did not abstract this book from the defendant's library. Mr. McCandless, is this your copy?"

"No," Harry said. "It would have the Wa-po-nah bookplate if it were mine. And mine was a well-thumbed book. This one is almost new."

Beaudoin laughed. "You see, Mr. Kilgore? I obtained this by my own devices, from an expert on such lore who mailed me the book from Washington at the beginning of the year. It was just coincidence, was it not, that the defendant also owned the book, also was familiar with this passage, and happened to use it as his inspiration in the murder of—"

"Objection!"

"That last remark will be stricken, Mr. Beaudoin," Hazledine declared. "The jury is instructed to disregard it."

Beaudoin did not seem displeased. "No further questions, Your Honor."

Harry came down from the stand. Kilgore felt inner turmoil now. Things had looked to be under control when Harry denied knowledge of the ring—but the bothersome business of the German anthropology text looked damning, and Kilgore had no idea how he was going to rebut.

He had only two witnesses left to call. Julian DuVivier came to the stand to testify briefly in support of Harry's claim to have returned to Wa-po-nah by one in the morning on the night of Honey's death. Beaudoin, in the cross-examination, tried vigorously to shake Julian's story, but the old man held firm. Kilgore successfully objected to any innuendoes by the prosecutor that Julian was perjuring himself in his master's behalf.

Kilgore said, "Julian?"

"Sir?"

"Was Honey Morgan alive when she left Wa-po-nah?"

"Indeed she was!"

"When Harry McCandless came back that night, was there anything remarkable about his manner?"

"No, sir."

"He was calm?"

Julian DuVivier's glance passed momentarily from Harry McCandless to the tragic figure of Dan McCandless in the first bench. He said firmly, "Mr. Harry McCandless was unusually calm and untroubled, Mr. Kilgore. If he were excited or distressed, I would have known. I don't think Mr. Harry could conceal the state of emotions from me. He never has."

"No more questions."

Strangely dissatisfied, Kilgore called his last witness for the defense—a saloonkeeper who testified that he had seen Harry's fraternity pin on Honey Morgan as long ago as September, and had questioned her at that time about it. She had told him it was a gift from Harry.

Hazledine said, "Is that all, Mr. Kilgore?"

"That's all. The defense rests."

"All right. It is now well past the usual lunch hour of this court. We will recess until thirty minutes past two, at which time the Territory may offer its rebuttal." He tapped his gavel. "The sheriff will take custody of the prisoner during the recess."

Harry was led away. Kilgore left for the office provided for the defense's use, where Sarah had brandy ready for him. His head was throbbing mercilessly. But he felt hopeful.

Dan McCandless entered with Clem. McCandless said bitterly, "I searched for the ring every day, Kilgore, and couldn't find it. And to think that the boy gave it to a piece of trash like that—"

"He's young, Dan. And very foolish."

"And my son. Do you think you've saved him, Kilgore?"

Kilgore managed a painful smile. "I'd say a tentative yes. Except for that stunt with the anthropology book, Beaudoin's not offered anything worth a damn as evidence. And the book alone isn't sufficient to prove anything. After the recess I'll ask Hazledine again to throw out the indictment."

"And if he doesn't?" McCandless asked fearfully.

"Then we proceed. Either we'll get a verdict in our favor, or else the record will guarantee a reversal on appeal. I tell you there's no case against your boy, Dan. And both Beaudoin and Hazledine know it."

McCandless shook his head slowly. "I wish I could believe that, Jake. But there's trouble ahead for us yet. They won't let Harry slip through their hands so easily. I'm worried. So terribly worried."

18.

THE MOMENT Kilgore saw the smiling faces of Beaudoin and the prosecution crowd after the recess, he knew that Dan McCandless' premonitions of disaster were about to be fulfilled. Beaudoin did not look like a man whose case was shattered. He had the glinting smile of a cougar about to leap on its prey.

He and Duer were conferring with Judge Hazledine now. Kilgore watched uneasily.

"What do you think they're up to?" Clem asked.

"I don't like it, whatever it is," Kilgore muttered. "That Beaudoin gives me a pain in my *good* ear. He's got something in mind, but what? What?"

When the court was called to order, Beaudoin arose and addressed the bench, glancing ironically at his opponent. Information had been received during the recess, he said, drawling for effect, which required that court and jury take a view of the various places mentioned in the testimony.

Kilgore was instantly on his feet, wincing with pain. "Take a view? View of what?"

"When we get there, you'll see!" Beaudoin said.

"In this cold?"

"Oh, what's that got to do with it?"

Kilgore said slowly, "Judge, the rules allow the jury to view the site of a crime, but it's an extraordinary remedy. I think we ought to know the purpose."

A wrangle ended with a firm ruling from the bench that the court adjourn to the following morning at nine o'clock. The jurors were advised to take warm clothing and the sheriff instructed to provide suitable clothing for the prisoner. Judge Hazledine arose wearily. "Mr. Kilgore, you may note any exception you wish. We'll go to Paraguay if that's where justice can be found. Our first view will be taken at Wa-po-nah. I imagine that your client's father has no objection?"

Dan McCandless slowly shook his head, bewildered by the turn of events—and then the judge was gone and newspapermen were running pell mell to the telegraph office, where the rattling keys began to distribute the news across the nation.

Confusion.

Kilgore could do nothing, could offer no explanation to Dan McCandless or to Clem. He stared in bewilderment at the smug Beaudoin and at the smiling Duer. Everyone in the room was reacting to the startling turn of events—everyone but Harry, who remained aloof, bored, thoroughly uninterested in the new development.

Kilgore left the courtroom quickly and, accompanied by Clem, went to his home. Though it was only three in the afternoon, the lawyer undressed and clambered into bed. His head ached numbingly. He had a fever. His eyes refused to focus properly. The exertion of the trial was taking its toll.

The tap on the door was repeated. There was no answer, and the door was opened. The gaunt, giant figure of Mc-Candless was sprawled in a great white chair of leather that faced a hearth of dressed stone. The bed had not been slept in.

"Mr. McCandless," said Julian gently.

McCandless drew a pair of stiff fingers across a strong jaw covered with white stubble.

"Julian?" he murmured vaguely. "Do you believe in retribution?"

"I don't know, sir," Julian said. "I think we get what we deserve, but I'm not sure what to call it."

"Yes, I suppose you're right. What's there?"

"Coffee, sir." Julian uncovered a silver platter heaped with scrambled eggs and bacon, crisp toast and fine silver. "You haven't much time, sir. There's a line of buggies coming from San Carlos."

McCandless gazed up at the serious, concerned face of the house servant. "How many?"

"Seven."

"Julian, what most concerns you about this visitation?"

Julian hesitated. "I'm just thinking, sir, about Don Alfredo. When he was alive, Wa-po-nah would never have seen a thing like this. Officers of the law inspecting the premises. He would not have permitted their presence."

McCandless was silent. "I'm afraid he'd sing another tune, Julian," he said finally. "Those people have got his grandson in their hands. It's quite different when you've given a hostage to fortune." He paused. "How is my wife this morning?"

"No different," Julian said. "Shall I pour?"

McCandless was dressed and waiting at the great portal to the house when the convoy of buggies drew up at the house and there debouched court and jurors and several newspapermen and curiosity seekers. Judge Abraham Hazledine, wrapped in a muffler of wool, snorting puffs of steam in the icy air, mounted the steps, followed by the lawyers of both sides.

"This isn't customary, McCandless," the judge began without preliminary. "Most cases don't call for a view of the premises—but we all want to clear up some matters. I've given instructions for decorum. Is it agreeable?"

McCandless said dully, "I suppose I've got to tolerate every cockalorum of the law who wants to bring his muddy boots through my house. I'm helpless to object. I've just got this to say—Hazledine, another day is coming and I'll know what to do. Meanwhile, I can't imagine what you hope to find."

"We'll soon see." Judge Hazledine stood in the great foyer and loosened his clothing while the rest of the party entered. The soaring Hispanic walls gleamed in the myriad colors of a great wheel of stained-glass windows which filtered the morning light. It was a scene of richness few had ever seen in their lives. Stamping and blowing their frozen hands, they murmured among themselves in low voices, conscious of the vast wealth indicated by the structure and its furnishings. A savage Goya painting stared down like a commentary on human cruelty and folly.

"Mr. Beaudoin, it's your play," Judge Hazledine noted. "Let's get the jury lined up. What's first?"

Beaudoin was standing in the foyer, wiping his mouth with a dandified air.

"First, let's get the defendant present during the procedure."

Father and son, the McCandlesses confronted each other in the great foyer. It was a moment of embarrassment. Neither spoke for a moment, and then Harry McCandless' eyes went to the floor.

"Sorry, Father!" he muttered.

"It's all right, son," McCandless said painfully. "You've got nothing to hide. There's nothing here for them to see but your home."

Beaudoin said, "Your Honor, I'd like the jury to take a view of the house."

Judge Hazledine said, "Any objections?"

"Just a minute," McCandless said. "I'd like everyone to keep out of the east wing. Those are my wife's rooms, and she's not well. I can't have you disturbing her."

Sheriff Mike Duer said uneasily, "I wouldn't dream of

disturbing Mrs. McCandless, Judge. It's just that the testimony covered the entire house—"

Kilgore had kept silent during the exchange, but at the sign of rising temper, he nudged Dan McCandless and drew him aside. "McCandless, I think you'd better offer to cooperate. It's got past the point where you can worry about feelings. Chances are, they'll skip any view of your wife's bedroom."

McCandless muttered. "Take charge, Kilgore," he said despondently. "I'm not fit to make any decisions. Let 'em do whatever they please. Julian!" he called out. "Take these gentlemen around."

"*Aquí, aquí*," Duer said to the Spanish-speaking members of the jury.

Led by Julian, the entire throng—judge, jury, and entourage—examined the house in a guided tour. The group was silent, grim and purposeful as each room was described by Julian. Harry McCandless walked through the ritual with an air of surprise, as though seeing the familiar walls for the first time. On the top landing leading to the attic, he tried an uneasy joke.

"Have you ever had a feeling, Kilgore, that you've been in a certain place before? That you're walking through a scene that you seem to remember?" A nervous smile played feebly over a sensitive mouth. "I have a conviction that I've been here before."

Kilgore growled at the frivolity, and then Beaudoin raised a finger. "What's up there?"

"The attic," Julian said.

Beaudoin pointed to a door.

"And that?"

"Mr. Harry's bedroom."

"Where sexual relations were had with the deceased girl?"

"Yes, sir."

Beaudoin signaled. "Your Honor, I'd like the jury to see the room."

More than a score of men were in the bedroom, staring at the walnut bookcases filled with learned books in a dozen languages that filled the walls to the ceiling, the fine paintings, the tanks of experimental fish, microscopes and scientific equipment and a hideous African mask carved in stinkwood— a rare wood from South Africa. A mutter of interest subsided as Beaudoin called for silence in Spanish and English. He pointed to a portiere and spoke with apparent foreknowledge.

"What's behind that curtain?"

"Why, nothing," Harry said uneasily.

Beaudoin said quietly, "Sheriff Duer, would you mind pulling that curtain aside?"

The door was set high in the wall; it was not more than two feet square, a door that might have closed off a laundry chute. On a signal, Mike Duer drew over an ornate bench and reached into the recess.

The Navajo rug was the mate of the one that had been wrapped around the body of Honey Morgan—the same size, five feet by four, and of the same general pattern and colors. It was stained deeply with blood. Kilgore went pale; Dan McCandless gasped in shock.

Judge Hazledine said, "Sheriff, you will impound this rug and have those stains tested to determine whether they are animal bloodstains or stains of human blood."

There was a moment of silence. "There's no need for that," said Harry McCandless finally. "It's human blood, all right. Honey Morgan's blood."

Kilgore whirled, glaring savagely at the boy to make him keep shut. But Hazledine said, "Are you making an admission?"

· "No, I'm simply telling you it's Honey's blood," Harry said dully, waving Kilgore away. "She had a bad nosebleed the night she was here. Doc Hewlitt corroborated that in his testimony. She was drunk, and fell down and bled all over this carpet."

"You didn't mention this nosebleed in your testimony," Beaudoin said.

Harry said, "No one asked me about it."

"And why did you hide the blanket this way?" Beaudoin demanded.

Harry said, "Because I was sure the sheriff would misunderstand if he found a bloody blanket."

Beaudoin persisted. "And how would you account for the *other* bloody blanket—the twin of this one, found wrapped around the corpse?"

Harry hesitated. "I don't know about that."

"Enough," Hazledine said. "These questions can wait for our return to court. There is another site to visit, is there not?"

"Yes," Beaudoin said.

"Have we further business here?" asked the judge.

They did not, and the party filed out. Kilgore felt drenched with sweat. Never before had a client of his gone to the gallows—but he had a strong hunch that the record was about to be broken. Harry's mystifying attitude, his lies and evasions, the incredible way Beaudoin and Duer plucked evidence out of the air, the general feeling against the defendant—all these were turning the tide against Kilgore.

The group was leaving the ranch now, setting out on some new journey. Kilgore sat back in his buggy, refusing to talk, silently suffering the twin agonies of his infected ear and his collapsing case. The prosecution party, in the lead, followed the main road out of Wa-po-nah and up into the hills toward the Sanchez farm. But halfway there they turned off the main road, taking an unmarked trail that led into the underbrush.

"What in thunder?" Kilgore wondered.

Beaudoin called a halt before the ruins of an abandoned house, well back from the main road. He said to the judge and the assembled listeners, "If we continue on this road, we will arrive at the Sanchez farm. But first, let's take a view of this house."

"What house?" Kilgore asked strongly.

"You'll see!" Beaudoin replied. "Mr. Duer, will you ask the jurors to follow? This way, Judge!"

It was an Eastern-style house of brick, which lay crumbling in ruins in the snow. An Eastern homesteader, Manley Pearce Duell, a poet and writer with a romantic interest in the West, had begun some years earlier to build the house in the pure mountain air with some vague notions about ranching—notions that had died under the harsh realities of cattle diseases and falling prices dictated by meat packers in Abilene, St. Louis, and Chicago. It lay midway on a direct route between Wa-po-nah and the Sanchez farm in the distant hills where the girl's body had been found. In a wooden form, covered with drifting bits of grass, was a crumbling whitish mass of friable substance.

"Your Honor," Beaudoin said, "it don't take any scientific tests to show that this stuff is builder's plaster. Just the kind of stuff that was found by Father Crespin in the poor girl's mouth. It just shows that she was brought along this way."

Kilgore said, "What of it? We know her mouth was stuffed with plaster. That don't make Harry McCandless any guiltier than before. We also know she had to be brought this way to get out to the Sanchez place. It's interesting—but how does it add up?"

Judge Hazledine said, "It does add to the record." He pointed out, "It does account for this mysterious substance. On the other hand, who was responsible?"

A shout of pure joy came up from the interior of the ruin. Mike Duer came lumbering out of the ruin, studying a small object in his hand. A grin of devilish exultation split his dark face.

"The ring! The ring!"

Indeed it was the ring! The ring—the Lucero diamond ring —had been found hidden in the corner of the ruin, wrapped in a silk handkerchief bearing the Wa-po-nah insignia and Harry McCandless' monogram!

Beaudoin said ringingly: "I think this demonstrates the guilt of the defendant conclusively and beyond doubt. He stopped here, hid the incriminating ring he had taken from the girl, stuffed his victim's mouth with plaster, and continued on to drop the body elsewhere. Then—"

"Enough, Mr. Beaudoin," Hazledine declared. "We will return to the courtroom to conclude this case."

Stricken, Dan McCandless howled in grief. An answering roar of rage came from the angry crowd.

"String the bastard up right here!" boomed a deep voice. "We don't need to finish the trial!"

"Get him! Get Harry McCandless!"

Mike Duer gestured, and instantly guns were facing the milling crowd. Behind the protective barrier, Kilgore clenched his fists until the nails dug deep into his palms; Dan McCandless, his face bloodless, gritted his teeth to keep from bursting into tears in front of these people.

Harry was white-faced and shaken and for the first time since the day of his arrest was silent. In the midst of hatred, he stood in the cold, licking his mouth nervously and holding his hands over his ears.

"Why? Why?" Dan McCandless moaned. "Why would my boy do this thing? Why should this happen to us?"

Kilgore sat back in the pitching carriage, nursing his throbbing ear, which was covered with a woolen scarf. It seemed to him that the wind cut through the protective covering—but the physical pain was no less keen than the pain of sympathy and grief for the stricken family. He felt close to collapse and struggled to keep his last ounce of strength.

"I don't see how you can be blamed," Clem Erskine ventured. "You tried a brilliant case, Mr. Kilgore. But I guess that's it—"

Kilgore's pain-tinged eyes were instantly wide with anger. "That is *not* it!" he said with wrath. "This case is far from over!"

Clem looked bewildered.

"Kilgore never throws in the sponge!" Kilgore said strongly. "Kilgore's fighting heart is indomitable. When the last appeal has been refused, when executive clemency has been denied, when the highest court in the land has refused redress—that is Kilgore's finest moment. Even when the trap has been sprung, even when the defendant's neck has been broken, even then Kilgore will not admit defeat. Kilgore will fight if only to vindicate the memory of his innocent client. No case is lost until Kilgore himself is lying in the grave! And even then, the memory of Kilgore's eloquence—the recollection of his fighting heart—the echo of his living voice heard throughout the land will speak the innocence of Kilgore's man! I have not yet begun to fight."

"Mr. Kilgore," said Clem earnestly, "you're a sick man, and I just don't see how you can finish this case. Dr. Hewlitt told me he's sure you've got a mastoiditis. In all this cold, you're endangering your life. I don't know what Miss Hilleboe will say."

Kilgore grunted. "Sarah Hilleboe is sure to tell me I've got to get up to Denver for surgery, or they'll be burying me as soon as the ground thaws out enough to dig. I know that croak."

"It's the living truth—"

Kilgore closed his eyes and shrank into the warmth of his sheepskin coat. "I've got a case to try," he said grimly. "Shut up!"

Kilgore entered the silent courtroom shakily the following morning and made his way to the counsel table, where Harry McCandless was waiting, flanked by deputies, manacled for the first time since the trial had started. Kilgore's legs kept wanting to give way under him. His face was flushed and feverish. One entire side of his skull seemed to be rotting away, to be turning into a soggy, putrefying mass.

He said in a barely audible voice, "Your Honor, the disclosures yesterday seem damning indeed. I ask for an adjournment of one week while—while reconsidering the new developments—"

"Refused," Hazledine said coldly.

Kilgore shivered. "Your Honor, there is a possibility that I will have a new witness—a witness whose testimony may have a strong bearing in deciding this case. The defendant's sister went to Denver three days ago to contact this witness. I have not yet heard from her. For this reason I ask the adjournment."

Hazledine shrugged. "Today is Friday, Mr. Kilgore. I'll grant your adjournment—until nine o'clock Monday morning. If you can produce your new witness by then, fine. If not, the case goes to the jury. This court stands adjourned until then!"

Kilgore's shoulders slumped. All he had now was the week-end. Carlotta remained silent. And there was only the slimmest chance that her journey would accomplish anything.

And who was giving the information to Duer? Who had told the prosecution about Eli Weingarten, about the bloody carpet, about the diamond ring? The victory had been in Kilgore's grasp—and then the blows had fallen like jests of the gods. It was all too mystifying. Exhausted, frayed, baffled, Jake Kilgore shuffled out of the courtroom, trying to conceal from the onlookers the extent of his weakness.

19.

A DAY had passed since the astonishing disclosures. Dan McCandless had taken the Saturday-morning train to Santa Fe. Now, at two that afternoon, he faced Governor Charles Tellegen in the governor's private office. Tellegen ordinarily did not conduct Territorial business on Saturdays, but McCandless had wired ahead, requesting the interview, and the governor had consented.

Dan McCandless had walked through hell for hours before making his fateful decision. Friday evening, at Wa-po-nah, Isabella had confronted him.

"My son will die," she said stonily. "He has committed this crime, and not even Kilgore can save him. But you can!"

"Me?" Dan McCandless asked.

Isabella's Castilian eyes were ablaze. "The governor would grant him clemency if you offered something valuable in return for the favor."

"Tellegen can't be bribed, Isabella."

"It would not be a bribe. You would offer the governor information—about a certain terrible crime committed in this

Territory twenty years ago. The murder of Don Alfredo Lucero!"

"No!" McCandless cried. It was a wail of despair, a horrible sound to come from a man so big.

"Your son, McCandless—the bearer of your name. He will die unless ancient guilt is expiated!"

McCandless shook his head with some of his old fierce strength. "It's no matter for Tellegen. No matter for the law at all. You know nothing about it."

"I know that Harry will die—and you alone can save him!" Isabella rose. "Think about it, Dan McCandless."

Alone, McCandless thought.

Harry will die. My son. My only son.

For three hours his only companion was a bottle of brandy, as he fought with himself, fought to sustain his courage. He could save Harry, all right—but only at the cost of betraying the code he had lived by. Only at the cost of his life.

Now he sat in an overstuffed chair, peering out of bloodshot eyes at the dignified and tranquil face of the governor of the Territory of New Mexico. McCandless said slowly, "There's no doubt any longer. The boy will be found guilty. Kilgore is holding out for miracles, but there's no hope for a favorable verdict. None at all."

Tellegen looked sympathetic. "Certainly you plan to appeal, Mr. McCandless?"

McCandless scowled. "We could appeal it right up to the throne of God, Governor. The verdict would still stand. As sure as we both sit here, that boy committed that murder. I tried not to believe it up till the last, but what they uncovered yesterday shakes my faith and destroys it. He's guilty."

The governor appeared uncomfortable. "Well, Mr. McCandless, I don't see what you expect me to do."

"Grant clemency," said McCandless starkly.

The governor paused. "In a case of this importance I'd have to contact the President for that. But I don't see how I can be expected to make such a request. And though I'm deeply sympathetic toward your personal tragedy, I feel that an exception—"

Dan McCandless gripped the corners of the broad desk and said, "I'm not asking an exception. I'm offering a *quid pro quo*. In return for the life of my son—for a Presidential pardon—I can offer testimony in another murder case of some importance to this Territory."

Tellegen said, "Please explain."

"I'll reopen the murder of Don Alfredo Lucero."

"Is this a joke, Mr. McCandless?"

"I was never more serious." McCandless was bathed in perspiration. A constricting band of fear tightened around his heart. He forced himself to go on. "The murder of Don Alfredo was a Federal offense, cognizable in the Federal court because it was committed on an Indian reservation. I was present at the murder." His hands shook convulsively. "I guess that makes me an accomplice in a way, after the fact. But I'll testify against the actual killer, who is a man quite well known in this Territory."

"You aren't talking about—"

"Yes. Joel Tilley."

Tellegen's eyes widened. "You've kept silent for twenty years, Mr. McCandless?"

"It was between Tilley and me, and no concern of the law. But I can't keep shut any longer. If I want to save Harry, I have to tell what I know about Tilley. I'm sure you'd welcome a chance to destroy the power of Joel Tilley in this Territory, Governor."

"Yes, of course. But—"

"Well, there's the *quid pro quo*. Give me Harry's life and I'll give you Tilley's."

"Do you realize that you'll be leaving yourself open for severe reprisals?" Tellegen asked.

McCandless shrugged. "They'll be reprisals against me, not against my family. I'll get only what I deserve. Will you grant the pardon?"

Tellegen pursed his lips. "When will the trial end?"

"I guess it'll go to the jury on Monday. They can't need much time for their verdict."

"I'll wire the President tonight. I can't interfere with the trial. But if the verdict goes against your son, I'll be able to grant the pardon."

"You're certain?"

"Absolutely, Mr. McCandless. I'll word my request in such a way as to show him I've given my oath. He'll support me. And in return—"

"Yes. I'll testify against Tilley. It's a deal."

"Your son will not hang, Mr. McCandless."

McCandless nodded abstractedly. Rising, he thanked the governor and left. He walked bleakly from the governor's mansion, knowing that he had just signed his own death warrant.

The wire was dated Thursday, and it was from Denver.

VANCE AGREES TO EXAMINE BODY STOP WE ARRIVE SAN CARLOS SATURDAY NIGHT HOPE ALL IS WELL STOP NEWSPAPER STORIES MOST FRIGHTENING

CARLOTTA

Kilgore's eyes gleamed. "He's coming! Vance, from Denver! He's going to have a look at the body!" Sudden excitement pervaded him. "Clem, get down to the station, it must be almost time for their train to be coming in. Sarah, get your dictation pad! I have to request a second autopsy on the Morgan girl! We're not licked yet, damn it all to everlasting brimstone! Not by a mile!"

Clem and Sarah exchanged puzzled glances.

"He's expecting a miracle," Clem muttered.

"It's the fever," Sarah whispered hoarsely. "He's half out of his mind, thinking that this Denver man is going to wave a magic wand."

"Kilgore will be disappointed."

"He'll be unbearable," Sarah said. She shrugged. "My conscience tells me to swear out a restraining order getting him out of that trial and to a doctor. But my common sense tells me not to, because Kilgore would slaughter me when he gets well."

"Sarah! Sarah!" came the booming roar. "Get yourself in here, woman! Has Clem gone yet? That train will be here any minute! We can't waste time!"

By quarter to nine on Monday morning, the little courthouse was jammed, and the overflow spilled out into the plaza. Word had gone around that this was to be the final day of the trial, and everyone had come for the exciting moments ahead —the closing speeches of the rival attorneys, and then the decision of the jury. Everyone wanted to see the look on Dan McCandless' face when the foreman stood up to announce the verdict of guilty.

There had been a mad struggle for seats the moment the doors opened. But one spectator who had not attended any of the previous sessions had managed to obtain a front-row seat in the prosecution group with no difficulty.

Joel Tilley.

Tilley sat quietly beside Laurie Morgan until Dan McCandless entered the courtroom. He rose, then, crossing the courtroom to the bench where the defenders sat.

For a moment the two men confronted each other—the short, bearded Tilley, the towering McCandless.

Tilley said gently, throttling his big voice down to a purr, "Dan, I want to talk to you."

"No one's stopping you, Tilley."

Tilley smiled frigidly. "Dan, I've got men with big ears close to the governor. I happen to know the substance of your chat with him."

McCandless felt a cold hand on his heart. "Your men ought to be congratulated, Tilley. Do they hide in privies, too?"

Tilley said smoothly, "Dan, if you were as smart as you used to be, you'd forget all about this notion of a pardon for your boy."

"He's my son. I aim to save him."

"You've told Tellegen you'll testify against me."

"Did I?"

Tilley's cheek muscles were throbbing. "There's no turning

back now. Whether or not Harry is found guilty, Tellegen will arrest me. And what will you do?"

"Testify. Regardless. I've had this thing on my conscience for twenty years, and it's killing me."

"It'll kill you if you get it off your conscience, too."

McCandless nodded slowly. "I'd rather die clean than die dirty. I'll testify. And nothing you can do will stop Tellegen from arresting you. I gave him a full statement already."

"I have friends, Dan. They'll take care of you for this."

There was a smile of relaxed resignment on McCandless' face. "I'll be waiting, Tilley."

With a black look, Tilley returned to his seat. Judge Hazledine had appeared, and was about to convene the court. Dan McCandless took his place at the table.

20.

THE DOOR swung open, and every head swiveled as Carlotta McCandless and Dr. Arthur Vance entered the courtroom. During their slow procession toward the front, Kilgore leaned on the defense table to support himself. He felt feverish, and every time a bit of cold air found its way through the courthouse windows he shivered. His face was beaded with sweat.

He waited. The audience discussed the new development busily. Dr. Vance took the stand and was sworn in. Carlotta sat beside Clem; Dan McCandless leaned forward, perplexed, while Pete Beaudoin nibbled a pencil, Mike Duer peered sullenly at the floor, Joel Tilley waited with folded arms.

Dr. Vance was a man of about sixty, solidly built and neat of appearance. His thick brown mustache was fastidiously trimmed, his suit crisp, his eyes clear, though he had had virtually no sleep at all. He waited on the stand, calm, perfectly sure of himself.

The courtroom was strangely silent. Kilgore eyed the jury a moment, then faced the witness.

"Where do you live, Dr. Vance?"

"In Denver."

"And what is your profession?"

"I'm a pathologist."

"Would you explain just what that is?"

Vance nodded. "A pathologist is a doctor of medicine whose specialty is the causes and nature of diseases, and of abnormal bodily affections and conditions."

"Might I ask where you took your degree?"

"Bachelor of science at Princeton, 1854. Subsequent studies at the University of Vienna and at the Sorbonne. Took my medical degree at Vienna in 1860. Three years in the General Hospital of Vienna, division of internal medicine. Appointed as *Privatdozent* in 1864. This is a teaching position of some prestige value. In 1866 I resigned to do hospital work in Paris, and I returned to this country in 1870. I practiced in New York for a number of years. Ten years ago I decided to move west, and have been practicing in Colorado ever since."

"And to which medical societies do you belong?"

"The American Medical Association, in this country, and I'm a corresponding member of the Reading Pathological Society of England."

Kilgore nodded. "I think we have established sufficiently your medical qualifications, Dr. Vance. Let me ask you now: have you conducted an autopsy upon the body of the late Honey Morgan?"

"Yes, I have."

"When?"

"Between the hours of midnight and four this morning."

"You found the body to be in adequate condition for meaningful observations, Dr. Vance?"

"Yes, sir. The unusually cold weather had kept the body in a fine state of preservation."

"Would you tell us some of your findings, Dr. Vance?"

The pathologist moistened his lips. "I first made examination of the deceased's heart, to determine whether or not the condition of enlargement might have been a factor in her death. I did this at your request, since you suspected she might have died of a heart attack. It was my observation that her heart condition was not serious and did not play a role in her death."

"Yes. This destroyed my hypothesis," Kilgore commented. "But what did you do next?"

"I next examined the skull of the deceased. I observed that the skull had been fractured and hematoma—blood clots—were present."

"Thus confirming the finding of Dr. Hewlitt?"

"Yes. Precisely."

"It was reasonable to conclude, then, that the girl's death was caused by a blow on the head which ruptured the dura mater," Kilgore said.

The pathologist nodded. "Yes. That would be a reasonable conclusion."

Beaudoin broke in. "Your Honor, if this new witness is merely going to confirm Dr. Hewlitt's findings, I don't understand how this constitutes proper rebuttal."

Kilgore replied, "New findings will be presented."

"You may continue with your examination, Mr. Kilgore," Hazledine said.

Kilgore turned back to the witness. "You say, Dr. Vance, that it would be reasonable to draw the conclusions Dr. Hewlitt drew?"

"Yes. Any general practitioner would be likely to arrive at the same conclusion. However, certain aspects of the body interested me, and I proceeded to delve somewhat deeper."

"Tell us of your findings," Kilgore prompted formally.

The doctor paused. "I looked beneath the extensive flooding of blood which had left the large hematoma, and I found the original cause of the outpouring of blood. This cause was an aneurism, a so-called subarachnoid hemorrhage."

"Would you put that in laymen's terms?"

"Certainly," Dr. Vance said. "It's a condition of spontaneous origin similar to a stroke."

Beaudoin was on his feet—but he was saying nothing, nothing at all!

Kilgore pressed on. "Of *spontaneous* origin, Doctor?"

"That's correct. It might have happened by reason of strong passion, or during exertion, or shouting. Or it might simply have been the finger of God touching the girl. There is no doubt that the aneurism was the cause of death. It killed her instantly. She must have dropped head-first, striking her head against a bedpost or table, causing the fracture and hematoma and other cranial injuries. There would have been considerable bleeding from the nose also."

"You would say, then, that the cause of death was natural, Dr. Vance?"

"Absolutely."

For a moment the courtroom remained hushed. Then, like a tidal wave rushing in over an unshielded island, a whisper began, rising to an outcry of disbelief. Death natural! Not caused by a blow on the head?

Beaudoin was shouting incoherently. Mike Duer looked poleaxed. Dan McCandless stared in dazed bewilderment.

"I object!" Beaudoin said strongly. "I demand that this testimony be stricken! How does he know that this aneurism, or whatever, didn't occur after Harry McCandless smashed her skull?"

Hazledine pounded for order. Kilgore said, "Let me put to you, Doctor, the attorney general's question: Could the aneurism not have occurred *after* death?"

"A dead person cannot have a stroke, Mr. Kilgore. There is no alternative possibility. The aneurism came first. The girl was dead before she struck the floor."

There was pandemonium in the court. Somehow, Kilgore made himself heard, asking if Beaudoin cared to cross-examine. The prosecutor shook his head. "Maybe later," he said. "I'd have to figure this out." Kilgore had struck like a thunderbolt of Zeus.

Kilgore said, "I ask that Dr. Spencer Hewlitt be recalled to the stand for further cross-examination."

It was an unhappy Dr. Hewlitt who blinked in the place vacated by the pathologist. Kilgore's questions were brief.

"Dr. Hewlitt, are you familiar with the reputation of the previous witness?"

"Of course. Everyone in the West knows of him."

"You'd be willing, then, to grant that his qualifications are superior to your own?"

The doctor gazed morosely about the courtroom and came back to the grim lawyer whose head was lowered with menace. "Guess so," he faltered. "But only as a pathologist. When it comes to general practice, I guess I might show him a few things we country doctors have got to contend with."

Kilgore growled with satisfaction and thrust out a weighty finger. "If he says that the deceased died as the result of an aneurism, are you prepared to accept his opinion as competent testimony?"

"He's competent, all right," Hewlitt muttered.

"Did you look for an aneurism?"

Hewlitt shook his head miserably. "Nope. Can't say that I did. I saw the fracture and the blood clots—the hematoma— and the signs of rape. I just naturally concluded somebody had walloped the poor little girl with a bat. It was pretty cold in that barn when I was working. Of course I should have looked further—"

"Not having looked further, would you care for an opportunity?" Kilgore asked hoarsely, wondering at the unreality of his own voice. "The body has been kept perfectly in this cold—"

"Might be a good idea," Hewlitt said with embarrassment. "Pathology is tricky, Kilgore. Anybody can make a mistake."

"How much time would you need?"

"Five minutes!"

Kilgore addressed the court out of the midst of blinding pain. "I ask for an hour's recess while Dr. Vance has a chance to confer with Dr. Hewlitt to investigate the true nature of the lesion that caused the poor girl's death," he said. "If it wasn't murder, let's find it out now."

One hour later Hewlitt resumed the stand, embarrassed and perspiring. He turned to the bench apologetically. "You know, Judge? I kind of wondered about a stroke myself, but I wasn't sure. Now I am sure. Dr. Vance put his finger on the exact cause of death." He paused to tug at a trembling mouth. "Guess I sort of made a mistake, Your Honor."

"I guess you sort of did, *Doctor!*" Kilgore said with savage contempt. "Your witness, Mr. Beaudoin!"

Beaudoin arose with burning eyes, pointed a finger, faltered and muttered. "No questions!" he said bitterly. "My big mistake was to depend on this drunken quack in the first place."

"Jesus, Pete—"

The doctor's whining protests were cut short by a rap from the bench. Judge Hazledine stared grimly at the press of faces —conscious of two areas of silence in the general mutter of anger and relief: the group about Dan McCandless, Spanish and Anglos in whom could be seen the dawn of hope; the grim bunch of hard-faced men who surrounded Joel Tilley. "I'll entertain a motion," the judge said harshly.

Kilgore faced the bench and stared through gathering darkness. He felt the steadying hand of Clem Erskine on his arm.

"Your Honor, I'll make it simple. All the medical evidence taken together shows that the Territory has failed to establish that the poor child's death was caused by any criminal agency. There has been an utter failure of proof of any corpus delicti as required by the laws and statutes of the Territory. Under the circumstances, I move"—he paused to glance at the white and unbelieving mask of anguish of Laurie Morgan—"I move that this tragic proceeding be resolved and that the jury be directed to enter a verdict of not guilty."

"No!" cried Laurie in a strangled voice. "My little girl! Oh, my little girl!"

Judge Hazledine waited for the sound of a woman's sobbing to subside before he turned to the prosecution side of the courtroom. "Mr. Beaudoin? Any objection to this motion?"

A moment of silence passed, and then Beaudoin arose and

walked forward to the bench. "Why, yes!" he said grimly. "I think there's enough here to go to the jury." He raised a hand to interrupt an outburst from Kilgore. "No motion has yet been made—or can be made—to strike out Dr. Hewlitt's earlier testimony, which showed a fractured skull and a criminal cause of death. And as for his retraction? I guess he's just been bulldozed by Dr. Vance—"

Judge Hazledine frowned. "Bulldozed or not, Mr. Beaudoin, he's your witness, and he's all you've got. Unless you're prepared to call for further medical evidence—"

"But is it all we've got?" Beaudoin stalked across the well of the courtroom to confront the white-faced defendant, who had received the turn of events with nervously darting eyes.

"Is it all we've got?" Beaudoin's voice rose to a pitch. "Harry McCandless has lied up and down since the day this case began. He's lied under oath. He's shown every sign of guilt a man could show. I say the jury should pass on this case! Not the court! I'm against a directed verdict.

"Once the jury has given its verdict," he concluded strongly, staring at the McCandless party, "and once it's pronounced judgment—I don't care what the court will do!" He returned to his chair and sat with folded arms, staring at the ceiling.

Mike Duer's grunt of approval broke the silence.

Judge Hazledine considered the matter, stroking his stiff Vandyke thoughtfully. "I'm afraid, Mr. Kilgore, there are aspects of this case that trouble me. There is an element that I fail to comprehend. If death was due to natural causes, if the deceased girl was felled by a stroke, why did someone remove the body so deviously into the hills? Who stuffed her mouth with plaster? What is this business about the diamond ring? I am led to conclude that some elaborate and diabolical hoax has been played on the court—but by whom and for whose benefit, I am at a loss to say. However, as long as there is a failure of medical proof, I am constrained to grant your motion—"

"No! No!" burst out a high-pitched, frenzied voice. "I killed her! I killed her!"

Harry McCandless had clambered to his chair to give himself greater height. Wild-eyed, shouting, oblivious of the touch of spittle in the corner of his mouth, he shouted at the bench. "I'm guilty, do you hear? I killed her! I stuffed the plaster in her mouth. Why won't you believe me? What else must I do?"

Dan McCandless arose with a stricken look. "Son? Oh, Sonny! Oh, my God! Don't say anything! They'll let you go if only you don't say anything—"

Kilgore cried, "Harry McCandless! Shut up, or you're dead!"

A dozen voices began all at once. Harry McCandless shouted through the banging of the gavel. "I've been trying to tell you all! Really I have!" A look of cunning crept into his eyes. "I told Mike Duer about the ring and the anthropology book. Didn't I, Mike? Tell them about that!"

Mike Duer said wonderingly, "So it was you that sent those notes!"

Harry laughed cunningly. "Of course I sent them! How else would you ever have guessed—any of you? The only reason we're in court now is because of me. Don't you see, Judge?" he turned back to the bench. "You mustn't let me go. Not now! Now when we're so close?"

"He's mad!" Dan McCandless shouted. "Don't listen to the boy! He never killed anyone—"

"Mad?" Harry threw back his head and laughed freely. "Mad? For the first time in my life I feel sane. Sane and clear! Do you think these people hate you, Dan McCandless? They don't know what hate is! Only the Luceros know hate! Real hate! Hate that goes back to the beginning! Hate! Hate! Hate!"

Kilgore turned and seized the wrists of the shouting youth. "Every word you're saying is being heard!" he said strongly. "Stop now! What are you trying to do?"

The courtroom went silent. Harry McCandless said in a childish voice: "I want my mother, Mr. Kilgore. I want to go back to her. I want to show her what I did." He gazed wonderingly at the bench. "You mustn't let me go, Judge," he said simply. "I must be allowed to die. It's the only way to show *him!* You won't let me go, will you?"

Tears were trembling in his eyes, childish tears of protest, as the sheriff touched his arm and motioned him back to his seat.

Kilgore stared at the suddenly infantile face with incredulity. The pattern of events suddenly was clear. Harry had seized upon the girl's sudden death and had transformed the cerebral accident into the basis of a suicidal scheme against his father. Kilgore wondered how much Dan McCandless had suspected of all this, how much McCandless had refused to believe.

Harry had planted the evidence—and *Harry* had tipped off Duer about Eli, about the carpet, about the ring. Small wonder Harry had deceived and tricked Kilgore, had given so many contradictory stories. It was all a game, a mad game the boy was playing—letting the trial drag on, doling out the evidence secretly to the prosecution, planning that the inevitable verdict would be death—death for him, but ruin and heartbreak for the father he hated!

But Kilgore had played his hand well. He had outplayed Harry without even realizing it. And Harry was saved from the rope now.

Judge Hazledine said quietly, "The motion for a directed verdict of acquittal is granted. The clerk is directed to make an entry to that effect. The defendant is discharged." He tapped the gavel formally. "This court stands adjourned."

"No, no," Harry McCandless said pitiably. "I won't go—"

Out of a vast abyss darkness swarmed and the chamber of silent faces swarmed and coalesced in myriad colors. . . .

"Kilgore!" Sarah Hilleboe cried.

The lawyer sagged, caught the rail, fell to his knees and smelled the dust and oil of the flooring. Clem Erskine was at his side at once. "Oh, Mr. Kilgore!" he cried in alarm. Troubled faces looked down.

"Fever!" Kilgore muttered. "Burning fever! Damn this, collapsing in court like a weakling! I—"

He winced, then shuddered as a fresh wave of pain shot through his skull. Clem's strong hands held him tight. Kilgore heard a confused hubbub of voices, saw Sarah, Clem, Carlotta.

"Take him home," a voice said. He recognized it as that of Dr. Vance. "I'll examine him straightaway."

Kilgore felt them lifting him, carrying him out. He railed inwardly at the absurdity of collapsing this way, in his moment of triumph.

He caught sight of a man standing alone. He caught Clem's arm and whispered, "Go to Dan McCandless. He'll need someone to help him."

The lawyer was borne out.

Dan McCandless shook his head when Clem approached. The big man wanted to be left alone with his heartache. He had seen his son's outburst—and then he had seen the United States marshal step briskly forward to place Joel Tilley under arrest for the murder of Alfredo Lucero. Tilley had left—but not before vowing revenge.

So it had all been to no purpose, McCandless thought sadly, this betrayal of the code on which his life had rested. Harry had not needed his sacrifice. McCandless' shoulders slumped. He had known the boy was unbalanced, perhaps unbalanced enough to kill—but he had failed to foresee the extent of Harry's sickness.

"Let me take my son home," Dan McCandless said. "Julian —help me—"

There had been a cold purpose in Harry's action, he thought blackly. Revenge. Revenge against the man who had benefited from the murder of his father-in-law for the sake of obtaining the Lucero Grant.

McCandless walked slowly toward the door, oblivious of the excitement around him, leading his party into the plaza. People who had scorned him yesterday rushed up to him, pumping his hand as though he had won a great victory, instead of losing all.

It was Harry who had won after all, McCandless thought. For now the murderer of Don Alfredo would be punished— and the informer, the murderer's accomplice, he, too, would be punished. It would not be long before Tilley's hired murderers paid him a call.

Dan McCandless knew where he would be at that time.

He would be in the malpais, by the white oak where Don Alfredo Lucero had been murdered. He would wait there, without a weapon, for Tilley's men to close in. And he would be calm, for this fate was that which he had earned.

The cold spell had ended finally, late in February, a week after the bullet-riddled body of Dan McCandless had been found in the badlands. Wa-po-nah was shuttered; a purchaser was being sought; the McCandless empire was in the hands of the receivers. Carlotta and Isabella McCandless were gone, taking their mourning elsewhere, traveling to Europe to forget the violence of the past weeks. Harry McCandless had been committed to an institution in San Francisco.

Jake Kilgore stood at the door of his law office. He was fully recovered now from his operation, and only the stubbliness of his sideburn where the doctor had shaved it served as a reminder of his recent illness. He stared out at the warming earth, at the golden sun and cloud-fleeced sky.

"Another month, Clem, and it'll be warm again."

"It's warm now, Mr. Kilgore. They say it'll hit close to fifty today!"

Kilgore spat. "*Fifty!* Clem, when Kilgore says *warm*, he means ninety degrees and above! The fine dry heat of New Mexico is what he means! And we'll be having that soon enough!" He glanced up at his lanky clerk. "The coming of the warm weather will be important to you, young man. Do you know why?"

"I'm sure I don't, sir."

Kilgore grinned broadly. "Because when it's warm, Kilgore likes to travel. And one of the first trips he'll be making will be to Santa Fe. He'll see the sights there. He'll pay a call on Laurie Morgan—and not at her sporting house—and try to patch up the wounds, if that's possible. And—incidentally—old Kilgore will move for the admittance of Clem Erskine to full membership in the Territorial bar."

Clem's eyes were shining. "Are you serious, sir?" He was thinking of the impression that his becoming a full-fledged lawyer would make on Carlotta when she returned in six months' time.

Kilgore snorted. "Erskine, I am *always* serious. But I enter the stipulation that I'm likely to change my mind if I find you slacking off."

"Oh, don't worry about that, Mr. Kilgore. There isn't a chance!"

"We'll see about that. And I think we've wasted enough time out here, Erskine. We've got a brief to prepare in this foolish damage suit the livery stable is instituting."

"Yes, sir."

"And while you're at it," Kilgore said, "I think the spittoon could stand a shine. It takes more than reading Blackstone and Gildersleeve and Prince to make a lawyer, Erskine. I want that spittoon to *gleam*."

And he turned and walked quickly back into his office, before Clem could catch sight of his broad grin.

www.ingramcontent.com/pod-product-compliance
Lightning Source LLC
Chambersburg PA
CBHW031420250626
47155CB00004B/1565